THE WAND & THE SEA

Also by Claire M. Caterer

The Key & the Flame

THE WAND & THE SEA

CLAIRE M. CATERER

Margaret K. McElderry Books

New York London Toronto Sydney New Delhi

For my mother,
Sally Scovel Caterer,
born under the sign of the fishes

MARGARET K. McELDERRY BOOKS
An imprint of Simon & Schuster Children's Publishing Division
1230 Avenue of the Americas, New York, New York 10020

MARGARET K. McELDERRY BOOKS
is a trademark of Simon & Schuster, Inc.
For information about special discounts for bulk purchases,
please contact Simon & Schuster Special Sales at
1-866-506-1949 or business@simonandschuster.com.
The Simon & Schuster Speakers Bureau can bring authors to your live event.
For more information or to book an event, contact the
Simon & Schuster Speakers Bureau at 1-866-248-3049
or visit our website at www.simonspeakers.com.
The text for this book is set in Impressum Std.
Manufactured in the United States of America
0515 FFG
2 4 6 8 10 9 7 5 3 1
Library of Congress Cataloging-in-Publication Data
Caterer, Claire.
The wand & the sea / Claire M. Caterer.—1st ed.
p. cm.
Summary: A year after their first visit to a parallel universe,
Holly and Ben Shepard and friend Everett return to find that
much is changed, and the fate of Anglielle is at stake unless Holly
can master Water Elemental magic in time to save the Adepts.
ISBN 978-1-4424-5744-7 (hardcover)
ISBN 978-1-4424-5746-1 (eBook)
[1. Adventure and adventurers—Fiction. 2. Space and time—Fiction.
3. Magic—Fiction. 4. Brothers and sisters—Fiction. 5. England—Fiction.
6. Science fiction.] I. Title. II. Title: Wand and the sea.
PZ7.C2687916Wan 2015
[Fic]—dc23   2014032582

FIRST
EDITION

I must go down to the seas again,
   to the lonely sea and the sky,
And all I ask is a tall ship and a star to steer her by,
And the wheel's kick and the wind's song
   and the white sail's shaking,
And a grey mist on the sea's face
   and a grey dawn breaking.

—John Masefield

Chapter 1

A Story Untold

Holly Shepard was unlike most twelve-year-olds in that she didn't at all mind sharing a cramped cottage bedroom with her pudgy, snoring, laptop-loving younger brother. It didn't bother her that she was four thousand miles from the place her parents called home, which was a little house in a little suburb in a big square of cracked land baking in the American Midwest. July was different here, in England.

Not that everyone in Holly's family appreciated this damp, chilly village. Her brother, Ben, preferred a place with more electrical outlets. Her mother would get wrapped up in work; her father tried to remember to drive on the left. When they had arrived yesterday, after fourteen hours, three airports, and one rental car, her mother was already regretting they hadn't rented a bigger cottage in a larger town, perhaps one that had a cricket team for Ben to join. (As if he would ever join a team of any kind.) Her father recalled that the grocery didn't carry the coffee he liked, and asked if her mother would pick up some in Oxford, near her office.

But Holly was bothered by none of this. Instead she woke up content and well rested in the limestone cottage in Hawkesbury, with its creaking plaster and dark oak planks that smelled of lemon. Holly hadn't left home. She had *come* home. And in any case, she didn't plan on staying long.

Holly tiptoed around the bedroom, careful not to smack her head on the eave, and grabbed her clothes to change in the bathroom. She skirted Ben's bed without waking him.

The world outside was sodden. The deep gray sky darkened the stone cottage, its white plaster walls glowing in the weak morning light. Holly slipped out the back door, ducked under the garden arbor ringed with hollyhocks, and sat down on the flagstone steps that led into a wide green valley. Through the mist she could just make out the shadow of Darton Castle on the far hill. It was a pile of medieval ruins now, like dozens scattered around the English countryside, but Holly remembered its cruel king and bloodthirsty knights. She pulled her poncho close around her. She had no desire to visit the castle. But the dense forest, which spilled through the west side of the valley, beckoned her. She double-checked her watch—which was also a compass—and then made sure the thin leather scabbard was buckled around her waist. The key—*her* key—was nestled inside.

It took Holly a long time to pick her way down the soggy hillside, and even so, her feet slipped and she slid on her backside the last few yards. She stood up and picked a muddy clump of leaves from one of her long braids.

Not the best beginning, but she was taking a long shot in any case.

The valley was alive with robins. Excited by the worm-yielding earth, they chittered along with warblers and bluebirds. A pair of rabbits noticed Holly and sped into the woods. But when she followed them, all the chirpings and chatterings ceased.

The woods of Hawkesbury were particular—silent, but full, like a dark theater crowded with a rapt audience. The air closed in as dank and close as a rain forest. Holly sighed. Walking through this deep green place was like being wrapped in a favorite blanket.

The iron key in its scabbard bumped along her leg as she hiked the path. She stopped, listening for the humming, the life of the forest reaching out to her. But she heard nothing.

It didn't matter. She *would* find a way to make the key work.

It had been a long year waiting to come back to Hawkesbury. Starting middle school had meant the end of recess and easy math. Her locker jammed on a regular basis. Her English teacher handed out tardies if you were thirty seconds late, even if it was because the school's one and only library book on Celtic mythology was stuck behind the section on anime superheroes. Her math teacher assigned homework every night and didn't give them time in class to work on it. ("That's why it's called *home*work, Holly," Ms. Knox said when Holly protested, and Holly's mother said, "That seems like a reasonable answer.") And though she tried to blend in to the cinder-block walls, Holly couldn't help asking questions and interrupting teachers and even getting the occasional lunchtime detention for "wasting the class's time."

Worst of all, the other girls had suddenly noticed her. Tracy Watson nicknamed her Pippi because of Holly's long brown braids. She cracked up every time Brittany King braided her own hair and then crossed her eyes, running her index finger up the bridge of her nose as if adjusting imaginary glasses. Holly knew what they were doing, but every time she glanced over at them through her own smudgy glasses, they shrugged at her with exaggerated innocent looks.

Holly had made friends with exactly one girl.

CLAIRE M. CATERER

Charlotte Devon, the shortest kid in the sixth grade, had frothy white-blond hair and arms so thin, she looked like she'd shatter if you touched her. Like Holly, Charlotte spent her free time in the library and even checked out books on fairy tales and King Arthur.

Holly almost told her about last summer.

They were sitting in the cafeteria and Charlotte was thumbing through *Fairy Tales of the Middle East* when Holly blurted out, "Do you think any of that stuff ever really happens?"

"What stuff?" Charlotte asked.

Holly steeled herself. "Magic stuff. Like in the books."

"Oh, sure it does. Look! I never saw a genie like this one."

"So you think it happens to real people? Did anything like that ever happen to you?"

"Is this like a joke?" said Charlotte. "I don't get it."

"No, I mean really. Maybe you saw something strange you couldn't explain?"

"Like a fairy in the woods who wanted to take me away to the fairy realm?"

"Yes! Like that."

"And then she'd give me something to eat so I'd be trapped in the fairy realm forever and be their prisoner?"

"Right!"

"And the fairies would steal the powers that only I had so they could come out of the shadows and reveal their true selves?"

"Exactly!"

Charlotte's face broke into a beatific smile. "No. We don't have any woods around here, Holly. So how would I get to the fairy realm? Hey, have you read this story about the snake master of Agadir?"

Holly sighed.

She didn't say anything to Charlotte about how she *had* met a fairy in the woods. And how the fairy had offered her something to eat. How the fairy had wanted to steal the powers that only Holly had.

She said nothing about a kingdom where a tyrant king had outlawed magic, where centaurs and magicians were the closest of friends, where a prince had held Ben captive and forced him to be a knight's squire. Where Holly herself was an Adept—a being of great magical power.

She didn't say a word about Anglielle.

Chapter 2

The Red Bird

A few minutes after Holly had entered the muddy overgrown path, the birds and squirrels took up their chatter. The dense canopy of oaks and beeches closed around her. She grasped a mossy sapling and pulled herself up along a slippery rise. In front of her a stream meandered through the wood, an offshoot of the river snaking through the valley.

But it didn't look like the stream she knew.

The narrow brook she had so easily crossed before had swollen, producing whitecaps as it churned through the forest. Holly dropped a twig into the water and watched it disappear in the current.

The brook wasn't safe to cross.

A harsh squawk broke over her head. A large bright-red bird sat on a low tree branch downstream. It glared at her and flapped its wings, showing their indigo undersides. Not a cardinal, or a hawk.

It looked like—though how could it be?—a parrot.

The red bird leaped onto an ancient tree that had fallen across the water. Holly stepped through the dripping undergrowth to reach it. The parrot launched into the air, screeching as if to say, *You're welcome.*

Holly considered crossing the tree bridge on foot, but it looked slippery. Instead she sat astride it and edged out to the center. *All this trouble,* she thought, *and I won't even be able to get through the portal.*

So what was she doing here?

She was the last Adept of Anglielle.

She never had figured out how someone who came from a world of jet airplanes and concrete and cell phones could wield the power of an ancient place of spells and sorcerers. But somehow she had magic within her. The closer she came to the portal, the stronger she felt that tugging, that homesickness. Hawkesbury felt more real to her than America. This forest felt more real than the lemon-scented cottage. When she reached Anglielle, something inside her would click like the tumblers of a lock aligning. She would find a way in.

Admittedly, the last year hadn't exactly been *magical.* The wand she had forged in Anglielle had reverted to the form of an iron key in this world, just like the one Mr. Gallaway had given her. But it still had power. She had seen it.

She had packed the key away last summer, pained at the thought that she might never see her friends in Anglielle again. Her own world was horribly ordinary, and her shoulder felt cold without the warm Salamander, Áedán, to protect her. She wasn't herself without him and Jade, the black cat. Feeling lonely one January day, she had stuffed the key into her pocket before going to school.

It was that most awful of months: only halfway through the school year, the weather cold and bleak, the new semester difficult. A phlegmy cough spread through the school and gave Holly a fever. Spring, let alone summer, was ages away.

Tracy Watson and Brittany King had chosen this day to sit near Holly's lunch table and talk in very loud voices about which Pippi Longstocking book they liked best, and when Holly didn't respond, they brushed by her seat and knocked over her milk with effusive apologies. That afternoon on the bus, Holly's friend Charlotte dropped her notebook and the girls scooped it up. They laughed at Charlotte's sketches of fairies and elves, even though they were better than what anyone else in school could draw. Charlotte bolted out of the bus with tears in her eyes. She'd be walking almost three miles home in the cold.

Holly tried to follow her, but the bus lurched forward,

and the driver barked at her to take her seat. The girls squealed as Charlotte trudged along, her head bent against the wind, and then Brittany dangled the notebook out the window. "Be careful!" Tracy screamed. "Don't drop it! It's a *work of art.*"

Holly gritted her teeth. The front of the bus erupted into chaos; the boys shouted, "Drop it! Drop it!" and everyone laughed. In her pocket, Holly's key vibrated, and a warm wave, like a lick of flame, washed over her chest and face. Her breath came in short, angry puffs. "Give it to me," she muttered, and gripped the key.

A familiar shock of energy zoomed up from her heart down into the key and back again, charging her hand like a battery. She glared at the notebook, the key buzzing in her fist like a trapped wasp. Brittany screeched as the notebook broke away from her hand.

But instead of falling under the bus's wheels, it rose like a feather on a breath of wind and wafted toward the center of the bus, where Holly slid her window open. The notebook slipped inside, hung in the air a moment, and dropped in her lap. The spiral binding was bent a little, but otherwise it was fine.

The kids stared gape-mouthed at Holly. But then she saw their internal logic kick in: A weird gust of wind had sprung up at the right time, and Holly had grabbed the notebook out of the air as it blew by.

Brittany gave a pouty sneer and spun around in her seat so fast that her yellow ponytail trembled. Holly smiled. The ponytail yanked abruptly downward, and Brittany glared at the boy behind her, who put up both hands in surrender.

That was when Holly had realized that the key still had power, even outside of Anglielle, and what was more, she still had the power to control it. She went home and returned the key to her dresser drawer, closed up in the glossy wooden box Mr. Gallaway had given her.

She never brought it to school again, but she didn't need to. Anglielle was there waiting for her, and whenever she doubted it, she ran her thumb along the faint red line, a scar she had received last year in Anglielle that stretched along her palm.

Now, as she stood in the Hawkesbury woods, the line wasn't faint anymore.

Holly shook her hand as she hitched along the tree trunk, snagging her jeans every few inches over the gushing stream. The longer she waited to return to Anglielle, the more the old wound pained her. It had changed from a barely noticeable pink line to an angry red streak, and when she raised her palm, she saw a drop of blood.

She had made a blood oath to Bittenbender, the fierce leader of the Dvergar, to return to Anglielle. Now that she was within reach, he wasn't about to let her forget it.

The Dvergar hadn't realized she didn't need an oath to call her home.

The minute she crossed the stream, a beam of sunlight cut through the forest canopy, illuminating an enormous oak tree standing like a sentry in the midst of a glade ringed by beeches.

She wanted to hug it, though it was too broad for her arms to span. The key buzzed in its scabbard and she drew it out, closing her eyes. She stood in front of the oak's knobbly trunk. *Please be okay. Please.* She opened her eyes.

The lock was still there. And still broken.

Melted, more specifically. In the center of the tree trunk was an iron plate with the elongated, backward S shape that had once been a keyhole. It was the only way in to Anglielle, that magical place where Holly was actually *somebody*. Last summer she and Ben and Ben's friend Everett had stood here as Holly's key had unlocked the oak. She was glad the boys weren't here now. Ben would be prattling about nothing, and Everett would be questioning whether she knew what she was doing, when he was the one who couldn't be trusted.

At least, she never *had* quite trusted him.

But when she'd opened the oak, he'd stepped through it along with her and Ben. And by unlocking the oak, Holly had revealed the keyholes in the beech trees surrounding it. At least one of the five had led them to Anglielle.

But there were only four beeches now.

That was the problem. The fire that had warped the lock on the oak had consumed the beech-tree portal, too. Now Holly held the key up to the iron plate, willing it to fix the twisted keyhole. But Holly's marvelous key, which translated languages and could levitate sketchbooks, which could work *magic*—even that wonderful key only clanged uselessly against the ruined lock.

She had come all this way, and waited so long—put up with her mother's lectures and Brittany King and fractions with exponents—she *had* to get back where she belonged. Holly pounded the trunk with her fist and put her mouth up to the lock. "Let me in! I have to get back in!" she called desperately.

A blast of hot air shot through the keyhole. It glowed like molten iron, and she jerked away. A blister bubbled on her lower lip.

Somewhere, some*when*, Anglielle's Northern Wood was still burning.

But how could it be?

She walked away from the oak tree, stifling an urge to kick it, and approached the circle of beeches. None of them revealed their keyholes. Until she unlocked the oak, the portals were useless.

"Why won't you *work*?" she yelled, flinging the key into the grass.

She didn't see where it landed and she didn't care. What was the point of knowing magic if eventually it stopped working? It was the same in all the stories. Kids get older, the magic disappears. Peter Pan let Wendy go because she wanted to grow up.

Holly hated the ending of that story.

But didn't she still have magic? What about Charlotte's notebook, and the scar on her own hand? That was real enough. . . .

It was all explainable. Maybe a gust of wind *had* lifted Charlotte's notebook. Maybe she'd scratched her palm on the tree trunk across the stream. *You're going to need to grow up,* Holly's mother often said. *Start taking some responsibility.* Girls like Brittany King had put away their dolls and puppets long ago, and here was Holly, trying to unlock a tree with an old key. Why?

Because she didn't belong here.

As she stood next to the oak tree, where somehow

suspended in time the Angliellan woods were burning, her world of locker jams and tardy slips and text messages faded away like part of a story she had read in a book a long time ago. The real world was ancient, truer, somehow. If she never returned to it, she would stay anchored to a place she had never really understood, knowing her home was just out of reach.

She laid a hand on the beech tree closest to the gap in the circle.

A hoarse screech startled her. The red parrot.

It perched on a low, fat branch next to her. And in its beak it held Holly's key.

Holly took a soft step in the parrot's direction.

It flapped its scarlet wings and screamed again, though it kept a firm grip on the key.

"I'm sorry," Holly whispered, as if the bird could understand her. "There's a nice parrot. Are you someone's pet? I do still want the key. So why don't you just give that back to me?"

It was a choice, after all. A choice about what you decided to believe in. That sounded like something Mr. Gallaway would say.

"He's the one I should talk to, isn't he?" she said, trying to keep the parrot's attention while she stepped a bit closer. "He'd know how to fix the lock on the oak tree."

The red bird blinked. It edged away from her along the tree branch.

"What does stupid Brittany King know about anything, anyway? The highlight of her summer will be finding toenail polish to match her swimsuit. That's right, isn't it, parrot?"

Holly's feet made no sound as she crept toward the beech tree, her voice almost as quiet. She cocked her head, keeping only one eye on the bird. She had read once that human eyes were threatening; fixed so close together, they were the eyes of a predator.

"I'm not a predator, am I?" she whispered.

Almost there. She could reach out and touch the bird now, but if she startled it, she'd never see her key again. Then a thought occurred to her.

"I have something even better than that old key," she said. She reached slowly into the corner pocket of her jeans and drew out a quarter. "Look, it's all new and pretty."

The bird's eyes flitted down to the coin in Holly's fingers, then back up to her face.

"It's all yours. Look, I'll just leave it right here. . . ." She eased her hand up to the branch and slid the quarter into a shallow knot. The parrot sidestepped away from her, hunched, and tensed its legs.

It was about to take off.

CLAIRE M. CATERER

"No, wait!" Holly cried. Her hand dove into her pocket. Amazingly, the parrot paused. Hastily, she dropped a second quarter into the hollow. It was like dealing with a capricious vending machine.

"*Caw,*" said the parrot softly, and dropped the key onto the ground.

Holly's shoulders sagged. The parrot snatched up the quarters and launched itself into the forest canopy. The sun glinted off its feathers, and Holly smiled, flooded with relief. She retrieved the key from the soggy grass.

She wasn't quite ready to give it up after all.

Chapter 3

The Five Elements

Everett Shaw stood in the back garden of Number Seven, Hodges Close. Glancing along the flagstone path through the spitting rain, he could just make out the hollyhock-covered arbor of Number One. He noted with satisfaction a plume of smoke curling up from the cottage chimney.

Holly and Ben had finally returned.

Everett opened the picket gate of Number Seven and peered into the screened-in porch attached to the house. He half hoped, as he always did, to find the oak chest that he had seen only once among the tables of seedlings and garden tools. It was the chest that held all of Mr. Gallaway's secrets, but Everett had never seen it after that time last summer, when he'd taken one of the large iron keys stored inside.

The key—the *wand*—that Avery had stolen from him.

Everett went through the porch and knocked on the kitchen door. It opened at once, as if the old man

CLAIRE M. CATERER

had been watching him through the window. He raised his bushy white eyebrows in question. "Yes? What is it?" he said finally, while Everett stood there, shifting from foot to foot.

"I . . . I brought back those loppers Mum borrowed from you." Everett held up the pruners.

"Very well, just put them there on the table." Gallaway jerked his grizzled chin toward the porch.

Everett did as he asked.

"Something else?"

"No, I . . . I guess not." Everett glanced down at the oak table, at the rectangular shape in the dust. A shape big enough for an old iron chest.

The old man grunted. "I suppose you'll want a cuppa. Come in then, if you must. Mind you don't drip on the kitchen floor."

Everett followed him into the cozy kitchen. Everett had grown almost an inch this year, and now he was a bit taller than Gallaway. The old man made a great show of assembling cups and saucers and teapot, as if he were being put to great inconvenience and didn't use them every day. He poured tea and opened an ancient-looking tin of shortbreads, pushing them in Everett's general direction. "So?" he said, his eyes looking a bit softer. "How is your mum? Feeling better?"

Everett shrugged. His mum wasn't ill, exactly,

but she had her good days and not so good days. Sometimes she was all bubbly and flitting about the house and making puddings. She seemed quite cheerful when Everett had told her about the Shepards coming back to Hawkesbury. But this morning she had deflated like a leftover balloon. She'd gotten the post and there was no check from Dad, which was already two weeks late, and that always put her in a mood. "Okay, I guess," he said to the old man.

"You give her that herbal tea like I told you?"

"Yeah, I think it did her good. She's run out now." Everett pushed the shortbread around on his plate. He didn't know how to ask what he wanted to; it wasn't as if Gallaway really *liked* him. It was Holly he liked talking to, and she had only just arrived in the village. "Have you . . . I mean . . . been walking in the wood lately?"

"What, in this rain? Not fit for man nor beast."

"I just thought . . . you know. Since Holly and Ben're back . . ." Hang it all, why did Gallaway have to be so hard to talk to? Holly said she'd told him everything about last summer, their time in Anglielle, Avery's betrayal, Everett jousting with the magic wand that had been one of Gallaway's keys. The wand Everett wasn't supposed to have in the first place. Maybe that's why Gallaway was so cross. He must know that not only had Everett stolen one of the magic keys, he'd lost it.

Well, a prince had taken it, but it came to the same thing.

"I have not seen Holly, nor any of the rest of the family," said Mr. Gallaway testily. He pulled out his raggedy red handkerchief and blew his nose. "I'd stay out of the wood if I were you. The stream is sure to be running high. Now, if you don't mind, Everett, contrary to popular belief, I *do* have things I ought to be tending to." The old man stood up, plucked a small pouch from a cupboard shelf, and handed it to Everett. "Give this to your mother. And come round again when she's out." Without another word, he grabbed his plaid cap and walked out, letting the door slam behind him. Everett was quite sure he'd done that deliberately.

When Holly emerged from the forest, it was already raining again. Up the hill, puddles dotted the back garden. The mist enshrouded Darton Castle. Holly checked the leather scabbard. The weight of the key inside calmed her.

She followed the flagstone path along the back gardens of Hodges Close. At the end of the path, she peered through a screened porch and smiled. Sheltered from the rain, the old man was stacking his seed catalogs.

"Come in out of the wet, if you've a mind to," he said without looking up.

Holly opened the door at once and shook off the

chill. After a minute the white-haired gardener put down his catalogs and gave her a half smile that extended to his deep-set blue eyes. He held out one liver-spotted hand. "I am happy to see you, Miss Holly."

"Me too," she said, shaking the hand. Then, throwing off her manners, she hugged him tight.

He coughed and turned away from her, sniffing. "Yes, well. Cuppa tea. Come inside."

She hung up her poncho inside the kitchen door while he gathered cups and teapot. "I wasn't sure we'd get back here," she said. "Ben and I've been at camp since June."

"I wasn't worried." Mr. Gallaway poured her a cup and set the bowl of sugar cubes next to her. "Your Everett has been hanging about the place, asking for you."

Holly felt her cheeks turn pink. "He's not *my* Everett. He's Ben's friend, mostly."

"And yet."

Holly watched a sugar cube dissolve in her teacup. "I wondered, Mr. Gallaway, if you had any idea how I could fix the lock on the oak tree. To get back into the glade."

The old man fished out a tattered red handkerchief from his pocket and rubbed his sharp nose. He raised his eyebrows at her. "Do you still have it?"

Holly knew what he meant. She pulled out the heavy

iron key and handed it to him. "It's not the one you gave me, you know."

Mr. Gallaway held the key up to the light, turning it this way and that. "No. But it will do. Look here." He pointed a trembly finger at the four loops of the clover-shaped handle. "Do you see? The four elements."

Holly had never really noticed it before. Along the edge of each of the four loops a tiny symbol was etched into the iron: a spiral, a circle with an S shape through the center, a teardrop bisected with a vertical line, and two squiggly lines. "Those are elements?" Holly said doubtfully.

The old man traced the teardrop. "This is fire. It looks like a flame, you see. And water, like the waves in the ocean. Do you see earth?"

"The circle? Like a globe?"

"Yes. Follow the seasons clockwise: Fire is followed by water, then earth, and finally air. If you recall, you last visited the glade at the festival of Midsummer."

"The season of fire," Holly said.

"Correct."

She rubbed the water symbol with her finger. A cold wave washed over her, like goose pimples, but very wet. She looked up; was the ceiling leaking? But the plaster, like her hands, was dry.

"If one were to go in order," the old man continued,

"then the element of water would hold the answers you're looking for."

That didn't make a lot of sense. "But the water season would be fall," Holly said. "It's summer now. It's not like I can come back and try again in three months."

Mr. Gallaway chewed on a shortbread he'd fetched from a tin.

Holly traced her finger around the cloverleaf. Then she remembered something she'd read. "But, Mr. Gallaway, aren't there five elements?"

"Ah. The aether. Not all the alchemists acknowledge it. But it is always there, in the center." He pointed to the diamond-shaped hole where the key's four loops joined. "While invisible, it unites the rest. It is the most crucial element of all, that of spirit. And spirit, you may know, has no season. Or rather, it is all seasons."

A wild clap of thunder rattled the windowpanes. Outside, the rain fell in cataracts down the wavy window glass. *Water.* Somehow, water would take her home.

Chapter 4

Coming Together

By the next morning, the Shepards had settled in at Hawkesbury. Holly's father drove her mother to the train station in Kingham and then retreated to the sun porch to work on several tedious-sounding writing assignments. Holly had hoped to visit the glade again by herself, but her brother, Ben, was already awake, his face buried in a bowl of something called Coco Shreddies.

"Everett just texted me," Ben said. "He's coming over. You're not sneaking off on your own, are you?" He nodded toward the backpack. "We're in this together, remember?"

"No, it's just . . . doesn't Everett kind of bother you sometimes? He did steal that wand—the key, I mean— from Mr. Gallaway. And he never even admitted it, or said he was sorry."

"So what?" Ben's face was turning red. "Anyway, you don't know what it was like in that castle. If it hadn't been for Everett—"

"You'd probably be dead," a voice said from the back garden.

"Everett!" Ben pushed Holly aside and opened the screen door. "Finally!"

Holly glared at Ben as the boy in the garden came inside and greeted him. Everett had grown a little, though he wasn't more than an inch or two taller than Holly. He was a year ahead of her in school, with unruly, reddish-brown hair and a rather nice face, at least when he was telling the truth. He gave her a half smile and held out a paper bag. "Brought you some scones. I think you like blueberry, yeah?"

"Yeah," she said, smiling briefly. "Thanks." It was awkward, seeing Everett again. He was all right, she supposed, but she never was sure she could trust him.

"So how's your year been? I thought you might e-mail or something." Everett sat down at the table.

"I figured Ben was doing that," Holly said, ignoring the hurt look on his face. "Plus, I had to use the computer so much for school . . ."

"She's a technophobe," Ben said through a mouthful of blueberries. "It means—"

"Yeah," Everett said, grinning. "I get it. But listen, have you gone back to the wood at all? I've been to that glade a dozen times this year, and I can't even see the lock on the oak tree. But then, you're the one who really knows how to work it."

Holly smiled. Okay, so he was being decent. Maybe he was just embarrassed about his theft. They were all older now anyway. "Remember, you can't see the lock unless you've got the key with you," she said, then explained what Mr. Gallaway had told her.

"That's pretty useless information," Everett said shortly. "How's water supposed to help us, exactly?"

"How should I know? It's just what he said."

"At least he actually *talks* to you," said Everett. "He's fine if I need to borrow a rake or something, but as soon as I mention one of you, he has someplace to go. He acts like I've *done* something to him."

"Well, you did—" Holly started, but broke off when Ben glared at her. But Everett *did* steal something from Mr. Gallaway: Was it any wonder he wasn't very friendly?

"Anyway," Holly went on, "maybe the three of us can figure it out. Something to do with water."

"I guess it's worth a try," Everett said, sounding unconvinced. He stood up.

"Wait a second," said Ben. "If we're going to the forest, and if we might find our way back to Anglielle, I'm getting some stuff together. For one thing, this time, I'm taking way more underwear."

Chapter 5

W *Is for Water*

For all of their preparation—packing backpacks, changing shoes, remembering compasses and pocketknives and Tylenol ("Trust me," Ben said, "we'll need it")—Holly didn't really think they'd get very far. Especially when, as soon as they entered the forest, a loud crack of thunder boomed overhead.

"Not again," Everett said, sounding nearly as whiny as Ben. "It's been raining nonstop for weeks here."

"Well, it *is* England," Ben said.

"No, but it's never been like this. We've hardly had a dry day all summer. It's like a ruddy monsoon all the time."

As he spoke, the wood darkened. The rain descended in sheets.

"I told you a mac was a good idea," Everett said.

A gust of wind tugged at Holly's poncho as she struggled to put it on, and another crack of thunder shook the trees at the same time a bolt of lightning lit up the gloomy wood. Suddenly the forest was alive with noise—the rain pounding on every leaf and trunk, the constant rumble of near and distant thunder, the stream churning like river rapids somewhere nearby. "Everett!" Holly yelled, grasping her hood around her face. "It's not safe!"

"We should go back!" Ben agreed.

"No, wait. Over here!" Everett dashed ahead and took cover between two broken trees crisscrossed over a rockfall. The overhanging vines formed a small cave. Holly and Ben ran in after him.

Inside it was steamy with three wet bodies. Holly wrung out her long braids one at a time and wiped her glasses dry.

"We're just asking to get hit by lightning." Ben pushed back his spiky black hair. "Holly, try working a juju on the rain."

"It'll pass," said Everett. "It always does."

Holly blushed. She was a little afraid to use her key in front of the boys, but it vibrated impatiently in its scabbard. She pulled it out. Closing her eyes, she visualized desert sands and camels and cracked ground, pushing the images through her heart into the key. A warmth in her chest traveled down her limbs into her hands, and the cold iron crackled hot beneath her fingers.

The thunder stopped, right in the middle of a rumble.

Holly's eyes flew open.

The rain had calmed to a light mist. The forest brightened, and the wind died down. What had been a raging storm was now just another drizzly day in Britain.

"Ha!" said Ben, ducking out of the cave. "What'd I tell you?"

"Like I said. It always passes." Everett stepped out and started back down the muddy hill.

Holly lagged behind as the boys walked on. Was Everett right? Was it just another coincidence? If it was, why was she furious with him?

"That wasn't just the storm passing," Ben was saying as she caught up. "That was *magic*."

"Whatever," Everett said.

Holly skidded a bit down the hill. "You're the one who wanted us to come here. Do you believe in this stuff or not?"

"I'm just saying not *everything* is magic."

"It doesn't matter," said Ben, stepping between them. "Let's just keep going, okay?"

They trudged through the dripping wood, the only sound the *squish-squish* of their boots in the mud, until the drizzle gave way to intermittent sunlight. Holly halted at the stream, which was even more engorged than it was the day before.

"That's the tree bridge I found." She pointed downstream.

"Oh yeah," said Everett. "I've crossed that way loads of times."

"Of course you have," Holly muttered.

Her cumbersome poncho slowed her down, and the boys got farther and farther ahead. At one point it snagged on a thorny shrub. She yanked it free and lurched forward. Her boot sank into the muck and stuck fast. "I'm coming!" she called ahead, though no one answered. Typical. She grabbed the loops of the boot and braced herself against a sapling, preparing to yank her foot free. But something caught her eye in the gurgling water.

Several smooth river rocks were embedded in the near bank, as if someone very small had built a stone spigot. Out of it poured a stream of clear water.

Holly peered at it—was it a pipe from a sewer line? But she could see none. She held out her finger to the stream, then drew it quickly back.

The arctic water burned her fingertips. Under her poncho, safe in its leather scabbard, the iron key vibrated. Holly pulled it out. Suddenly she heard the familiar hum that had been missing from the wood: a steady flow of current like from a live wire. Magic was still alive in this forest. And the key . . .

It started to pulse in a pattern—a short buzz followed by two long vibrations, then a distinct pause. Over and over, *buzz-vibrate-vibrate*. As if she'd set it as a ring tone.

It was calling her.

"Hey, are you coming or what?" said a whiny voice beside her.

She startled, nearly dropping the key into the rushing current. "Gosh, Ben, way to sneak up on a person."

"We've been waiting at that tree bridge forever. Are you stuck?"

"I'm listening."

"What's going on?" called Everett.

"She's *listening*." Holly refused to look at Ben, though she knew he was rolling his eyes.

Everett walked up and took hold of Holly's hand— the one closed around the key. She wanted to shake him off, but he stood very still. He was listening too.

"Can you feel something?" Ben grabbed her other hand. Holly remembered how this worked; they could only feel the key's vibrations through her. "Wow!"

"Hush," said Holly.

"No, wait," said Ben. "It's like . . . it's Morse code."

The other two stared at him. "Since when do you know Morse code?" Everett asked.

"They use it on Planeterra Six, the deluxe edition." Of course he was talking about his favorite computer game. "See, in order to enter the alien king's mother ship, you've gotta crack this pass code, which is set in a series of dots and dashes. As if that wasn't hard enough, you have to negotiate with this six-eyed dude from Alastra, who's got a complicated social ritual—"

"Ben!" Holly interrupted. "Do you know what this means or not?"

"Yeah, it's a *W*. Just the letter *W*, over and over again."

The three of them fell quiet as the key continued to pulse.

W . . . for *water*?

"See these weird rocks, like a pipe or something?" Holly said. "The key is trying to tell us something about the water, like Mr. Gallaway said."

A shrill screech sounded above their heads. The red parrot landed on a high branch, looking at her very hard with one black eye.

Telling her something.

Holly dropped the boys' hands and thrust the key beneath the stone spigot. The water poured over it, freezing it to her fingers. She gritted her teeth; the key was still pulsing its letter *W*, faster now. She couldn't pull away until it was finished, but finished doing what, she didn't know. Her breath, coming in fierce, pain-racked gasps, began to smoke. A sheet of ice crept over her hand.

"Holly, stop!" Ben cried.

"Don't," said Everett. "She has to keep going."

"It's freezing her to death!"

"Just wait," she said through her teeth. "It's okay." But tears started from her eyes, solidifying into ice crystals on her cheeks.

Then, just as she felt she would have to let go, a weak heat stirred in her chest. It fluttered like a dying flame, then sputtered down her wrist into her fingers, and the ice began to melt.

The key went silent.

Holly pulled away from the icy water, and the hot, delicious sun warmed her blue hand.

The parrot squawked with satisfaction and flew away.

"Are you okay?" With one finger, Ben touched the back of her hand, which was turning pink.

"Yeah. I think so." Holly took a shaky breath. Her jaw hurt from clenching it.

"We ought to have stopped you," Everett said. "It went on too long."

"No, it's all right. Look."

She held up the iron key. One of the symbols forged on the loop—the water symbol—glowed with a blue light. Holly cupped her hands around it against the sun, and the glow brightened.

"Cool," Ben whispered.

"It's ready now," said Holly. "I think it will open the oak tree."

Chapter 6

Quenching the Fire

The boys didn't argue with her. They helped her pull her boot out of the mud, and the three of them followed the stream back to the tree bridge. Although Everett walked across it easily, Holly insisted that Ben straddle the tree trunk, because, as she reminded him, he had failed to learn to swim at camp last month. "Not so loud," he whispered fiercely, glancing at Everett, but he did as she asked.

Holly stuffed her poncho in her backpack when they reached the glade, and just as she started to say, "I can't believe how hot it is," a cloud enveloped the sun and a cold breeze whipped up.

The key vibrated again in her hand. She hadn't put it away.

Ben and Everett hung back, letting her step up to the oak tree alone.

Suddenly she wished that one of them would stand beside her. In a way she liked that things were always

　　　CLAIRE M. CATERER

up to her, but she couldn't help wondering why that was. Why *she* was the Adept, the only one left. Ranulf the centaur had told her that the king had exiled the Adepts native to Anglielle years ago, but he couldn't explain how Holly, a human from another world, could wield their magic. Nor could Almaric, the magician who had befriended her.

As she stepped closer to the oak tree, the iron key extended in front of her like a sword, the hum of the forest rose in pitch, and the key matched it. Her heart quickened. The water symbol glowed faintly on the key, then undulated, like a real wave. It made her feel a little—could she be?—*seasick.*

The breeze stiffened. The sky darkened.

Once again the forest fire glowed orange through the oak tree's ruined keyhole. Taking a deep breath, as if bringing two live wires together, Holly touched the key to it.

It fused there, and Holly couldn't let it go. An icy gurgle of water flooded through the warped keyhole and over her fingers. Her boots sank in the mire up to her ankles as the glade became a bog. A chill wind whipped her braids about her face, and again her hand went numb; the orange glow began to fade.

The lock stretched like pulled taffy, first so long and skinny that the keyhole narrowed to a slit. Then it shrank back, short and fat, and Holly heard a familiar whooshing sound: ocean waves crashing on a rocky beach. A hundred other noises followed, gurgles and splutterings, rainfall, bubbles, and the *drip-drip-drip* of water falling off leaves following a cloudburst. Finally, all at once, the keyhole righted itself with a kind of sigh.

Holly had fixed it.

She felt rather than heard the boys tiptoeing up behind her. Everett took her hand so he could see the lock properly. "You did it," he whispered. "It's perfect."

"Just like it was before," Ben said, too loud, as usual.

Holly tried—and failed—to keep her mouth from turning up in a self-satisfied smile. Of course her magic still worked. After checking that everyone had hands joined, she drove the key into the lock and turned it forcefully.

The three of them planted their feet in the marshy ground, knowing what was coming next: The earth trembled and the oak tree split apart in a bolt of lightning to form a rectangular doorway. They stepped through.

The earthquake stopped.

The lightning didn't.

All at once the clouds dipped low into the forest, creating a strange twilight in the glade. Thunder cracked all around like bombs going off, and Ben clamped his chubby hand around Holly's arm like a lobster. Everett stumbled, sending them all sprawling as a bolt of lightning singed the grass. The rain descended in torrents.

"What'll we do?" Ben yelled above the deluge.

"Find a tree, and fast," Everett said. They staggered to their feet. The water rose to their ankles in the boggy ground. The rain poured over them like a waterfall, and the four beech trees surrounding the glade whipped wildly in the gale. One of them would take them to Anglielle now that Holly had unlocked the oak.

"I don't know which one to choose!" she shouted.

"Go clockwise, like Gallaway said!" Everett pulled the group over to where their portal had once stood. He pointed to the beech to the right of the empty space.

Holly squinted through the rain at the tall, skinny tree. A small keyhole had appeared in its trunk, just like on all the beeches. A rune carved below it looked like a right triangle without a bottom bar, but that meant nothing to Holly. As she gazed into the upper branches, they swayed and undulated, like . . .

Like water.

Another bolt of lightning crackled down, narrowly missing them, and the thunder's sound wave threw them toward the tree trunk.

"Just do it!" Ben cried.

Holly thrust the key into the lock. Ben gripped her arm tight, and Everett took hold of her other elbow. She turned the key and waited for the rumble of earth and the blinding flash that would transport them to Anglielle.

It didn't happen exactly that way.

Chapter 7

Survival Skills

The ground trembled, but the blinding flash was just another bolt of lightning that struck beside them with a resounding *boom* that sent Holly lurching toward the beech. She fell through a wide fork at the tree's base, Ben and Everett tumbling messily behind her, until the three of them ended up . . . someplace.

She couldn't breathe.

Or see.

Her limbs felt strangely heavy. The boys' hands slipped away from her, and Holly scrabbled for them in slow motion. And then she noticed that her feet weren't on the ground either, but bicycling in thin air.

No: in thin *water*.

A light glimmered above, and the water materialized around her. As the light brightened, she saw she was in a murky underwater place filled with rocks and plants and a few long silver fish who wiggled by. She tried to cough, swallowed a mouthful of water, and then, unable to see the others, kicked her way toward the light above.

She gulped cold air and coughed until her ribs ached as she flailed her arms. Where were the boys? Was this some kind of water kingdom? She wasn't in Anglielle—how could she be?

Rain pattered on her face. She breathed deep, tried to calm down. She scissored her legs again, treading water.

Through her spattered glasses she saw that she was in a forest, heading rapidly downstream through a stand of tall grasses and water lilies. She tried to grab one as she floated past, but her hands slid through the slick leaves.

Her hands. The key!

She floated down a fork in the stream into a still pool, and grappled with her backpack, which weighed her down. There, tangled in the straps, was the key— or rather, the wand.

For it was always a wand here.

She *had* to be in Anglielle.

But then, where were the boys?

"Holly! Holl—"

The voice was small and strangled. Holly whipped her head around, searching the trees. *Please, let him be on the bank*. It was Ben.

Ben, who couldn't swim.

Holly paddled toward the bank, flung the backpack among the trees, and shoved the wand back into its scabbard, buckling it in tight. "Ben!" she cried. Her eyes roved through the rushing water.

"Holly! Here!"

She nearly cried with relief. There, clinging to an overgrown root of a beech tree, was Ben's face just barely above the water. Every few seconds, a wave washed over his head, and he sputtered. But he kept hold.

"Hang on! I'll get you out!"

If she could get herself out.

Downstream, she saw Everett, dripping on the near bank, draped over a skinny tree trunk flung across the stream. She let herself drift and grabbed hold of the trunk as she passed, then hauled herself ashore.

Everett's reddish-brown hair was plastered to his head, his ruddy cheeks scratched and bleeding. His chest heaved as if he could never draw enough breath.

"Are you okay?" Holly asked.

"Yeah . . . Ben . . . in the . . . water."

"I know. Stay here, I'll help him."

It sounded brave when she said it. But as she flung herself from one tree to the next, peering through the mist, she wasn't so sure. "Ben!" she called. "Say something!" But she heard nothing but the stream tumbling by.

Then, a sound. She stopped, listening.

"I said, if you'd stop screaming, maybe you'd hear me," said a small, sullen voice a few feet away.

"Ben! Hang on." *Learn to swim, why can't you,* an angry voice inside her said. But she ignored it and groped her way through the forest until she saw his chubby arms wrapped around the tree root. She reached down. "Grab my hand."

She braced one arm around a shrub, ignoring the thorns that tore at her sleeve, and strained the other hand to reach him. His slippery fingers grasped weakly at her wrist. But he was weighed down—his backpack was snagged on another tree root.

"How can I take it off?" he said. "I can't let go!"

"Here." Everett came up behind Holly, dragging a long, ropey vine with him. "Lower this grapevine down. Ben, tie it round your waist. We'll pull you up."

"Give it to me." Holly seized Everett's end and ran to the trunk of the beech tree. She looped it around and tied a half hitch.

"What are you, a sailor?" Everett asked.

"I know how to tie knots, okay? It's a useful survival skill." She took the other end and wound it around her legs and waist in a makeshift harness.

CLAIRE M. CATERER

"Hang on, you're not going down there." Everett grabbed her arm. "You'll never make it."

"He can't drag himself out, either." Whatever Everett might think—and Holly hadn't forgotten his opinion of what girls could and couldn't do—he'd have to save it until after Ben was on dry land. She squished through the mud and sat on the bank. Well, relatively dry land.

"Here." She tossed the loose vine back at Everett. "Ben, I'm coming down."

"And just how's this gonna work?" he asked.

"Pull the slack, Everett! First of all . . ." Holly slid into the water and looped the taut grapevine around one hand, bracing herself against the stream bank. She pulled out her Swiss Army knife and sliced the backpack free, then heaved it up into the forest. Then, grasping the grapevine, she worked her way around to take hold of the tree root just in front of her brother.

"I'm secure, Ben. Now let go and take the vine with both hands. Then Everett will pull you up. Ready?" she hollered up.

"Anytime!" He played out a little slack, and the grapevine settled in the water.

Ben stared at her, goggle-eyed. "I'll have to climb *over* you, Holly."

"Or learn to swim right now. *Which*," she couldn't help adding, "you should've done at camp."

"*Okay*, I'm going." He grabbed hold of the grape-vine and braced one foot on the tree root, his short arms trembling, and then plopped like a fat trout onto Holly's back. His boots skidded over her back and onto her head, smearing mud across her braids and into her neck as he scaled her body like a mountain. Holly gathered up the grapevine's slack as the rushing water tugged at her feet.

"Just a bit farther," Everett said above her head. "That's it . . . I've got you. . . ."

And then, a mighty heave, and she heard the sat-isfying squish of Ben's chubby body landing flat out in the mud.

Now *that* was funny.

"Come on, Holly, you're next," said Everett, pulling the vine taut again.

Holly braced her feet against the tree root and hauled herself up. Everett pulled her the last few feet until she, too, landed in the mud.

For a moment the three of them sat, panting. The rain misted over Holly's glasses and wet silt dripped down her forehead.

"This is a fine welcome," Everett said at last.

Ben threw one arm over his sopping backpack. "So much for packing extra underwear."

Chapter 8

The Black Hollow

Their seat on the drizzly stream bank was a far cry from the warm, sun-dappled forest they'd landed in last summer. The three backpacks were torn, muddied, and waterlogged. The only bright spot Holly could see was that at least her glasses weren't broken, and her wand was safe.

It was cold, besides.

"Look at the trees," Ben said. "I don't think it's summer here."

The forest was bathed in golds and reds, and many of the trees were nearly bare. A thick layer of fresh leaf fall covered the ground.

"It's late in the day, too," said Holly, pushing herself to her feet. "We'd better start walking before it gets dark."

"Just where are we walking *to*?" Ben asked. "Is this even Anglielle?"

"Yes," said Everett. "It's the Northern Wood. Look

there." He pointed away from the stream to a barren rise. "That's where the fire was."

He started up the hill. Holly took Ben's hand to help him up the slippery incline.

"I can make it," he said, though he didn't drop her hand.

"I forgot," she said, nudging him. "That was some pretty fancy climbing in the water."

Ben grinned. "You're easier to climb than that rock wall at home."

"Up here," called Everett. "I see something."

He was standing on top of the hill. The wide hollow was littered with a blackened mess of stumps and burned bracken. Holly's stomach turned.

"This was my fault," she said in a small voice.

"How is it *your* fault?" Ben asked.

"Avery's the one who lit everything up," Everett added. "It's a wonder the whole wood didn't get torched."

But she did feel responsible. She had bungled the Vanishment spell, bringing Prince Avery and the knight Grandor with them. And she'd put her friends in danger. "I don't even know what happened to Jade and the others. What if they—"

"That's what I was talking about," Everett broke in. "What's that shiny thing?" He pointed at a bright orange glow at the edge of the burned-out clearing.

"Maybe some fallen leaves?" Ben suggested.

"Áedán," Holly said softly. "It has to be." She stepped through the shrubs, then slid a few feet down the hill into the valley and ran over to the far side.

The Golden Salamander couldn't speak to her, but he was part of her. She knew he would wait for her return. She pulled back the shrubbery, ready to scoop him up.

But Áedán wasn't there.

It was just a trick of the light. A shaft of sun had broken through the clouds and shone on an old gold pendant. Holly stood still, her chest hollow. Why had she come? No one was waiting for her. Perhaps no one was even alive to wait.

"Is it that salamander thing?" Ben stumbled down the hill behind her.

She turned away, unable to say anything.

"It's something else," said Everett. He picked up the pendant. It was hexagonal, about as big around as a pocket watch, and bright gold. The surface was engraved, divided into four quarters.

"It's like your key, Holly. Look." Everett held the pendant out for all of them to see. Etched around the circle were the symbols for air, fire, water, and earth. A small purple stone joined them in the center.

"I think this is proper gold. But it must have been here for ages." Everett's eyes glinted in its reflection.

Holly took it from his hand to get a closer look. A thin stream of black smoke was seeping out of the pendant. "Is this a locket? What's that smoky stuff?" She pressed a button on one side, but the catch wouldn't open. The smoke drifted around her head and dissipated. A soft, dark whisper wafted by, and a melancholy chill swept through Holly. She held the locket to her ear, but she heard only the wind blowing through the scattered leaves. She handed it to Everett. "Here, you take it. I don't like it."

Everett put the chain around his neck and tucked the locket into his shirt. "I think it's cool."

"Whatever." Holly began to wonder if this really was Anglielle after all, despite how familiar the blackened valley looked. It felt off somehow. Where was everyone? "I don't know what to do. We're miles from Almaric's cottage, and it'll be dark soon."

"Can't you do that disappearing spell?" Ben asked.

"The *Vanishment*. It's too dangerous. I have to visualize the path exactly, and I only have a rough idea of where the cottage is." And, she thought, she wasn't quite ready to attempt a spell that difficult yet.

"Hang on a tick," said Everett. "Holly, didn't you call that centaur bloke last time? Maybe you can do it again."

CLAIRE M. CATERER

"Ranulf," Holly said.

"You don't have a wand for nothing," Everett said. "At least give it a go."

If there was one thing Holly could've asked for—besides dry clothes—it was that Everett would quit trying to take charge. Especially if he was going to be right all the time. She bit back the disappointment of not finding Áedán. If anyone was left in Anglielle, the wand would find them. She pulled it out of the scabbard.

Now in its wand form, the key was more powerful. It didn't just buzz like an angry insect; it thrummed, warming her stiff fingers. She flexed her hand around the shaft, welcoming it back. It had been more than a year since she'd held the wand. She had forged it herself, with the Wandwright's help, out of a switch from a redwood tree. Long and straight, it fit her hand as if it had grown there. The smooth purple amethyst stone nestled in her palm; small etched carvings twined around the shaft, pictures that changed even as she looked at them.

Right now one symbol dominated the wand. Two undulating swirls: the water.

She closed her eyes, picturing the centaur, his chestnut flanks and wild brown curls. *Ranulf, can you hear me? I'm back. I'm right where you left me.*

She felt the warmth surge inside her, shooting out through her fingertips; she knew the wand was working. It emitted no spark, but she could feel something like an invisible charge, reaching out—

And fading away.

Ranulf was nowhere.

"Well?" Ben asked tentatively.

Holly turned back to the boys, swallowing a stupid lump before it turned into tears. "I felt the wand reaching out, but it didn't . . . it didn't go anywhere. It's like he's just *gone*."

"Not gone," said another voice. "Captured."

Chapter 9

The Coracle

The boys looked around. "Who's there?" Everett called.

"Shush," said Holly. She stood very still. She knew that voice.

"Your Ladyship," it said, just over her head. Curled up on the nearest tree branch was a large black cat with bright green eyes. Holly broke into a smile. She wanted to tug him down from the tree and hug him. But he would never have allowed it.

"Jade!" Just saying the name made her feel warm. The large cat was her familiar—a being who augmented her magic and who was forever loyal to her. Jade wasn't always the most polite, but he had never failed to help her.

"At your service." The cat walked down the length of the branch, then eyed the two boys.

"You remember my brother, Ben," Holly said.

"I do," the cat acknowledged. "The brave squire at the king's tournament. And the young knight, as well."

Jade wrinkled his whiskers in Everett's direction, as if a bad smell had just wafted by.

"Everett's our friend," Holly said.

"Of course, Lady Holly. May I say what a relief it is to find you again in the kingdom." The cat's voice, like his coat, was silky and well groomed, with a lilting, slightly Gaelic accent.

Holly suddenly recalled Jade's words. "Did you say Ranulf was *captured*?"

"Imprisoned." Jade's eyes turned steely. "In Reynard's dungeons."

Holly paled. The king was not known for mercy.

"We cannot bide here." The cat leaped neatly from his perch and onto the damp leaves. "I heard your wand's call and came to direct you to safety."

"But what about Almaric?" The magician was old and frail. "He's all right, isn't he? And Bittenbender, and the others?"

"Come quickly."

"Hang on," said Everett. "Where's it we're going, exactly?"

"A safe haven," Jade said, and darted through the trees up the hill, back the way they'd come.

Holly followed the cat, motioning to the boys behind her. She heard Ben say, "It's okay, he's Holly's friend, remember?" and Everett replied, "It's rather hard to tell *who* one's friends are here, remember?"

Holly stumbled through the forest to keep up with Jade. He slipped through the trees back to the brook, which they followed for almost ten minutes before it branched off in two directions. Jade stopped.

"I remember this," Holly said. "Ranulf and I followed this fork northwest. Can we cross it?"

"Nay," the cat said. "We voyage."

Ben came panting up behind them. "Did he say *voyage*?"

Jade nodded at a stand of nearby rushes. Holly pulled them back and found a funny, bowl-shaped craft moored to a willow tree. The little boat was made of tightly woven branches, with a single narrow board nailed across the middle as a seat.

Ben's face turned an unhealthy shade of white, and Everett snorted. "Are the three of us meant to fit in a coracle?"

The cat stepped carefully over the wet stream bank. "I came to transport the Lady Adept to safety. I was unaware there would be"—he sniffed—"*passengers.*"

Everett said something else in a miffed tone, but Holly wasn't listening anymore. Just beyond the willow tree where the coracle was tied, she glimpsed something else. This time she didn't want to announce it. Instead she walked through a stand of cattails to a leafless oak tree. At its base lay a ring of smooth river rocks, and in the center a small fire blazed. Curled up in the flames was the tiny, amber-colored Salamander. He stirred at her approach, opened his bulbous golden eyes, and leaped from his nest onto her shoulder.

Holly jumped back, half expecting to be burned, but Áedán's sticky feet were only pleasantly warm. "You're here!" she said, smiling. "You're all right."

The Golden Salamander nestled against her neck; he and Holly shared a contented sigh. He could not speak, nor was he a pet; he was her protector, a creature she had freed from his nest at the Wandwright's home more than a year ago. For all of that time, Holly had felt the chill of his absence on her shoulder. But she was whole again now. His essence, born of fire, fueled the magic in her. She was a child of the fire too, like her namesake, the holly tree. Somehow she was more *herself* with Áedán by her side.

Suddenly remembering the others, she stepped back to the coracle. "Look, Jade! I found him! Almaric was right."

"Áedán has slept these many months waiting for your return," the cat told her.

Ben's eyes lit up at the sight of the geckolike creature. "I told you he'd be okay." He raised a single finger but then pulled it back. "Is he . . . slimy?"

"No, you can pet him. Carefully."

Holly was impressed with how gently Ben ran his tentative finger over Áedán's head.

"Look," Everett broke in, sounding peevish, "if we're going to *voyage*, we'd best get on with it."

"We must make haste," Jade agreed, and leaped into the stern of the coracle.

"I don't guess anyone's got a life jacket?" said Ben.

Everett and Holly just stared at him.

The coracle dipped and nearly capsized as Everett stepped into it. He sat in the middle to balance the boat. Ben joined him, his face turning a greenish color as if he were already seasick. Ignoring this, Holly followed him, then pulled the craft to the bank and untied it.

As soon as the boat was free, it shot away from the shore. At first Holly thought the white-tipped current was driving it, but then she realized they were rushing *upstream*.

"Holly, slow it down!" Ben cried.

"You will not need to navigate," said Jade. Glancing back, Holly saw the cat was balanced perfectly, his whiskers blown back against his cheeks. "The coracle is a very old one of Almaric's, given to him by one of the Water Elementals."

"Holly, face the front!" Ben snapped.

For several minutes no one said anything, as every-one's attention was fixed on keeping their seats. Like a tube pulled from a motorboat, the coracle bounced along the surface of the water, rattling its passengers' shoulders and landing them painfully on their back-sides. It whipped from side to side, lurching around boulders and tree roots. Holly's stomach roiled, and she could tell Ben was close to getting sick. Everett sat up straight, like a ship's mast, though his face was tight.

Holly concentrated on the trees as they flitted by on the shoreline. The wood looked much as she remembered, though the air was damp and cold. Through the treetops she glimpsed a low cloud cover. Golden-leafed beech trees glowed in the autumn light, and flocks of migrating birds took flight as they sped by. A hawk screeched overhead and Holly took a deep, chilly breath. She could not deny that she was wet through, that her hair was matted with mud, her feet freezing, her backpack a wreck. But the air—the *feel* of Anglielle, a world suffused with something that was also inside her—held a rightness she couldn't explain to Ben or Everett. She didn't think of her mother or father, or her comfortable bed or the little village of Hawkesbury: Here in this cold, misty misery, in her coracle sailing to a place no one could tell, she was home. And she was happy.

CLAIRE M. CATERER

Chapter 10

The Sea Hag

Everett knew that a coracle was meant to drift along a quiet stream or pond, helped along by a paddle, carrying *one* passenger and perhaps a fishing pole. The way Holly's cat friend was doing things they might've been in a speedboat. Everett's fingers ached from gripping the pine seat as the craft churned through the white water, threatening at every moment to hurl them all into the rushing stream, which had swollen into a narrow river.

He wasn't used to cats who spoke, whatever strange things he'd seen in this kingdom (and he had seen plenty). The last time they were in Anglielle, he and Ben had spent most of their time in the king's castle with a group of unfriendly knights. Everett had met one little fairy, a fire Elemental, but she hadn't been very nice in the end either. Holly, on the other hand, had met centaurs and talking cats and strange ladies who fashioned magic wands out of thin air, and what's more, everyone had considered Holly a hero—the last of the Adepts, which were a race of sorcerers. But Everett had been taken for a criminal. His own hold on magic had been all too brief, thanks to the fire Elemental.

He'd spent the last thirteen months getting past all that. He tried to come up with ways to help these Exiles that Holly talked about, the ones the king was so keen on hunting. Everett had once thought that perhaps they *ought* to be hunted, because the prince Avery had said so, and he seemed like such a regular bloke. But he had betrayed them, standing by as one of his knights tried to skewer the three of them. So while Everett told himself he wanted to be on the right side this time, he also thought that putting Avery in his place would be a pretty sweet side benefit.

The river narrowed again to a stream, and the coracle slowed. The trees grew closer here, nearly touching over the surface of the water. They were deep in the wilds of the wood now. Everett could see no discernible paths, only the tiny trails worn by chipmunks and badgers. But this was where the coracle stopped moving altogether, and at a few words from Jade, Holly let the boat drift to shore and lashed it to a tree.

It was noticeably darker outside than when they'd set out. Everett's watch was no use, for it still read ten

CLAIRE M. CATERER

in the morning. His stomach lurched as he stumbled onto the bank. "'Scuse me," Ben said, and shoved by him. He was promptly sick at the foot of a birch tree.

Everett's head ached, but at least his stomach was returning to normal. He pulled the backpacks out of the boat and handed them around, then followed Holly, who followed the black cat, up the bank and through a stand of birch and oak. Yellow leaves drifted all around them.

"We're close, aren't we, Jade?" Holly sounded excited. Everett couldn't imagine anything much existing this deep in the forest, but in another few minutes they had rounded a bend and gone over another hill to find themselves in a quite civilized clearing. At the edge of it, two enormous trees grew very close together, or perhaps they were one tree with two trunks; and in between them was a low, arched wooden door that looked as if it had sprouted out of the ground.

"Almaric!" Holly cried. She ran ahead and around the giant tree to a small side window. "Almaric, it's me, Holly!"

The door opened, and Ben nudged up next to Everett. Neither of them had met the old magician before, and they weren't quite sure what to expect.

An old, plump woman was certainly not it.

She looked more like a fat brown mushroom than

a person, almost as wide as she was tall, which wasn't very. Her blobby nose stretched across plump cheeks, and her bulbous gray eyes were set wide apart on a chinless face. She wore a formless, gray-green robe, the color of which matched her hair, hanging in a lanky, slimy mass around her shoulders. The smell wafting from her was like bad fish or rotten eggs. Or both.

"Almaric!" Holly called again.

"I wouldn't put much store by doin' that, dearie," said the old woman in a burbly croak. She waddled into the glade and craned her nearly invisible neck toward the window.

Holly turned to her. "I . . . Where's Almaric? Who are you?"

The woman poked one of her stubby fingers into her ear. Having extracted a small slug, she held out her hand. "Nerys. Sea hag. Howdy do?"

When Holly didn't respond, Everett nudged Ben and stepped forward. "Hallo," he said, trying to sound cheerful. "I'm Everett and this is Ben. That's—"

"The *Lady* Holly," Jade cut in, glaring at Everett. "The Adept."

"Ooo-hoo! That's right, he said you'd be comin' soon! Nerys. Sea hag," she repeated, and showed off a very few jagged teeth.

"Yes, sorry, nice to, uh . . . meet you." Holly looked as if she was trying not to breathe too close to the sea hag. "But where's Almaric? Doesn't he live here?"

"No, not so much, as I'd say."

"What? Why not?"

"Why, 'cause he's dead, that's wot."

The color drained from Holly's muddy face. She glanced at Jade, whose eyes grew round, and the two of them dashed into the cottage.

The old woman ignored them and grinned at Everett. "You lads fancy a glass o' kelp wine?"

Chapter 11

The Dead Magician

Holly and Jade glanced wildly around the cottage's front room. The stone fireplace was cold, and the kettle hanging there hadn't been filled in an age. Even the chintz-covered furniture was dusty.

"The bedroom," Holly said, and dashed to the back of the cottage.

There, on a bed shaped like a crescent moon to fit the round walls, lay the magician, his white hair and beard as bushy as Holly remembered. His bare feet poked out of the linen robe edged with embroidered leaves. The blue eyes were closed, the wrinkled hands folded on his chest.

"Oh, Jade . . ." Holly's eyes brimmed with tears as she approached the bed. "How did this happen? Was it that woman?" A hollow coldness filled her chest. Ranulf was gone, Almaric was . . . she could hardly even think the word. . . .

"Stand aside, Lady Holly." Jade leaped onto the bed.

He touched his nose to Almaric's, then sniffed around his eyes and cheeks.

"Jade, please don't." It seemed disrespectful, and too much like something an ordinary cat would do. But Jade only spared her a disdainful look and placed a paw firmly over the magician's nose.

"What're you—" Holly started to say, but the old man suddenly flailed about, coughing and spluttering, and his eyes flew open.

"What in blazes!" he exclaimed, leaping to a half-sitting position.

Holly gaped at him. "Almaric? Are you . . . all right?"

"Lady Holly!" The magician sprang off the bed like a young man and put a hand to his hair, smoothing it down. "How wonderful to see you! Jade, did you—"

Whatever he'd been about to say was muffled in Holly's impromptu hug. She knew she would embarrass him—in fact, he blushed and scrambled about for his walking stick, which he located next to the bed. "Yes, well . . . good work, Jade, finding Her Ladyship. Awfully fine of you."

"Ranulf's predictions were quite accurate," Jade said coolly. He leaped onto the nearby dressing table and preened his whiskers.

"But wait," Holly said, still confused. "Were you . . . You *weren't*, were you?"

"Dead, you mean? I do apologize," Almaric said cheerily. "A small ruse. It's a magician's talent. I simply couldn't abide that woman any longer. The, ah . . . well, her personal . . ."

"Smell?" Holly provided.

"To put it bluntly." He beamed at her, his blue eyes nearly disappearing into his cheeks. "But never mind! Now that you have returned to us, things can be put to rights."

"The two lads have arrived with Her Ladyship, Almaric," said Jade. "One is her kinsman; the other"— he paused to swipe a paw across his face—"is the traitor."

"Oh no," Holly said, shaking her head. "Everett was a prisoner, like Ben."

"He worked with stolen magicks," Jade said.

"Now, Jade," Almaric broke in. "That is all in the past."

"He did steal that key—the wand—from Mr. Gallaway. But he doesn't even have it anymore. Prince Avery took it." Holly paused. However Everett had acted before, they were all a year older, weren't they? And everyone makes mistakes sometimes. "I think he's all right now."

Jade sniffed and twitched his tail.

"They're waiting outside. We really ought to get them out of the cold."

"My very thought," Almaric said. "And if I may say so, with all due respect, Your Ladyship . . ." He hesitated.

"You could all do with a wash," Jade finished.

What Holly really wanted to know was what had happened to Ranulf, and how long had she been away, and who was the sea hag, and a hundred other things. But Almaric would hear none of it until the three of them had taken turns in the bath, which was heated with a spell he was quite proud of. Their clothes were clean by the time they were finished. Even then Almaric refused to say another word until the kettle was on and a large potful of stew was simmering over the fire. The sun was going down as they settled into the soft chintz chairs opposite Almaric's low table and sipped the wild-scented tea he gave them.

"Now," Holly said at once. "What's happened to Ranulf?"

"Raethius of the Source appeared to the Mounted not three months gone," Almaric said. "He demanded their knowledge of the stars to predict your return. When they resisted, he captured Ranulf. He has been held in the king's dungeons ever since."

"And this Raethius guy controls the king, right?" Ben asked.

"He controls all of Anglielle," said Jade, "but he takes little interest in the mortal kingdom and is rarely at the castle. The subjugation of magic is his passion. When last you were in Anglielle, Raethius was on one of his journeys. He did not learn of your visit until long after you had gone. But when he did hear of it, his rage was so great that it destroyed one of the castle towers. So say the falcons."

"I don't understand," said Holly. "What does Raethius care about me?"

Jade held her gaze with his own steady green eyes. "You are the last Adept. He knows that much. You are a threat to the king's power, and a threat to the king is a threat to his puppeteer."

The group fell silent. Even with Áedán on her shoulder, Holly felt a cold finger of dread dance down her spine.

"I . . . I can't worry about him," she said. "We have to focus on Ranulf. How can we get him out of there?"

"It's suicide to storm the castle by force," Almaric said. "But if we could bewitch the guards somehow, we may have a chance."

"Maybe there's a spell I can learn," Holly said. "Some kind of sleeping spell, or—"

"I know the very one!" crowed the sea hag. Everyone startled; Holly had almost forgotten she was there, for she had been sulking in a corner ever since the word *bath* had been mentioned. "It takes but one word, and the knights'll drown on dry land. Their lungs fill with seawater, they gurgle and gasp, then drop right in front o' yer eyes!"

"That sounds pretty good," Ben said.

"No, it doesn't," said Holly. "It sounds pretty awful. This isn't one of your video games, Ben. Those knights are real people—and remember, Loverian saved our lives. Do you really want me to drown them?"

"Most of them would kill us as soon as look at us," Everett put in.

"So we're supposed to be as bad as they are?"

"'Tis a war, dearie, not a tea party," said Nerys.

"There's got to be another way. Almaric?"

Holly knew he had limited knowledge of Adept magic, but some was better than nothing. With the Adepts themselves gone, Holly had to learn on her own.

Almaric eyed Jade, fidgeting. "Yes, Lady Holly. I may know of an alternative."

Chapter 12

The Few Options

"Absolutely not, Almaric," said Jade, baring his teeth. "We agreed. We dare not invoke such a creature."

"We didn't *quite* agree, Jade. She could solve both our problems, killing two birds with one powerful stone. She could help us rescue Ranulf first of all, and then—"

"Hang on, *who* could help us?" Everett asked.

"We be callin' up the sea witch!" Nerys said, clapping her pudgy hands. "This very night, the night of Samhain, when the veil 'twixt the worlds is thinnest, we'll call her and she'll have ter come, innit?"

"What's the night of sow-en?" asked Ben.

"Samhain. It's like the Celtic Halloween," said Everett.

Almaric had risen from his chair and started serving the stew. Jade followed him. "You know this is folly," he said.

"Ranulf and I discussed it months ago," said the magician.

CLAIRE M. CATERER

"Why?" Holly asked. "What did Ranulf want with this . . . sea witch?"

"Before he was taken," Almaric said, "Ranulf and I had talked of a plan to begin the overthrow of the king."

"Really? What kind of plan?"

"The Exiles' numbers are fairly strong, but without the power of the Adepts, they remain scattered and frightened. It's difficult to rally the troops, if you will. Of course, Lady Holly, your own powers are formidable. But if we could find the rest of the Adepts and bring them home—"

"You could finish the king for good," said Everett.

"And more to the point, we would have a chance at defeating Raethius." Almaric pulled a stool up to the table and began eating. "Bring down the Sorcerer, and the king is as good as deposed."

Nerys snorted. "I don't see the Adepts makin' a speedy return."

"They are imprisoned on an unknown island," Almaric said, as if he'd explained this several times before. "The details aren't clear, but we know they vanished off the Iardan coast by boat when Reynard's knights attacked their settlement. No doubt their exile is Raethius's doing."

"And there's, like, a cloaking spell hiding them?" Ben suggested.

"Ranulf and I believe," Almaric said, "that if we could sail close enough to the Adepts' island, we could detect it, even if Raethius has hidden it. With the lady Holly's help, we could break through the barrier. But we have no craft nor sailing knowledge—"

"That's why we're callin' the sea witch!" Nerys crowed. "No shame in it, dearie! It's what I do."

"Just wait," Holly said loudly, and everyone quieted. "Jade, tell me what you think."

The cat's tail bristled. "We have no sea chart pointing us to the Adepts' location. But conjuring the sea witch is not to be taken lightly. She is dangerous and unreliable. How do we know she would help rescue Ranulf in the first place? Once freed, this is a genie that will be impossible to put back in its bottle."

"She's a genie?" Ben asked eagerly.

Jade sniffed at him. "I was making a point."

"And I say our options are very few," said Almaric.

"What about the others who could help us?" Holly asked. "Like Fleetwing, or maybe Bittenbender?"

"As I say, I'm afraid the Exiles are somewhat scattered," said Almaric. "Not all of them believed you would return, Lady Holly. We have not seen Fleetwing since Midsummer. The changeling has vanished. Even the Mounted have kept themselves hidden. But Hornbeak the falcon has gone to find them, as well as

Bittenbender. Some of his own people, the Dvergar, are also held in the castle dungeons. He may be willing to help us, now that . . ."

Holly squeezed her hand into a fist, touching her fingertips to the long scar down her palm. "Now that I'm back."

"But we need more magic than brute strength to overcome the castle guards, and that the sea witch can give us." Almaric looked hard at Jade. "Regardless, this is our only chance to conjure her. Once Samhain has passed, she will be unreachable."

"Enough talk." The sea hag rocked back on her stool until the momentum set her upright on her squat legs. "The moon is near risen. If the sea witch's to be called, the time is now. You lot, begone, so's I can prepare." She shooed Almaric away, but then pulled Everett by his sleeve and gave him a watery grin. "Not the lads. Ye can help me."

Almaric stood up and lit a small glass lantern, then motioned to Holly. She grinned at Everett, who scowled back, and followed Almaric into the glade, with Jade at her heels.

They settled on the tree stumps that served as Almaric's patio furniture. "You're not taking cold, Lady Holly?" asked Jade.

The air was chilly, but the little Salamander on

her shoulder warmed her enough. "It's fine."

"But something troubles you."

How could she explain it? She had hoped this would be easier. But what had she expected? Strolls through the forest with Ranulf? A quick, painless battle to dethrone the king? More than that, she hadn't even thought about . . .

"Raethius," she said in a voice just above a whisper. "Jade, how bad are things? Tell me the truth."

The cat looked at Almaric, who shifted in his seat, looking away. "The Sorcerer has grown in power, but he shows signs of desperation. He has had the magic-folk subdued for years, but then he heard of your visit and the stirrings of an uprising. We hear rumors that dark creatures have appeared from the Gloamlands at his bidding. He poisoned a school of freshwater merfolk in one of the northern lochs. An enclave of the Dvergar was found on the moors, their bodies gutted—"

A wave of nausea washed over Holly. "I just don't understand it," she said. "Why would he do this? Raethius is a sorcerer. Why does he kill the magicfolk?"

"We're not certain," said Almaric. "So little is known of him. Some say he came from the Gloamlands himself—the lands in the wilds of the north. Some think he may have Elemental blood. But it is clearly

CLAIRE M. CATERER

his mission to subdue the magicfolk, to divide us and leave us cowering in the woods."

"I believe his aim since the beginning has been to amass the kingdom's most powerful magicks for some other, darker purpose," said Jade. "Why else would he travel so often? The mortalfolk are not his concern, and he uses Reynard's knights as fodder. He searches for something." Jade raised a whiskered eyebrow at Holly. "Something he fears you will prevent his obtaining, perhaps."

Áedán huddled close to Holly's neck with a shiver.

The cottage door opened and the sea hag popped her head out. "We're as ready as ever we'll be, Yer Ladyship. Or will ye stay in the gloamin' till dawn?"

Chapter 13

Calling the Sea Witch

Everett was less than happy about being drafted for sea hag duty. He had the feeling, as the others left him and Ben alone with Nerys, that Holly thought she was entitled to plan everything. Everett thought it should be more of a democracy. Yet here they were, getting ready to conjure some kind of witch who everyone seemed a bit wary of.

It seemed to Everett like a very bad idea.

At Nerys's direction, he started stacking Almaric's wicker furniture in one corner. Maybe Ben was used to Holly taking charge, but Everett wasn't. Hadn't he managed to keep himself and Ben alive the last time they were here? No one—not even Ben—knew how close Everett had come to making a horrible bargain with the Elemental. The fiery little person who called herself Sol had agreed to give Everett the magic he needed to earn his and Ben's freedom, but in exchange she wanted Holly—for what purpose, Everett was never quite sure. But when he didn't deliver her, which of course he *couldn't* do, Sol snatched the magic away from him. Although he knew he had done the right thing, he had felt the loss ever since. That wand had made him special, made him *someone*. He liked that feeling just as much as Holly did.

He wasn't sure what this old magician knew about him, though Jade clearly didn't like him. Everett was hoping that this time around he might prove himself and get to do a bit of the magic that Holly was always going on about. He set down the chair he was carrying and pulled the chain from inside his shirt. The gold locket gleamed at his touch. This, at least, was all his. No stolen wands or agreements with dodgy magical creatures. Idly, he tried to spring the catch to open the locket, but it held fast.

A finger of smoke oozed from inside it and circled him, as if something inside the locket were burning. But the gold didn't feel hot. Everett squeezed his eyes shut. His head felt thick and dizzy.

"This table ain't movin' itself," Nerys called to him.

Everett glared at her, but he dropped the locket inside his shirt. He took a deep breath; his head cleared.

Ben helped him move Almaric's low table to the center of the room. Nerys covered it with a black cloth and opened her rucksack. Out of it she took a small skull—it might have been a monkey's, Everett told himself, but he could see it was probably a child's—and a very sharp silver-handled knife. She laid the knife crosswise to the skull, which she placed in the center of the table. She cut a long, thick rope to a length of about three feet, and laid it parallel to the knife. Finally she arranged five black beeswax candles around the other items.

Everett watched all this in silence until Ben nudged him aside. "Do you think this is okay? She's kinda—I don't know—black magicky."

"We don't have much choice, do we?" Everett whispered back. "Anyway, they're Holly's friends, right?"

"*She's* nobody's friend, far as I can tell," said Ben, eyeing Nerys. She was busy sprinkling something shiny on the surface of the altar. "And what's this about a sea witch? Isn't a sea *hag* bad enough?"

"All ready, methinks," Nerys said. She gave them a hard look as if she'd heard everything they'd been saying, then walked out and called the others in from the clearing.

"It's now or never," she said as everyone gathered around the table. "Time grows short."

"Of course, Nerys," Almaric said, smiling nervously. Everett noticed that Nerys had spread several gold coins, like doubloons, among the other objects.

"The sea witch only comes with a price," Nerys said, following his eyes. "Now then. All take hands round the altar."

Holly and Jade exchanged a look, but they did as she asked.

"I don't like this," Ben muttered.

"Not to worry, Ben," Almaric said, smiling. But his wrinkled hand, clasping Everett's, was sweaty, and the old man's eyes roved back and forth from the door back to the altar. "All will be well."

Nerys stood up on her waddly feet to light the candles, then rejoined them at the altar, completing the circle. Clearly, Ben wasn't crazy about holding her pudgy, algae-smelling hand, but she snatched his up and held it so tight that he winced.

"Eyes closed," she commanded, and then began to chant:

> *"Beyond the land, we call to thee*
> *Come over swell and over sea*
> *Pull the anchor from the sand*
> *Bide a time upon the land*
>
> *Sea witch of legend, ship of yore*
> *Whose voyage wide, from shore to shore*

Will steer us true, to isles of gloom
By witch's compass, witch's broom

Come hither, to the magic elm
Where dwelleth those of earthly realm
And bring ye aid, what we desire
Through the storm, through muck and mire."

Though the chanting was soft and lulling, at the end Nerys threw up both her flabby arms and cried in a louder, deeper voice than Everett would have believed possible:

"Now come!"

At once, a strong, wet breeze blew through the window and extinguished the candles. Ben whimpered and a chill snaked down Everett's back. He heard a soft gasp from Holly. Almaric said nothing, but grasped his hand tight; and the moon went dark.

Inside the cottage Everett could see nothing. Even the fire in the hearth had gone out, leaving a thick, palpable gloom. Outside, a gust of wind rocked the elm trees and shook the cottage. Rain followed immediately, the same sort of relentless, bucketing rain that had plagued Hawkesbury all summer. He heard a great burbling, as from the overswollen stream, though the sound was too loud for that, almost like waves crashing on a shore. The earth trembled. The front door flew open with a bang at the same moment the moon broke from the clouds, backlighting a dark figure who stood in the lashing rain.

It growled: "Who's callin' us out in this infernal weather, then?"

The fire bloomed in the hearth again, flooding the room with a weak light, and in stepped a squat, dark-haired little man with a fierce scowl and a battle-axe propped over one shoulder.

"Is't the Adept?" the creature said. "'Cause she owes me."

Chapter 14

The Sea Hag's Lesson

Holly jumped as Nerys pushed away from the table. "Earthfolk!" she spat. "What the devil is *he* doin' here? The sea witch don't mix with Earthfolk! Of all the nerve." She padded squishily over to her stool. "Spell's broken, thankee very much, I *don't* think."

Almaric dropped Holly's hand and stood up. "Nonsense, Nerys. I've invited Bittenbender here to help us! And . . ." He looked questioningly at the Dvergar, who grunted and jerked a thumb behind him. Two other men, neither of them any taller than Ben, entered the cottage. Both were bearded, though one of them, who had a shock of very red hair, was clearly younger than the other, who was dark like Bittenbender and wore a squashed hat over a low, beetling brow.

Bittenbender waved them forward. "This here's Swikehard"—he indicated the dark-haired Dvergar—"and our ginger's Wiggers. He's not long a man, but good in a fecht, all the same."

Bittenbender's was the first familiar face Holly had seen that didn't prompt her to give him a hug. "This is my brother, Ben, and our friend Everett," she said. "This is Bittenbender, leader of the Dvergar."

"I recall 'em," said Bittenbender. "The cause of all the trouble, if memory serves."

"Or you might say," said Almaric, "the catalyst that brought us all together. Had we not united to rescue these boys—"

"Then some of my men would still be with us." The little man scowled at Holly. "Did ye know about *that*? The king has been hunting us ever since the Battle of Midsummer, and here I am again, coming to Yer Ladyship's aid."

In Holly's experience the Dvergar did very little that did not benefit himself. "We're glad you're here," she said, trying to mean it. "But what about the sea witch?"

"The spell's cast. She'll come when she's needed, if the magic wasn't broken too soon," Nerys said from her sulky corner.

"But she ain't here yet?" said Swikehard. He slid a dark look toward Bittenbender.

"Then this mission's a lot o' blethers," the leader said. "Where's yer *magic*, Lady? Ain't that meant to be worth somethin'?"

A loud argument erupted on all sides. Almaric

berated the Dvergar for not showing Holly the proper respect; Bittenbender bellowed that he wasn't sending his men to get slaughtered; Ben said they were ready to take on the knights, whatever the cost; and Holly tried to quiet them all down. But what actually got everyone's attention was the Dvergar throwing his dagger into the center of the table. It stuck upright and thrummed.

"Tha's better," he said grimly. "Here's our position, *Lady* Adept. We'll stay the night and no longer. Iffin ye can't come up with a real plan by nightfall tomorrow, we're heading back to the settlement." He sheathed the dagger and motioned to Swikehard and Wiggers. "Come on, lads. We've no problem sleepin' in the glaur. Although"—he looked pointedly at Almaric—"we'd not say no to a nippy."

Almaric groaned and rummaged around for a bottle of something dark to give to the Dvergar. Once he'd brought it to them and returned, Holly said, "We can't be sure the sea witch is coming. We'll have to figure out another plan, and fast, or Bittenbender and his men won't stay to help us either."

"Don't jump down my throat," Ben said, "but what about that other idea? The—drowning thing."

"*No.*" She glared at Ben and looked for a moment very like her mother.

"Okay, okay. Then what about some other spell? Almaric, didn't you teach Holly that Vanish-me thing? You must know some other ones."

"I have my own spells, of course, Ben. But a magician's magic is quite different to the Adepts'. You must understand, I was a friend to them—as much as they *had* friends—but they guarded their spellwork jealously. I happened to see the Vanishment performed, but I hardly have a catalog of spells at my disposal. That is . . ." He trailed off, then busied himself with the kettle again.

Jade narrowed his green eyes. "What is it you're not telling us, Almaric?"

"What? Nothing, nothing. The tea is about ready, I think."

"Blast the tea," Everett said. "If you know something that can help us, out with it."

"No, indeed. It was forbidden for magicians—for *anyone*—to study the Adepts' grimoires. Obviously, I would have had no such access." The old man cleared his throat and blinked nervously at the sea hag. "However, Nerys . . ."

"Thought ye didn't like *my* spells," said Nerys, squeezing a slug from one armpit. "Besides, Samhain's nearly past and I'm dryin' out. Gots to be gettin' back to the sea, I do."

"Nerys, please," said Holly. "Do you know anything

I could use that wouldn't kill the guards? Maybe just put them to sleep?"

The sea hag rocked herself off her stool, puddling the floor. She jabbed a fat finger at Holly. "You. Alone." She jerked her head toward the door.

Holly followed her outside, under the dripping trees. The moon was nearly full, but hidden mostly behind the clouds again. Off to the other side of the cottage, Holly could hear the Dvergar's noisy snores. Nerys sat down with a squish on one of the tree stumps and invited Holly to join her, as if it were her house.

"About time you and I had a little girl talk, dearie," she said. "These others—the magician, the lads, even the Dvergar—not real magicfolk like the two of us, eh?" She nudged Holly with one slimy elbow. "Here now. I gots a giftie for ye."

She reached into the folds of her foul dress and pulled out a remarkably dry circlet made of small purple flowers. "It's the heather, like yer own wand contains."

Holly glanced down at her scabbard, surprised.

"Ye can't hide it, dearie. The water herb calls out louder'n a willow whale, innit?"

"This is very nice, Nerys." Holly didn't want to offend the sea hag, but she was more interested in spells than accessories just at the moment.

"It grants ye power over the water element," Nerys

said. "Ye've not got much time ter be learnin' new spells, and this charm will give yer magic a boost. Put it on now, an' I'll show ye the spell I've in mind. It calls the water. See here." Nerys closed her eyes and mouthed a few words. A cluster of raindrops trembled on the yellow leaves of a nearby pin oak. They pulled together like quicksilver, flew through the air, and poured in a stream over Nerys's head.

"It casts a waterfall," Nerys said as the water sluiced off her. "It'll hold those it touches in a trance, if it's done right."

She snuffled, then blew a snail out of one nostril and tossed it in her mouth. "Ye'll need to practice it. The sea hag don't need to speak a spell aloud, but Adept magic's different. Commit the words to yer mind: *tubhair eas*. Try it on me. I'm dry as a stone."

Holly pointed the wand at the trees and thought of the heather, and the words *tubhair eas*. Then she uttered them.

The wand bucked in her hands, and a shower of rainwater shook off the branches. It didn't gather in a nice stream as it had for Nerys, who frowned at her. "The heather. Put it round yer neck." She pointed at the circlet of flowers, which Holly still held in one hand.

"Don't, Lady Holly." Jade crept out of the cottage doorway into the moonlight.

"And who asked you, then?" Nerys jerked her head around and snarled. A cloud of steam rose off her shoulders. "I was meant to speak with the Adept *alone*. She's born of fire, innit? She holds the Salamander."

Nerys gave Holly a slimy grin and laughed to cover her anger. "Fire Adepts do have their problems with water magic, Lady. Fire and water—they don't mix. I'm jus' tryin' ter help. Ye can't call the water otherwise, without practicin' the craft day and night. I was made to think ye didn't *have* all day and night."

"And I say the Adept will not be donning your charm." Jade leaped onto the tree stump, sniffed at the heather circlet in Holly's hand, then pointed at her belt loop. "Attach it there."

Nerys fixed Jade with her bulbous eyes and Holly backed away. Whatever help the sea hag was giving, Holly would follow Jade's advice first. She tied the heather flowers to her belt loop, raised her wand, and uttered the spell again. This time a silver snakeling of water flew through the air and doused Nerys, who glared at Holly and Jade both. "Well," she said finally. "Guess my work is done, then."

Chapter 15

To the Castle

They were a tense, strange party that crept through the woods the following night. Hoofstone, a palomino centaur, had arrived an hour before. He carried Holly, Everett, Jade, and Bittenbender. A russet centaur named Brune carried the others. Ben, who was very allergic to horses, had taken his medicine but still sniffled constantly until Wiggers whispered, "Put a sock in it, can't ye?" Ben, Holly observed, deliberately wiped his nose on the back of the Dvergar's leather tunic.

Holly had spent the day practicing the few spells she knew. As she worked, she could hear the boys on the other side of the clearing. The red-haired Wiggers was helping them with their swordplay. This sounded something like, "Hey, you don't have to poke so *hard*" (Ben) and "I *am* feinting, quit nagging, you little git" (Everett) and "Ef ye cannae even *heft* a sword, ye've no hope of swingin' one" (Wiggers).

Now, riding through the night on Hoofstone's back,

Holly touched Nerys's charm on her belt loop. She was glad to have it, even if it felt a little like cheating. She agreed with Jade; she was glad the sea witch hadn't shown up. Only the king or Raethius knew where to find the Adepts' island, and without their nautical charts, searching for it seemed like a pointless voyage. But Holly still needed someone to train her, and no one else knew the Adepts' spells. For now she was on her own.

Once the centaurs had cleared the woods, they broke into a gallop along the edge of the forest leading to the castle. Holly was forced to wrap her arms around Bittenbender to keep from falling off, and the crossbow on his back cut into her chest. Also, the smell wasn't particularly pleasant.

Within the hour Holly spied the harsh stone fortress rising on its rocky cliff. A river fed the moat that ringed it. The falcons were right: Raethius had reduced one of the castle's four towers to a pile of rubble. Her ears ached from the cold wind, and she eyed the sky warily. The huge, round moon threw stark shadows across their path. They may as well have announced themselves with a bullhorn.

"Courage, Lady Holly," Jade whispered as the shadow of the gatehouse towers fell across them. "It is an Adept's greatest asset."

CLAIRE M. CATERER

Actually, Holly thought that magic was an Adept's greatest asset, and she still wished she knew more about it. But they crept silently along the length of the moat, their sounds muffled by the gently coursing water. Bittenbender tapped on Hoofstone's shoulder. "Right, now. Stick to the plan. After ye cross back, the two of ye wait, hear? No chargin' in. We're not takin' the castle, after all. We'll need ye only if the Adept's spell fails us."

Hoofstone nodded. "For Ranulf."

Bittenbender drew his dagger. The other Dvergar followed suit. Ben's sword screeched as he pulled it out, and Swikehard shoved him. "Keep quiet!"

"Leave him alone!" Holly raised the wand to Swikehard's face.

The Dvergar muttered an oath, and they stepped along the bank of the moat toward the gatehouse. The drawbridge had been raised for the night, and the water shown black in the shadows of the gatehouse towers.

Now came Holly's part of the plan. *Please don't make me look like an idiot.* She nodded at Jade and raised her wand.

It trembled over the surface of the water as she closed her eyes. A comforting warmth spread up to her chilled ears and back to her stiff fingers. She pictured gathering the water, and uttered the sea hag's spell: *"Tubhair eas."*

The whole group skipped back from the moat as a silver wave collected itself and flew out of the water. "Wow!" said both of the boys together. Even the Dvergar's faces shone as the moonlight struck the wave's tip.

"Halt!" cried one of guards on the far side of the moat. He was hidden in the shadow of the gatehouse, but Holly saw the shape of the crossbow he raised. "Who comes, in the name of the king?"

"That's Pagett," Everett whispered.

Just as he spoke, the snakelike tube of water paused over Pagett's head. Then in a rush, it descended. They could just make out the moon's reflection. The knight spoke no more.

"Halt, I say!" came another voice, but a second wave poured over the top of the first.

"That one's Gervase," Ben said. Now all they could hear was the constant rush of the waterfalls over the knights' heads.

Holly hoped Nerys was right, that they were only enchanted and not drowned.

She nodded to the centaurs. The Mounted slipped silently into the moat, their heads just above the water.

Holly almost cried out at the shock. Though not deep, the water was icy. Jade winced and shook his fur. Ben's teeth chattered as he clung to Wiggers on Brune's back. Silently, they forded the moat. As they drew up to the lip of the gatehouse, Holly saw the two knights behind a giant cascade of water. It tumbled over them back to the moat and over the top again like a perpetual fountain. Behind the glassy water, the knights' eyes were closed, but they seemed to be alive.

Holly knew the spell wouldn't hold for long. She pulled herself up into the gatehouse, then helped Ben and Everett as the Dvergar dismounted. The centaurs nodded to Holly and crossed back to the other side of the moat. They were far too big a group, Holly thought; it was only a matter of time before someone coughed or Ben sneezed, and every guard came running.

Past the gatehouse they walked under a portcullis into a narrow passageway. It was open above to a kind of catwalk. Another portcullis loomed over the far end of the passage. Holly knew the iron gates could be lowered with a single blow to the winch chain, trapping all of them in the castle. She was sure she heard footfalls above on the catwalk, but when she peered into the gloom, she saw no one.

They walked more or less single file, with Everett in front. He knew the castle layout better than anyone, because King Reynard's castle was a mirror image of Darton Castle in Hawkesbury back in England. Holly followed behind him. She wanted to keep her wand extended, but Bittenbender hissed, "D'ye want to tell the whole castle we've got an Adept with us? It's weapons ye'll be needing, lass." Holly stowed the wand and pulled out a small dagger instead. They glided silently as a group beneath the second portcullis and into the castle proper.

Now, Holly thought, *we're in real danger.*

Chapter 16

To the Dungeon

The whole plan seemed foolhardy now. If they had split up, they might not be noticed—kids walking around the castle would be mistaken for pages, and the Dvergar were short enough that they might be too. But with all of them together . . . and yet, how else could they proceed? Swikehard and Wiggers brought up the rear, their swords drawn, and Ben stuck so close to Holly that the point of his sword kept poking her shoulder blade. Everett led them through several passages until they stepped into the arched walkway surrounding two sides of a silent, moonlit courtyard.

They halted at a sound from the arcade just opposite them.

"D'ye call this food for a prisoner?" It was a gravelly voice belonging to someone used to shouting a lot.

Everett turned back to Holly, his green eyes so round, they took up most of his face. *Grandor,* he mouthed.

Holly recognized him: the knight who had tried to

kill them—more than once. The little group shrank into the shadows of the arcade.

"Sorry, my lord," came a smaller, squeakier voice. "But it's for—"

"What matter who it's for? He's a prisoner, same as the rest. Do we feed him from the king's table?"

"N-no, my lord, from my own supper only."

"That be folly, Dart. A squire needs strength. A traitor needs none. Bread is his fare. Now go."

The group shrank behind the arcade pillars as the knight strode into the courtyard. A chill danced across Holly's shoulders, even where Áedán warmed her skin. The moonlight glinted off Grandor's chain mail and his dark hair. A cruel scar quivered down his cheek; one burly hand twitched against his scabbard. Holly held her breath, willing him to walk away. A moment later his footfalls faded into the shadows.

"That was close," Ben whispered.

"The lad looks easy enough to deal with," Bittenbender said. "If he's the only dungeon guard—"

"He's just a squire," said Everett. "And an all-right bloke at that."

"He's not even armed," said Ben. "We're not killing any kids, and for sure not Dart."

"Ben's right," Holly whispered. "Nobody hurts him. That's final."

"So ye're the general now, lass?" Bittenbender said in a low voice.

"She is the Adept," Jade hissed. "There is no further discussion."

The Dvergar fell back with his men and they muttered darkly among themselves. "Are you sure we can trust them?" Ben whispered to Holly.

"We don't have a choice," she said.

For the next few minutes, they crept along in silence, the only truly awful part coming when they had to cross the moonlit courtyard, as Dart had done ahead of them. The entrance to the dungeons lay on the opposite wall.

Between them and the entrance yawned the broad, unyielding face of the keep.

The freestanding monolith in the center of the courtyard housed the great hall, where the royal family hosted everything from banquets to executions. Somewhere underground, passages connected it to the main castle, but from here, it looked completely separate. Though it was long past the hour of feasting, Holly feared its windows were not empty.

"We must proceed as if we belong here," said Jade. "And not all together."

They traveled in pairs, crossing the courtyard, then crouching in the keep's shadow while Holly continued to the dungeon entrance on the far side.

Holly kept an eye on the keep, but its windows were dark. *People walk across the courtyard all the time,* she thought. *No one will think anything about it.* And yet, when she and Bittenbender shuffled across the open space, her heart hammered like an overexcited drummer, losing the beat and catching up to it a measure later.

At last she reached the doors to the dungeon. Holly shielded the lock with her body and drew out the wand. *Finally*, she felt it saying, its restless tremble resolving into a clean, strong hum. It twitched in her hand like an anxious horse at the starting gate. She took a deep breath.

"*Osclaígí!*" she said in a strong, fierce whisper, touching the wand tip to the lock.

The tumblers turned with a satisfying click, and Holly lifted the crossbar. A trickle of sweat ran down her spine as Áedán shifted position. She stepped inside. The others tiptoed across the courtyard, two at a time, and slipped in behind her.

Jade, winding around her ankles, put a velvety paw against her shin. Holly tried to think of some of the knights' names in case she was stopped. Grandor, of course. There were others. . . . She had met them only the once, when they had taken her before the prince. . . .

Loverian.

His name suddenly came to her, and then his face, which made her smile. He was young, with a strong chin and dark eyes and curling brown hair that brushed his neck. He had tried to speak up on her behalf to the prince, and later he had saved her life, when Grandor had nearly sliced her in two at the Battle of Midsummer.

"Are we standin' round here all night, then?" Bittenbender nudged her with the flat of his dagger. "Let's find the prisoners."

Everett led them down another corridor to a tightly winding staircase that descended into the dungeon like a long black snake. "We'll break our necks going down there," said Ben.

"Wait," Holly said. "I've got a light." She pulled off her backpack and rummaged in it for the lantern Almaric had given her. At least, she thought he had given her one.

"Ye mighta thought of that afore now," said Swikehard, and Bittenbender chuckled unpleasantly. Her face grew hot as she threw things aside looking for the lantern. How could she have forgotten it? Wasn't she supposed to be the leader?

A sharp *scratch* came from behind her, and Wiggers held up his own round light. "Will this do, Lady?" he asked. The other two Dvergar sniggered.

Holly thanked him and stepped to the front of the group and started down the steps. It wasn't enough that Ranulf was suffering, maybe *dying*, in his dirty cell somewhere below them, nor that somewhere in the castle, a full garrison of knights was ready to cut them down. No, she had to add being inept into the bargain. She carried a wand she could barely use, hadn't planned ahead, and half her party didn't respect her. She had heard the term *fearless leader* before, and it was not one she could apply to herself.

"We have no leisure for such thoughts," came Jade's voice, almost inaudible beside her. She didn't know how he had read her mind, but it wasn't the first time.

The lantern threw tall, jumping shadows on the close walls as they descended the stone steps, which continued for several minutes before ending in a dank, holelike space. Everywhere the lantern light shone, the rough-hewn stone walls dripped with damp from some unseen source.

"This passage goes on for a little, then turns a corner to the dungeons," Everett said. "Then there's an open space with cells that go off in different directions."

"If yer right," one of the Dvergar muttered.

As he spoke, they came upon the last turn. A dim light shone around the corner. Holly swallowed hard and beckoned to Bittenbender. "There must be a guard," she whispered.

"Nae fer long." The Dvergar slipped back against the wall and into the shadow.

"Don't kill him. Just knock him out."

"This is our bit," said the little man, gesturing to his friends. "You do yer own." With that he rounded the corner.

Holly forced herself to stay still, though she didn't trust the Dvergar to do as she asked; a moment later Wiggers appeared and motioned to her. He led the way to the dungeon cells.

She winced, though they weren't any different from what she'd expected—a length of filthy, cramped spaces, lit only by a single lantern hung on the opposite wall. Off to one side a knight sat slumped, senseless, in a chair. A cold finger of dread touched Holly, but then she saw Swikehard looping great lengths of rope around the chair. He spat on a handkerchief, wadded it up, and stuffed it into the knight's mouth. "Happy now? Takes twice the time to do it this way." He knocked the knight's chair over for good measure and handed a ring of keys to Bittenbender.

"Find the lads," said the little man, and he and the other Dvergar spread out.

Holly traveled down an empty length of cells to the

center, where she could barely make out a huddled form in the gloom through the bars. "Ranulf?" The smell of the place was horrid, a mixture of waste and sweat and fear and despair. The bundle in the corner only moaned in response. Holly touched the cell door with her wand and muttered, *"Osclaígí."* The lock clicked and the door swung open.

Holly held up the lantern, and Jade slipped in ahead of her, approaching the centaur. The dim light illuminated the sharp planes of his sunken cheeks and the fresh cuts and bruises on his chest. His breath came in shallow puffs. "Jade, is he all right?"

The cat prodded Ranulf's cheeks gently with his paws, and then did a funny thing she had never seen him do before: He breathed on Ranulf's face in little puffs of air. The centaur stirred at last and opened his eyes.

"Who goes there? What—"

Holly nearly cried hearing his voice, however raspy it was, for it was still deep and carried its Gaelic lilt. His eyes, however dulled, lit up when he saw Jade, and then widened when Holly crouched down next to him. "Lady . . . Lady Holly. You mustn't be here. He is coming for you. You must go. . . ."

"No way. Everett! Help me get him up."

It took both of the boys and Holly together to help

Ranulf to his feet, which was an awkward business because his hooves kept slipping on the stone floor, and no one much wanted to be kicked, even accidentally.

"Can you walk?" Holly asked doubtfully.

"What of the guard, Lady?"

"He's . . . taken care of."

"Holly, we need to go," said Everett.

"Ranulf, are these the only cells?" They crept out and peered through the dark down the line.

"Nay, there be another passage beyond—at least two Dvergar prisoners that I know of," Ranulf said.

"I'll see who else is there," Everett offered, and took off down the corridor.

A minute or two passed, but there was no sign of Everett or the Dvergar. "I'd better go check on him," Ben said.

"Ben! Come back here!" Holly whispered fiercely, but he was already gone. Why couldn't the boys stay put for once? They all needed to stick together.

The centaur leaned against the cold stone wall. "Go after him, Lady Holly. I will bide here."

She didn't like leaving him, but Jade crept ahead of her in the dark and she followed. But before she had reached the corner, her lantern light fell on a huddled form in the last cell.

"*Loverian?*"

Chapter 17

His Highness

Everett followed the dungeon passage around the corner just as Bittenbender came out of the gloom at the far end with Swikehard and Wiggers. Two other Dvergar clung to them, barely conscious, bruised and asking for water. "We got what we came fer," Bittenbender said. "Did ye find the Mounted?"

"Ranulf, yes, he's—"

But whatever he'd been about to say vanished from his throat. From behind Bittenbender, a figure emerged, and Everett froze in place, a chilly sweat breaking over his shoulders.

Prince Avery.

The prince hadn't changed much. He would be fourteen now, Everett quickly calculated, but he was still quite skinny and no taller than Everett himself. He wore a simple scarlet tunic with a high collar that brushed his curly blond hair, and leggings with hose. His deep-set blue eyes, which he usually trained in a kind of haughty, I'd-just-as-soon-squash-you-as-a-bug sort of disdain, right now were wide-open circles of utter shock. Even his voice, in his surprise, forgot to sound princely.

"*Everett?*"

Avery wasn't even looking at the Dvergar, who froze in their tracks for a split second, and then, as if they had anticipated this, sprang into action. Swikehard and Wiggers drew back, melting into the shadows with the men they had freed, and Bittenbender seized Avery from behind, pinning his arms. Everett could tell from Avery's wide eyes that Bittenbender's dagger was probably pressing into his spine.

"Ain't this a pretty prize?" said the Dvergar in a low voice. "Now mayhap we can make some real bargains with the king."

"What—" Avery started, and then gasped as Bittenbender gripped him tighter.

"Don't hurt him," Everett cried, then wondered why. What did he care what happened to Avery? He'd betrayed them, pretending to be his friend and Ben's, and then tried to turn them over to the king. They'd all be dead if it hadn't been for Holly and Ranulf. Still, for a minute, seeing Avery look so scared, Everett couldn't help feeling sorry for him and remembering how they had been friends, if only for a short while.

But then his anger bubbled up all over again. "I mean, we need him alive."

"Too right that is." Bittenbender kicked at Avery's legs, frog-marching him forward.

Suddenly Ben appeared around the corner. "What's going on? Did you find the—*wow*." He stood almost comically frozen midstride. But then his face bloomed red, and with his sword drawn, he was really quite frightening, even given his size. Avery backed away, stumbling over Bittenbender, who kicked him again.

"I—if you please, may I—"

"Shut it," Bittenbender said, and jerked his chin at Ben. "Gag him. We're takin' him along. Swikehard, get some rope."

Everett was surprised how quickly Ben whipped out a handkerchief, his face still grim with that awful expression. "On yer knees," Bittenbender said, and the prince complied. His eyes were wide and wet, as if he were biting back tears. Ben shoved the handkerchief into his mouth and yanked it around the back of his head, pulling it so tight that Avery winced. But before he'd gotten it tied, Avery bit down hard and head-butted Ben, who sprawled backward, knocking into Swikehard coming forward with the rope. Bittenbender, caught by surprise, loosened his grip, and Avery twisted out of his arms. The dagger flashed, and Avery cried out, but he'd suffered only a shallow scratch across one arm. The prince rolled out of the way, Bittenbender cursed, and Everett ran to help Ben up.

"I'm okay, just get him," Ben said, panting.

They turned back to see Avery cornered at the far end of the dungeon, his hand on a long rope. He had pulled a dagger of his own, though it looked no bigger than Holly's pocketknife. It trembled in his hand.

"Stay back," Avery said, his voice shaking. "This bell will summon the king's knights in an instant."

"Dinnae be daft, lad," said Bittenbender in a low voice. He pulled a crossbow off his back and aimed it at Avery's chest. "Ye'd drop dead afore any knights came to yer aid."

"One more step, and I shall call them. Let me speak. I have no wish to harm thee."

"There's a likely story," Ben said. "He's a liar, always has been."

Again, Everett felt a surge of pity for the prince. Ben was right; he *had* betrayed them. But even when it had happened, Avery taunting them from astride his stallion, Everett hadn't quite believed it. There was a bitterness in his voice then, a sense that he was doing something he *had* to do, not something he wanted to do.

"Let him talk," Everett said now. "He won't get two steps before we kill him anyway."

"Ask the prisoners—the little men," Avery said quickly. "I have been naught but kind to them. The man-horse as well. I have brought food—"

"Ye hadn't brought much, from the look of 'em," Bittenbender growled.

Avery seemed to realize the truth of this, and backpedaled. "I did my best, good sir. It has not been easy—but I wouldst aid thee—"

Swikehard spoke behind them. "We got no time fer this, Bittenbender. I say gut 'im while we have 'im."

"You will need maps!" Avery cried, and they all halted. Even Ben looked more confused than angry.

"Maps for what?" he asked.

"Nautical maps. I—I have heard the Mounted and the other prisoners, whispering of a voyage to find the Adepts. But the sea is vast, you have no chance of finding them—"

"And ye ken where they be," Bittenbender guessed, inching forward. Avery tightened his hand on the bell pull.

"I—I do not, but I do know where the king keeps the seafaring charts. If any documents show the Island of Exile, it must be they." Avery was babbling now, his chest heaving as he eyed the Dvergar's crossbow.

"Don't trust him, it's a trick," Ben said.

"But he's right," Everett said. "Even Almaric said

the island would be hard to find. And Avery *has* seen the king's maps. He talked about them last year, remember, Ben?"

"*I* don't remember. But then, he wasn't pretending to be *my* best friend."

"What choice had I?" Avery broke in. "The king had decreed I betray you—but I *did* want to see your world—"

"Haud yer wheesht!" Bittenbender said. "Here's the bargain, Yer Highness: ye'll come wi' us, under *our* terms. Ye'll find these maps fer us and hand 'em over. One wrong move and I'll slit yer throat without a second thought."

"It's a trap," Ben said desperately. "He'll lead you right to the king, or the knights, or whoever."

"It'd be worth it," said the Dvergar. He gestured with his crossbow, and Avery moved away from the bell pull. "He kens well that I'd be happy to give me own life if I could gut *him* first." He yanked Avery by one arm. "Now bind him fast."

Chapter 18

The Suicide Mission

Holly held her lantern up higher. Could this prone figure be the knight she had just been thinking of?

Loverian's shoulder-length brown curls were matted and bloody, his cheeks bruised, and he held one arm at an awkward angle that told Holly it was probably broken. The young knight looked up at her, surprised out of his weariness. "Lady Holly," he said, his voice raspy. "Leave this place at once. 'Tis not safe."

A wave of nausea washed over her. "You're here because of me. Because you defended me in the Battle of Midsummer, when Grandor attacked."

"I . . ." The knight's voice caught in a coughing spasm, a wet, dangerous sound.

"Jade, we have to get him out of here. He's sick."

The cat's green eyes glowed in the lantern light. "My lady, we cannot shelter a king's knight."

"But he saved my life!"

"As you saved mine," the knight said in a low voice. "Our score is settled. Leave me to my fate."

"No way." Holly pointed the wand at the lock. *"Osclaígí!"*

The lock fell open. Holly darted inside and slipped one arm under Loverian's uninjured shoulder. "Okay, on three . . . I don't think I can lift you by myself. . . ."

"Lady Holly." Gently Loverian disengaged his arm from hers. "I cannot go with you. Your familiar speaks truth. I am a knight of the realm."

"But that's just *wrong*," Holly said, raising her voice. "You don't owe the king anything. Look what he's done to you!"

"I battled an ally in favor of his enemy," said Loverian. "I ought to have been beheaded at once."

Jade hissed in the dark. "There is no time."

Holly dashed her hand across her eyes. She couldn't be crying, not about a king's knight. But neither could she leave him to die in the place. But at a steely look from him, she backed out of the cell, and he pulled the door gently shut.

"Will . . . will you be all right?"

Loverian only bowed his head.

"Lady Holly," said Jade, his voice uncommonly gentle. "We must go."

"I know." She wiped her nose, turning away from

Loverian. She couldn't bear to look at him. "But where are the others?"

"We be here," came a rough voice down the corridor, and Holly saw Bittenbender's lantern bobbing along in the darkness. "And we got ourselves a guest."

An icy dread pierced Holly's chest when she saw Avery, and she could hardly believe her ears when Bittenbender said he was going to lead them to the nautical maps. "Are you crazy?" she said, and everyone winced at her furious whisper. "Just throw him in one of the cells. Ranulf can barely stand up, and the Dvergar aren't much better. I can't drag them all over the castle."

"You don't have to," said Everett. It figured he'd buddy up to Avery again, as if he'd totally forgotten that the prince had tried to burn them alive in the forest. "Take Ranulf and the others back to Almaric's. We'll stay and get the maps from Avery."

She turned to Ben, who put his hands up. "Don't look at me. I think it's nuts."

"But he's the only one who knows where those maps are," Everett insisted. "We'll never find the Adepts without them."

"That's what *he* told you," Holly said. "Forget it. We're not doing it."

Bittenbender stepped around Avery's back, bringing his dagger to his throat. "And *I* say we *are* doin' it, lassie. He's too big a prize to let go. Dvergar settlements will be marked on the king's land maps, and I've a mind to take those as well, if there be any."

"It's suicide," Holly said, struggling to keep her temper. "Ranulf, what do you think?"

She hated to ask him. He leaned against the dungeon walls, his every breath a rasping chore. He raised his good eye to her. "You may well exchange one set of prisoners for another. His Highness . . ." Ranulf winced as some bruise pained him. "His Highness cannot be trusted."

"It's not up fer a vote," Bittenbender cut in. "Ye got two choices, Adept. I kill 'im here, or I take 'im wi' us."

Avery's face went white, and he made some gurgling noises through his gag. His wide blue eyes pleaded with her.

"Lady Holly, think on it." Jade kneaded her ankle with one soft paw. "Without maps, our quest is doomed, even if the sea witch arrives. We would be more likely to find a single acorn in the Northern Wood."

"Maybe . . ." Holly searched her brain for some other idea. "Maybe we could come back for them?"

"And breach the castle a second time? Nay. The time is now."

Holly shivered in the damp air. She hated this. She couldn't let Bittenbender kill Avery, and if he *did* know where to find the sea charts . . .

"All right," she said, turning back to Bittenbender. "I came here to free Ranulf and the others. This other idea is on your head. But you do it on your own. Ben and Everett are coming with me."

Bittenbender's lips curved into a nasty grin. "Suits me. Wiggers, go with the prisoners and be assured they get out all right. Swikehard, you'n me'll follow His Highness to the maps."

"No!" Everett pulled Holly aside and whispered. "Don't you see? They'll just kill him once he hands over the maps. Then they'll tell you that he double-crossed them."

Ben joined them. "He's right, Holly. Avery doesn't stand a chance if we don't go along."

"*You* said the plan was nuts. What do you care about Avery, anyway?"

"Nothing," Ben said, straightening his back. "I just don't like to see people—*kids*—get killed in cold blood."

"But . . . But . . ." She was supposed to keep them safe. It was her job.

"But you cannot," said Jade quietly. How did he always know what she was thinking?

"Fine. Do what you want." Holly put one arm around

Ranulf's waist, letting him lean on her. "But I am not breaking back into this castle to rescue you guys. You got that?"

"Just do your bit," Everett said. "We'll get the maps."

In spite of her anger, she gave Ben a quick hug, and looked Everett in the eye. "You won't have a wand, you know. And not many weapons."

"It's okay. Bittenbender and Swikehard will watch out for us," he said.

Holly shook her head. If only she could believe that.

Chapter 19

Splitting Up

It figured, Holly thought, that the boys would go off on some impossible quest and leave her to do the real work, which was getting the prisoners out of the castle. But at least the smaller group was easier to manage, especially with Ranulf. She and the Dvergar might fade into the castle walls, but there was no disguising a centaur. They had to get out as quickly as possible.

Still, she couldn't help feeling she should've done more to keep Ben with her. She was supposed to lead them, and it was her job to protect her brother. But lately he'd started acting like he didn't need protection.

She could hardly spare any of this much thought as they climbed the winding stone staircase back up to the heart of the castle. It was tough going for Ranulf, who paused at every landing and heaved great, rattling breaths. More than once Jade leaped onto his back and puffed into his face as he had done in the dungeon cell; this seemed to revive Ranulf enough to move on.

CLAIRE M. CATERER

Meanwhile, Holly was half dragging one of the Dvergar prisoners, a man called Onck. Wiggers brought up the rear with Kepswich, the other prisoner. It was a long trip up the staircase.

It was much worse going out than coming into the castle. Ranulf's hooves echoed off the stone floors. The corridors somehow stretched longer than before, but they didn't dare move too quickly, for fear of sounding like an attack of cavalry. The rescued prisoners could only shuffle along, the Dvergar occasionally moaning as they went, even though Holly and Wiggers took turns whispering, "Quiet!" as loud as they dared.

As it turned out, she needn't have worried. They met no one until they reached the moat, where Holly again cast the *tubhair eas* spell over the castle guards. The centaurs spied them and slipped into the moat. In a few moments they had crossed the water and stood shivering on the far bank.

"But where are the others?" Hoofstone asked.

"It's a long story. They'll be coming soon," Holly said, hoping she was right.

The centaur gazed across the moat at the enchanted guards. "We watched when you cast the spell the first time, my lady. It lasts only a few moments."

Which meant the guards would be on alert when the boys came out.

"They had to make things more complicated," she said, her anger covering her fear. "Now what do we do?"

"Brune and I will stay, Lady Holly," said Hoofstone. "And see that the lads escape safely." He pulled his longbow from his back.

Holly hated to put the centaurs at risk, but it seemed the best plan. She thanked Hoofstone, then led Ranulf and Wiggers, along with the two Dvergar prisoners, to the edge of the wood.

"But it be a fair walk back to the Elm," said the little red-haired man. "How will the prisoners bear it?"

"No worries," said Holly, sounding braver than she felt. "I can do the Vanishment spell. I learned it last year." She didn't mention to Wiggers that she'd only succeeded in doing the spell a few times. "Now, gather around. Everyone needs to be connected." Holly took hold of Ranulf's hand, and she felt Jade's velvety paw on her knee; the Dvergar each took an arm or shoulder. She pulled out the wand and took a deep breath.

She had learned by now that the bigger the spell, the more quiet and concentration she needed. In her mind she counted off everyone who needed Vanishing—herself, Wiggers, Ranulf, Jade, the other two Dvergar—and took a moment to note where each of them had grabbed on. She visualized the route to Almaric's Elm. For a few moments, everyone's eyes were shut tight

CLAIRE M. CATERER

and they breathed as one being. Holly raised the wand, picturing the cottage as clearly as she could; then she shouted: "*Im—*"

But a cold, sharp blade at her neck kept her from finishing the spell. Her eyes flew open. The knight Grandor stood in front of her, with three more armored men behind him.

Chapter 20

The Chamber of Maps

Everett had tried his best to look brave as Holly disappeared down the corridor, holding her lantern ahead of her. The gentle *clip-clop* of the centaur's hooves faded above their heads as the group ascended the staircase. A gloom fell once they were gone.

"I hope they'll be okay," Ben said. For once he sounded not whiny, but genuinely worried.

"Let's get the maps," Bittenbender growled. He prodded Avery forward with his dagger. The others trudged after them, and Everett began to think this was a very bad idea after all. Bittenbender might gladly give his life to take out the prince, but Everett wasn't ready to do that—nor, he thought, was Ben.

At the top of the stairs, the Dvergar ripped the gag from Avery's mouth. "Now," he snarled, "ye'd better pray ye steer us true."

Avery took a minute to cough and compose himself, trying to gain back some of his royal carriage, but his voice trembled. "R-round yon back corridor, through the courtyard. In the—the keep."

"In the *keep*?" Ben squeaked.

Everett's heart fell. The keep was the most dangerous part of the castle. They'd be trapped there.

"I have the key," the prince reminded them, indicating the ring on his belt. "'Twill be quick work, I assure you."

"Quick work under the king's nose," said Swikehard.

"At least it isn't far," Everett put in. "Let's just get it over with."

"Oh, it'll be *over*, unless I miss my bet." Bittenbender gave Avery a shove. "Lead on."

Despite what he'd said, Everett had hoped the maps room would be in some deserted corner of the castle, where they could stay out of everyone's way. As they walked through the moonlit courtyard, he wondered what was to prevent Avery from shouting at the top of his voice. But then, Avery had always put himself first. He'd never risk it.

"I hope we're not being stupid," Ben whispered as Avery opened the tall iron door to the keep with a trembling hand. He led them past the great hall, which yawned dark and empty, and up a corner staircase.

"We must ascend two floors, then to the Chamber of Maps on the east side," Avery whispered.

"And the king?" Swikehard asked. "Where be *he*?"

"He has retired for the night."

"What about the queen?" Ben asked.

"My . . . my mother is not well. She never leaves her chamber at this time of year."

"What's that mean, *this time of year*?"

"It means she is not your concern." The look he turned on Ben stopped even the Dvergar in their tracks for a moment. Then Avery shivered, blinking, as if regaining himself. "It be safe enough. The king's chambers are in the west wing of the main castle, not here."

Everest thought that was unlikely. A king sleeps in the strongest part of the fortress. But he and Ben followed the two Dvergar, who prodded Avery up the stairs.

"In case you forgot," Ben whispered, "he double-crossed us before."

Everett didn't answer. He didn't tell Ben the real reason he'd gone along with the prince's cockeyed plan; perhaps he didn't even know it himself. But somewhere buried under his regard for Holly and his friendship with Ben was a bitter seed that had sprouted the year before: Holly and her wand.

He tried to tell himself that the wand didn't matter, that the fact that everyone here thought Holly was so

special was fine by him. But there had been a wonderful couple of days of glory last year when everyone had
looked at *him* with awe and wonder as he threw knights
from their horses and conjured dragons out of thin air.

With stolen magicks, a voice whispered.

Everett had only imagined it—the voice of the
fiery Elemental who had imbued his stolen wand with
power. Her voice had gotten into his head somehow,
and he heard it often, whenever he felt especially low.
He wished someone here tried to make him feel better
about himself instead of worse.

Maybe that was why he needed to trust Avery.

They gained the second floor. The prince motioned
to his left and winced as Bittenbender shoved him forward. The keep was square, and small compared to
the main castle, so it wasn't long before the corridor
turned a corner and faced three large, imposing doors.

Everett felt something tremble against his chest.
Curious, he pulled the chain out of his shirt. It was
the gold locket he'd found in the wood. The water and
earth symbols were glowing, and the pendant tugged
on its chain as if it were alive.

"Well?" Bittenbender was saying. "Which door is it?"

The locket pulled Everett toward the center door.
"It's this one." He shoved the chain back into his shirt-
front.

"How do you know that?" Ben asked.

"He speaks truth." A sheen of sweat gleamed on Avery's forehead, even as his breath smoked in the chill air. "This door leadeth to the chamber of maps."

"Then get it open." Bittenbender motioned to Swikehard, who stood aside to keep watch. Avery fumbled with the keys. "Afore the sun rises, Yer Highness," said the Dvergar in a low voice.

"In a moment," the prince snapped. Ben and Everett exchanged uncomfortable glances. Neither of them wanted to see Bittenbender lose his temper, and Avery wasn't used to being ordered about.

Everett's locket settled warmly against his skin. He smiled to himself. He didn't know how it worked, but he didn't care. The locket was special. That was all that mattered.

"Ah! Here," Avery said with relief, and the door swung open.

It was a cozy room, the natural cold tempered with gold and red tapestries and fine woven rugs. A dying fire burned in the stone fireplace, which was topped with a mahogany mantelpiece; sharp-beaked ravens were carved along the columns on either side. Tall bookshelves crowded the shadowy corners. Dominating the center of the room was a broad oak desk littered with open books. A lantern on the desk was still burning.

"Someone's been here," Bittenbender said. "And not long ago."

"Let's get this thingy and get out of here," Ben said.

"The nautical maps be under lock and key." Avery unlocked a tall wooden cabinet near the fireplace, revealing a secretary desk. At least ten rolls of parchment filled the pigeonholes. Everett pulled one out gently and spread it open.

Unlike the monochrome antique maps Everett had studied at home, these were decorated in bright colors. In the corners, square-rigged ships sailed with dragons at their prows. Their blue and silver flags bore the symbols from Holly's key: the spiral, the flame, the wave, the earth. The same symbols that were etched on the cover of Everett's locket.

Ben peered over his shoulder. "Is that the one we need?"

"I say take 'em all," said the Dvergar. He started stuffing rolls of parchment into Everett's satchel.

Avery's eyes widened. "But if *all* the charts go missing—"

"This desk hasn't been opened in a long while," Everett said. "Surely no one will notice."

"But the dust will be disturbed," Avery said. "My father is certain to wonder at the cause."

"I should say so," came a deep voice.

Everett's chin jerked up. A figure emerged from the back of the room. He must have been sitting hunched there in the dark among the bookshelves, his heavy cloak camouflaged in the gloom. A hard, bristly dark beard threaded with gray masked his face; Everett knew him at once.

The king.

CLAIRE M. CATERER

Chapter 21

The Wand Fails

Holly didn't dare swallow. The blade was so hard on her throat that one movement would open a vein.

"Now let's have that wand," said Grandor softly, holding out his callused palm.

She couldn't perform the spell, not with the knight touching her, or she would Vanish him along with the rest. But she wouldn't—she *couldn't*—give up the wand.

"At once, or forfeit your life," Grandor said. He turned the sword blade's edge to her skin.

Holly felt Áedán, the Golden Salamander, gather his power. But before he could act, the knight's sword flew from his grasp. It glowed as if the moon still glinted off the blade, though it had landed in the dark turf. The hilt righted itself, and turned, as if looking for something.

"Here, Claeve-Bryna," said Ranulf. The sword leaped into his hand, emitting a trail of sparks.

It was Ranulf's battle sword, no doubt lost when he was captured. Of course it had sought him. Just holding it seemed to give the centaur strength, and he lifted his head. His protruding ribs heaved with the effort, but he raised the sword over Grandor.

At that moment several things happened. Another knight's sword clanged against Ranulf's, and the centaur shoved Holly behind him. She fell against Wiggers and Kepswich, who tumbled to the ground like dominoes. The other prisoner, Onck, pulled Wiggers's dagger from his belt and staggered forward; the other knights charged back.

Holly struggled to her feet and pulled up Wiggers, who cursed when he found his dagger missing. "Fall back, Lady!" he shouted to Holly, and grabbed the longbow off her shoulder. He took one of her arrows and shot it into the crowd of knights.

It was hard to see anything. Wiggers and Onck got lost in the melee of armored men; Ranulf ran back and forth in the small clearing, his sword throwing sparks; the knights bellowed. Holly tried to fight her way to the front, but she couldn't get beyond Ranulf, and then she felt Jade's claws in her ankle. "Tarry here, Lady Holly," he said. "It is Ranulf's task to protect you."

"I'm supposed to be protecting *him*," she said, and

CLAIRE M. CATERER

scrabbled around in the grass for her dropped wand. Finally she snatched it up and pointed it at the nearest knight. "Stop!" she cried, and waited for the blaze of power to streak down her arm and out the wand tip.

But nothing happened.

"I said, stop!" she cried again.

For an instant the wand trembled and warmed in its familiar way, but then it cooled again; she wasn't making the connection with it. Ranulf had already felled one knight with his sword, and a few of the others were falling back to the castle. Then Hoofstone the centaur, still hanging back in the trees, charged forward and shot an arrow into the brawl. He was sure to shoot one of their friends.

"No, Hoofstone!" Holly shouted. She closed her eyes and focused the wand again.

Clear the way, she thought. This time the wand's strength bloomed in her hand, and a spark flew from it, scattering the others. Holly darted into the breach to find Grandor and Ranulf locked together. Someone had given the knight another sword. Holly brandished the wand in his face.

"I said, *stop.*"

Sweat dripped down one side of Grandor's face, catching in the long scar that extended to his jawline. His chest heaved as he pushed against Ranulf, who, though taller, was weakening. The knight turned a dark eye on her. "So you did."

"Walk away," Holly said. "We won't follow you."

She could tell from Ranulf's expression that he wouldn't have promised any such thing. But Grandor, instead of letting go and skulking off, held her gaze and smiled. "It seems that I've the upper hand here, lass. You're not full skilled with that weapon."

Holly blushed but said, "Do you want to test that theory?"

Her legs were shaking beneath her, and it was all she could do to keep the wand steady in her hand. He was right; the wand wasn't working well, or she wasn't working well with it. But now that she stood opposite him, her focus was on one place only—his chin, where her wand pointed. The thought of concentrating all the wand's power on the knight's face turned her stomach. She could kill him.

"This beast," said Grandor, shoving a fist into Ranulf's chest, "is *my prisoner.*"

Holly remembered the sticky feet clinging to her shoulder. "All right, Áedán," she whispered, and a bolt of fire shot from the little Salamander's foot.

He could not harm, but only protect; and Holly knew he would enclose Grandor in his protection as well. But as the curtain of fire rose around them—Holly,

CLAIRE M. CATERER

Grandor, and Ranulf—the others skipped back, the Dvergar uttering creative curses. The knight's head darted around frantically, looking for a way out.

"Leave me go, sorcerer," he gasped.

"Without the prisoner," Holly insisted.

"Leave me *go!*"

Holly whispered to the Salamander, and the fire curtain vanished, leaving her eyes dazzled with the afterimage.

Grandor backed away, the tail of his tunic singed. The other knights had already fled back to the castle. "You cannot escape, Adept. A greater power awaits you. This time you shall meet him. Mark me: You shall not bide long in this world."

Chapter 22

His Majesty

Although there was no way for him to know this, Everett's thoughts were echoing Grandor's at that very moment: He would not bide long in this world. In fact, he reasoned, none of them would, except perhaps for Avery.

Before Bittenbender knew what had happened, King Reynard rose behind him and reached a riding crop over his head and braced it against the Dvergar's neck, holding him fast. Bittenbender gurgled, his arms pinwheeling as the king pulled the crossbow off the Dvergar's back and tossed it aside. He regarded Everett with a dead stare that flickered toward his scabbard. Understanding, Everett drew his own sword carefully and laid it on the writing desk, and motioned to Ben, who copied him. The king found Bittenbender's dagger and added it to the pile.

The king flicked his dark eyes at the prince. Avery dropped at once to one knee, and Everett did the same, pulling Ben down with him. Reynard shoved the Dvergar away and onto the floor, where he fell, coughing. The king stood in front of them and spoke in a graveled but dangerously soft voice.

"Your Highness. Pray make thy companions known to us."

The prince raised his chin briefly. "Your Majesty . . . We were . . ." He trailed off, his voice hitching. The boys were very close together, and Everett could feel Avery trembling next to him, nearly as much as Ben, who had started to wheeze. He needed his asthma inhaler.

Bittenbender raised his eyes and spoke more bravely, Everett guessed, than he felt. "His Highness is our prisoner."

"Is this true?" asked the king, still addressing Avery.

"Y-yes, Your Majesty," Avery managed to say.

"It is true that my son, His Royal Highness Prince Avery, Lord of the Midland Peaks, Duke of Crow's Wing Moor, heir to the throne of Anglielle, has fallen prisoner to two children and a beast of the Earth?"

The prince's cheeks bloomed bright red and his chest heaved. He bit down on his trembling lip. "Yes, my lord. It is true."

"And these lads are the same who betrayed Your Highness at the Battle of Midsummer?"

"Yes, my lord."

"Yet again their kinswoman, the Adept, is absent," mused the king softly. "Curious." He walked a semi-circle around the four of them. His boots, smelling of fresh polish, made no noise on the woven rug. He passed once in front of them, then twice; and then with a sudden movement he cracked the riding crop across Bittenbender's face, and the Dvergar collapsed, moaning. The king planted one boot on the Dvergar's neck and jerked his chin at the prince. Avery handed Bittenbender's dagger to Reynard, who cut the prince's bonds. He handed it back, and Avery turned and brandished it at Everett. It shook in his fingers.

"The prince," said Reynard, "is no longer thy prisoner."

Ben's breathing grew more ragged, and the king's attention turned to him. "Stand," he ordered.

Ben obeyed with some difficulty. His legs were shaking badly, and he had started to cough, but still he didn't reach into his pocket for the inhaler. The king walked slowly behind him and then, just as suddenly as he had struck Bittenbender, he tore the jacket off Ben's back. In a moment he had the inhaler in his hands. He threw the jacket to the floor.

"This device"—he leaned down into Ben's white face—"it can aid thee, nay?"

Ben could barely draw air, but he nodded. Everett

stole a glance at Avery, who looked like he might be sick; he was breathing hard, staring at Ben.

The king pumped the inhaler once into the air, watching the mist dissolve. Then he held his hand out toward the fireplace. "If I were to destroy it, thou wouldst die. I have seen this ailment before, though younglings in my world do not reach such an advanced age as thee."

Tears sprang to Ben's eyes, and he struggled to speak.

"Please, Your Majesty," Everett blurted out. "Just let him have it."

Reynard ignored him. "But thou art of another world, nay?"

"Father . . ." Avery said in a shaking voice.

"Silence." With a backhanded toss, the king threw the inhaler into the hearth.

"No!" Everett darted forward before he could stop himself. He grabbed a fancy brass shovel standing next to the fireplace and scooped the inhaler out of the coals. Luckily, it had fallen short of the flames. The inhaler looked all right, but would it still work? He blew on it, trying to cool it, then turned back as the king bellowed.

It was Bittenbender. The Dvergar, playing at being abject, had grabbed the king around his ankles and tackled him to the floor, knocking Avery over too. The dagger fell out of his hand. Everett heard the crack as Reynard's elbow hit the flagstone hearth. At the same moment, Swikehard burst through the door and jumped on the king's chest. Bittenbender joined him and wrested the whip from the king's hands; he turned it sideways and braced the wooden shaft against Reynard's neck.

A horrible, raspy sound came from Ben's throat.

Everett darted forward and shoved the inhaler into Ben's mouth. Ben winced—the plastic was probably hot—but he pumped it once, then twice. Everett stood twisting his shirttail, his lips dry, his heart almost stopped. *Please, just work. Let him be okay.* . . .

Ben heaved a gasping breath. Relief flooded his face as the color started to come back.

"Quick!" Bittenbender shouted. "The dagger!" He pressed the whip harder into the king's neck.

"Nay, Dvergar." Avery snatched it up and brandished it at Bittenbender. "Leave the king."

Everett glanced desperately from one to the other. Bittenbender was struggling to hold the king in place; Swikehard had his arms pinioned. Reynard might still throw them off, or he might choke. Everett didn't like the idea of killing the king, but what choice did they have?

Then he remembered his own sword. He snatched

it off the desk, grabbed Avery by his tunic, and pressed the blade to his neck. "Drop it," he said.

"Nay," the prince said in a low voice. "I have a plan."

"Your only plan is to drop that knife," Everett said tightly.

The dagger clattered to the floor.

Bittenbender lunged for it.

"Stop!" Everett kicked the dagger aside, stepping on the Dvergar's fingers. "Your Majesty, turn over. Avery, tell him."

"Father . . . please . . . do as he says." The prince sounded close to tears.

Casting a sidelong look at Everett, the king relaxed. The Dvergar rolled him over, and Everett kicked the dagger out of Bittenbender's reach. "Tie him up."

Bittenbender scowled at him. He pulled a length of rope from his belt, but then suddenly he seized the brass shovel Everett had tossed aside. He raised it.

"No!" Avery shouted, but the shovel came down on the king's head.

Reynard slumped on the floor, senseless. Avery struggled in Everett's arms, but Everett held him off with the sword. "It's okay. He's not dead, is he?"

"This ruddy thing couldn't kill a rabbit," Bittenbender said with disgust, throwing it into the hearth. "He probably won't be out long, neither." He nodded to the other Dvergar. "Best make sure we're not disturbed," he said, and Swikehard took up his post outside the room again.

"The maps," Everett said, struggling to keep his voice from shaking. He shoved Avery toward the writing desk, where the open satchel still sat. "Put the rest of them in that bag. Be quick."

He couldn't fault Avery's speed. The prince bunched the parchment into the satchel, not pausing to fold them carefully. His hands trembled and he sniffled, biting back tears. Ben was still collapsed on the floor, his chest heaving, but he was breathing all right. Bittenbender stuffed a handkerchief into the king's mouth and tied his hands, pulling the ropes brutally. When he was done, he climbed off the king's back and picked up the riding crop. He slashed it across Reynard's face. "There's partial payment fer all ye've done to my kind," he snarled, then scampered off to find his dagger.

"Everett, His Majesty must not be harmed," Avery said, handing over the satchel.

"Shut it, you. Ben, can you walk?"

Ben nodded, getting shakily to his feet. He twisted the rope around Avery's wrists.

"Right, then. We'll be getting on."

"Oh, we're gettin' on, all right," said Bittenbender

from the corner of the room. He had found his dagger, and he ran across the room to where the king lay sprawled in front of the fireplace.

"Bittenbender, no!" Everett cried. It was stupid, perhaps, but he couldn't bear to watch the king die in cold blood, even as hateful as he was.

"This ain't yer fecht, lad," growled the Dvergar, and leaped onto the king's back, the dagger held high above his head. But before he could bring it down, a broad orange spark cut across Bittenbender's hand, knocking the knife away. It skittered across the stone hearth.

"What the—" came Ben's croaky voice, returned at last.

Avery had twisted away from him and pulled a thin wooden stick from his cloak, which he now grasped in his shaking hand. He slashed the air with it, and another spark cut low across his father's body, missing the Dvergar by inches. Bittenbender, his eyes round, sat astride the king as if on a prone horse. He couldn't speak.

"My wand," Everett said at last.

It was the wand Avery had taken from him last year. It was still wrapped in red silk, the lady's favor that had granted the wand power. And it still worked—for the prince, no less.

The king moaned.

"Off him, Earth man," said Avery. He brandished the wand, and Bittenbender obeyed him. "Leave the king alive, Sir Everett, and I will go with you as promised. But leave the king alive. I am your prisoner. You have what you desire. Now leave us go."

In a coughing hiccup, Everett's voice returned to him. "Uh . . . yeah. Right. Come on, let's go. The king isn't to be harmed. You've got our word, Avery. Ben, tie him up again."

"But how did he—"

"Just *tie him*," said the Dvergar, pushing past Ben and snatching up his dagger. "He's got *our word* now, dunnee?"

Everett took the wand from Avery and pocketed it. How could it still work? Surely the power the little Elemental had given it would have worn off by now. Or was she working with Avery, too? He searched the room for the fiery creature, but he saw nothing but the dying firelight and the prone king, trussed on the flagstones, conscious now and kicking as if he could break the bonds the Dvergar had tightened so mercilessly. Their swords drawn again, the four of them left the Chamber of Maps.

Chapter 23

The Murder Hole

Everett and Ben and Prince Avery and the Dvergar were able to sneak down the corridors silently for some time. Everett fancied he could hear the king crying out, but Reynard was well gagged, and it was only Everett's imagination that made it seem otherwise. He wished the maps room wasn't located in the keep; they had a horrible number of passageways and staircases to cover before they were anywhere near the castle entrance. Still, they passed through the fortress undisturbed.

Until.

They had finally entered the wide corridor leading to the gatehouse when a loud boom told them that someone had burst into the castle from some other entrance. "The north gatehouse," Avery whispered. "It must be one of the garrison."

"It seems ye've called up yer lackeys after all, Yer Highness," said Bittenbender, who had been letting

Avery take the lead and now jerked him back close.

"Don't be daft, how could he?" Everett said. "We've been together the whole time."

A thunder of footsteps told them the knights were nearly upon them.

"Quick! In here." Avery threw open a low door near the inner portcullis, and the five of them crowded into a tiny room that Everett soon recognized from the smell.

"Is this a *bathroom*?" Ben whispered. "Gross!"

"Shut it," Everett hissed back.

They all fell quiet, though they would likely have never been heard over the shouting and trampling of heavy boots that echoed past their hiding place. Everett recognized Grandor's voice. "'Tis the Adept, I say!" Grandor hollered to one of the other knights. "Not a moment gone, in the wood just the other side of the moat. She's broken out the Mounted, and the two Earth men."

"Very well, Sir Grandor," said a calmer voice, who Everett recognized as Tullian, the leader of the castle garrison. He seemed to be addressing a group. "Bryce, check the dungeons. See what Loverian can tell you. Gregory and Anselm, secure the east wing. Grandor, follow me to the main gatehouse."

Everett nudged Avery. "Can we get out by the north gatehouse?"

"We should never gain it afore the knights find us, and it will be well guarded by now."

"If Holly's spell is still working, we can slip through the main gatehouse," said Ben.

Everett felt sick to his stomach. It would be all too easy for Avery to break away from them and call Grandor and his men straight to them. In fact, he reasoned, this must be exactly what Avery was planning to do.

Ben opened the door a crack.

"What're you doing?" Everett snatched at his sleeve.

"Someone's got to see what's going on, and I'm the smallest." Ben slipped into the shadows just off the portcullis. He crept forward, peering through the passage.

"Well?" Everett whispered.

"Ummm . . ."

"*What?*"

Ben slipped back into the water closet. "We've got a problem. The spell's broken, and there's knights all over the place."

"Crikey," said Everett.

"We have to leg it," said Bittenbender. "The shortest way out."

"Through the main gatehouse, then," said the prince. "All be chaos and disorder there."

"We'll be takin' His Highness," said Bittenbender.

No one argued that point. Everett darted out and cleared the first portcullis, holding short of the second. Glancing up at the catwalk, he remembered what this passage was called: the murder hole.

The Dvergar scuttled out next as one awkward, lopsided figure, Bittenbender holding the prince's ropes while Swikehard jabbed his spine with the dagger. Beyond the outer portcullis, Everett could see Grandor searching around the moat while Tullian gave Gervase and Pagett a tongue-lashing for being tricked.

"We must have been enchanted, my lord," Gervase kept saying. Everett watched as Bittenbender prodded Avery ahead of him, staying in the shadows. They would have to dive into the moat and swim for it. Everett wondered how they'd manage to hold Avery's head above water.

Unless, Everett thought suddenly, Bittenbender shoved him under.

The Dvergar's wily little eyes shifted from one knight to the other as he crept along the gatehouse wall. Everett saw what would happen: The Dvergar would drop Avery in the water, and when the knights scrambled to save him, Bittenbender and Swikehard would clear the far bank. Everett's and Ben's chances were slim at best.

"Cut the winch! Lower the portcullis!" someone hollered from inside the castle.

"Ben, come on!" Everett shouted. There was little point in being stealthy now. Where *was* he?

"Do not be a fool, lad," he heard then. "Step away from the winch."

Everett slid against the wall of the murder hole closer to the inner gate. Oh no. Ben was frozen midstep, standing in front of the winch that raised and lowered the portcullises. He was *guarding* it.

"You don't want to mess with me," came Ben's small voice. "The Adept's my sister." With a trembly rasp, Ben drew his sword and held it in front of him. Ben backed up as the knight approached. Everett recognized him—Bryce. He was only nineteen.

"I have no wish to harm you, but the castle has been breached," Bryce said, wielding his own sword. "Now step away."

Everett stole a glance back at Avery and the Dvergar. They had snuck by Tullian, but they would be spotted as soon as Bittenbender shoved the prince into the moat. But Everett couldn't stop what Bittenbender was doing; he had to get Ben through the passage before the portcullises came down.

Ben was shaking, both of his hands tight on the hilt of his sword, but he stood his ground. Everett inched closer. What could he do? He was already halfway out, and if he went to help Ben—

But he had to. With a great yell, he darted forward, praying the element of surprise would gain them a moment; he grabbed Ben's hand and pulled him toward the murder hole. The knight raised an ax to the winch.

Ben slid through just as the inner portcullis crashed down.

"Whew, that was—" he started to say.

Everett tugged on him again. He knew what would happen next: Bryce would lower the second portcullis and trap them in the murder hole.

Everett heard the crack as the ax fell on the chain.

The iron grill above them released.

He yanked Ben's left arm, the right one flailing.

The grill fell, and one of the points clanged against Ben's sword blade.

"Leave it," Everett said just as Tullian and Gervase looked up in surprise.

"My lord! His Highness!" cried Gervase as Bittenbender shoved the prince into the water. Everett jumped in after him, then remembered, even before Ben said it.

"I can't—"

"Come on!" Everett cried.

Ben scooted closer to the edge of the moat. Gervase

had already dived in after Avery, and Tullian was running toward Ben now, his sword over his head.

Which may have been the motivating factor.

Ben jumped.

Everett, treading water, scooped him up by the shirt collar. Ben gasped, his arms whipping back and forth in the air. "Ben, it's okay," Everett said desperately; "just hold on to my satchel. I'll get us across."

It was like the old fable of the scorpion riding on the frog's back. Ben clung to his shoulders with both hands. The moat was only twenty feet across, but Everett couldn't make any headway. He fought to keep his head above the surface. Ben yanked at Everett's sleeve, and pulled something free. Everett turned to see a red scarf drift across the water.

The lady's favor. And with it, the wand he had taken from Avery.

Everett made a mighty grasp for it, but the wand sank out of his reach, pulling the red scarf with it. He dove after it.

Everett strained to see, but the water was black. He heard Ben cry out in a muffled tone, and he panicked. Ben was sucking in water. He grasped Ben's collar and hauled him to the surface.

The scene was even more chaotic now. Knights with torches darted back and forth, throwing reflections off the water, which churned like a stormy sea between Ben's thrashing arms and the knights struggling to rescue Avery. The bank looked miles away; Everett hollered as Ben pulled him under again.

A swift kick cracked his shin; it was Avery, he thought, for Ben was on his other side. Everett pushed Ben away to get to the bottom; his best bet, he thought, was to kick off and propel them both to the surface. But even underwater, Ben was fighting him, and Everett couldn't hold his breath any longer; his lungs were burning.

In horribly slow motion, they sank. Everett kicked, but not with the strength he'd envisioned. Everything was so heavy—his legs, his satchel, Ben's body, which had gone alarmingly still. The locket around Everett's neck floated in front of his face.

Strange colored spots, like miniature fireworks, appeared behind Everett's closed eyelids; or were his eyes open? He wasn't sure anymore. He wasn't trying to breathe. He had given up breathing.

They drifted.

Then, deep beneath the moat's muddy bottom, the earth trembled.

It reminded Everett of something—what? His mind drifted back to the forest in Hawkesbury, to the oak tree that had split apart as if in an earthquake. Maybe

CLAIRE M. CATERER

if he died here, he'd wind up back in that wood; he'd be home. And after a long, tired walk, he'd enter his own front room on Clement Lane, where his mother would be making tea. . . .

His shin ached where someone had kicked it.

His whole *body* ached. Someone had yanked him away from his mum's kitchen and thrown him onto a hard, splintery surface, when all he wanted was to go back home.

And someone was shouting, almost nonstop.

"Thar's three of 'em, are ye blind? Pike, cut the sails! Hove to! Hove to! Mind the trees, or I'll lash ye to the foreyard! Now starboard two points, lads! Oggler, see to the prisoners, yeh feckless rogue!"

Then he heard gasps and coughs to either side of him before a broad hand came down on his own chest and pumped it. A rush of water shot up through his throat, along with the sour remains of whatever had last been in his stomach. He flipped over like a fish and threw up on the surface of . . . something.

Finally he coughed, gasping, thinking it felt better to drown than to be saved, and he opened his eyes.

He was . . . *couldn't* be. On the deck of a *ship*?

Next to him lay Ben, spluttering as well, and Avery, on his other side. Leaning over them, then stepping nimbly away from the vomit, was a burly man with a black eye patch slung across his bearded face. He wore baggy trousers and a voluminous shirt, stained all over with sweat and the leavings from a late supper. He regarded them with one roving green eye, keeping his balance as the ship creaked from side to side.

"Where . . ." Everett managed to say. How long had he been unconscious, that he'd been kidnapped to sea?

Avery sat up on trembling elbows and pointed to the sky. "Look there, Sir Everett! 'Tis not the sea at all!"

As Everett followed his shaking finger, he nearly passed out again. They were sailing, all right—two masts loomed above them in the black sky, with lanterns swinging from their crossbeams—but there was no water.

They were sailing through the wood.

CLAIRE M. CATERER

Chapter 24

The Lost Boys

For all Holly knew, the boys had been captured by now, and she doubted they had found the nautical maps the prince had promised. She had managed to bring everyone back to the Elm safely, if a bit clumsily. As if Grandor's appearance were just an annoying interruption, she drew her wand again and had the others gather around her. The Dvergar grabbed hold of the arm she laid gently across Ranulf's back, and Jade huddled close to her as she gathered strength for the Vanishment spell. With a single word, she transported them.

"Imigh!"

It wasn't an especially graceful bit of magic. The mist that sprang up around them was sharp and cold, and when it cleared, they tumbled in a heap in a patch of mud just inside the Elm's clearing. But they *had* arrived. She had managed that much.

Jade shook his coat in front of a small campfire

burning next to the cottage. "The number of times I have had a bath this week," he grumbled. "It almost makes one grateful for rain."

But Wiggers only shook his wet hair and brushed off the worst of the mud. "We Dvergar ne'er mind the glaur," he said, smiling at Holly. He grasped her hand in both of his. "All thanks, milady. We won't soon forget it, and I'll be tellin' Bittenbender so myself." He beckoned to Onck and Kepswich. "Come along, lads. The missus'll have bree and tea on the hob."

With that, the little men disappeared into the wood.

A moment later Almaric burst out of the cottage carrying a large pot and a long-handled ladle. He greeted Holly hastily but did not even inquire about the others. He set the pot over the fire and brought Ranulf over to it. The centaur seized the ladle with both hands and gulped from it, after which the magician filled a wooden bowl. Ranulf drank down the lot.

Holly winced again at his bruised body. "Is . . . is he going to be all right, Almaric?"

"Right as rain by morning, Lady Holly, you'll see. I've brewed several infusions that will fix him straightaway."

"My thanks, Lord Magician," said the centaur, looking up at last.

"Not at all. But . . ." Finally Almaric glanced about. "Where are the others? Not captured, surely?"

"Not exactly," said Holly. "It's a long story."

"Another time, then," said the old man. "Forgive me—I must tend to Ranulf." And with that, he led the centaur around the back of the Elm to the little shed where Holly had bathed earlier.

"Come, my lady," said Jade, walking to the cottage door. "Out of the rain."

For it had started again.

The cottage was dark; the sea hag had disappeared. Holly lit a lantern as Jade settled on the hearth and commenced his bath. With very little effort his coat was dry and shiny again. Holly sat nearby with a cup of tea she'd made from an almost-cold kettle.

"Perhaps a rest," the cat suggested as she stared at the dwindling flames.

"I won't be able to sleep until the boys are safe," she said. "I can't believe I let them go ahead with their stupid plan. Now Avery's probably got them locked up somewhere, and I'll have to find a way to rescue them. *Again.*"

Jade regarded her with steady green eyes, looking for all the world like an ordinary cat.

"At least they weren't there to see what happened with Grandor. Or what *didn't* happen, more like. I couldn't do anything. I couldn't shoot, couldn't do a spell, couldn't make the wand work—I should've gotten us out of there right away, but I'm so . . . so . . ."

"Untrained," the cat finished.

"I was going to say lame."

Jade glanced at her feet.

"It's an expression," Holly said, rolling her eyes.

Jade resettled himself. "One task of a familiar is to serve as an Adept's mirror. An aid in seeing your true self."

"You mean my true lame self?" Holly kicked at the braided rug beneath Almaric's table.

"If it be so."

"Gee, thanks."

"Lady Holly, you must look at your situation honestly if you are to learn from it. I will not deny your performance was less than impressive. You were not able to keep the group together. You did not fully harness the wand's power—"

"I *know*."

"But you *were* successful. Your aim was to rescue Ranulf and the Dvergar. This you have accomplished."

Holly's spirits lifted a little. Getting Ranulf out of the castle was the brightest spot of the whole experience.

"And you were able to perform the Vanishment, which is an advanced spell. You have learnt well."

"But I've hardly learned *anything*. I didn't know any

kind of spell to use on Grandor. Yelling didn't do much good."

"At times an Adept's emotional state can call up heretofore unknown spells or talents. You saw this at the Battle of Midsummer."

"But why couldn't I do that tonight? You've known Adepts before, Jade. What am I doing wrong?"

"You are doing for yourself," said the cat, "and thus have no way of correcting your mistakes. I can only guide you; I cannot teach the craft. You need to apprentice."

"But there's no one to teach me."

It was a lonely feeling, one she hadn't felt as keenly before. As much as the others wanted to help her, they couldn't. The Adepts themselves were lost in exile; even their writings had been destroyed. Everyone expected amazing things from her, but what good was having power that she couldn't access or control?

"What are we going to do about the boys, Jade?" she said at last, toying with the wand in her lap. "How will we find them?"

The moment she spoke, a great cracking noise, like a giant breaking walnuts, resounded through the cottage. Holly and Jade exchanged a puzzled look, then ran outside.

Several of the trees around the clearing had broken off at their stumps, lying like huge jackstraws in the dark, damp forest. Almaric was standing on the edge of the mess, arguing furiously with someone. An enormous dark bulk loomed behind them, but Holly couldn't make out what it was, nor who Almaric was yelling at. But a moment later the figure gently put aside the old magician and walked toward her, dragging a few other, shorter people. Holly peered into the blackness. Just then the moon shifted out of the clouds and lit up the glade.

It was a tall, slender man, dressed in a long, fitted coat with flared sleeves and waist. He wore breeches and high boots, and beneath the coat, a white shirt strung across with a cutlass and all manner of scabbards. Beneath his tricornered hat flowed a mass of long black curls. He shoved his charges into the moonlight and grinned at her. Everett and Ben, along with the prince, tumbled out of his grasp onto the damp ground.

"There, Lady Adept. Mayhap these be the lads ye're askin' after?" called the young man.

No, not man, Holly thought, unable to speak. *Pirate.*

Chapter 25

Words with a Pirate

Holly sat in the warmth of Almaric's now quite crowded sitting room, listening to the boys explain what had just happened to them. Gathered around the hearth with her and Jade were the old magician, the young pirate, and the three boys. She jumped up when they had finished talking and ran to the window, through which she could just glimpse the looming shape that sat at the edge of the glade. "You mean that"—she turned back to the pirate—"is a *boat*?"

"Did ye, or did ye not, call up the sea witch?" said the captain.

"Yes, ah . . ." Almaric stuttered a bit. "I suppose we did, yes."

"Then ye've no cause to complain when she shows."

Holly was confused. "But where *is* she?"

"That be the *Sea Witch*, past yon oak tree," said the pirate proudly.

"It *is* the ship, my lady," Almaric explained.

"We conjured *that*?" Ben said. "Cool!"

Almaric hastened to explain to the captain that it was the sea hag who had done the conjuring, and they certainly hadn't expected the ship to appear in the forest, knocking down trees left and right.

The pirate held out a leathery hand to Holly. His fingers were joined with a transparent webbing, like a frog's. "Morgan, captain of the *Sea Witch*."

"So you came up out of the moat?" Ben said, breathless. If Holly hadn't known better, she'd have thought he had opened a brand-new version of Planeterra Six.

"Aye, lad," said Morgan. He tapped the mug that Almaric had given him, and the magician gave him a sour look before fetching whatever it was that he wanted. "We came as summoned. When we saw men overboard, Oggler hauled ye three on deck."

"That moat can't be more than five meters deep," Everett said, sounding confused.

"Oh, Ev, it's not a *regular* boat, is it, Captain?" said Ben, as if he knew all about it.

"The *Sea Witch* is like no other."

Holly tried to picture it: The great ship rising out of the moat, throwing spray onto the castle gatehouse as the knights scrambled out of the way. And now they were stuck with Avery, who sat staring at the floor.

His blond hair had started to dry in the warmth of the hearth and was curling at the edges. Why had the boys brought him along?

"Well?" Holly nudged him. "What happened to Bittenbender and Swikehard?" She felt a sudden surge of loyalty to the Dvergar. She didn't really like them, but at least they weren't one of the enemy.

The prince made an attempt at a withering stare. "I see no cause to speak with thee."

"I seen the Dvergar, if that's who ye mean," the pirate cut in. "Just as we surfaced, the little rogues gained the shore and ran off into the wood. Fine friends, them."

"A friend to the Adept, perhaps," said Avery.

Almaric gave the prince a stern look. "I think it in your best interest to treat Her Ladyship with due respect, Your Highness."

"Yer *Highness*?" The captain gave a low whistle. "So that's who we've captured, eh? Ye'll be greeting the dawn from the yardarm, laddie, if any of the crew find out."

"They just left you there to drown," Holly muttered. Another picture formed in Holly's mind: Ben flailing in the water while the Dvergar fled through the trees. "If I ever see them again . . ." She couldn't steady her voice. She wanted very much to have Bittenbender in front of her, to see what the wand could do to him.

"Hardly men of honor," Avery confirmed.

"What d'you expect?" Ben said. "You've enslaved and slaughtered their people. They're hardly going to be your best friends."

"It's not as if you haven't betrayed *us* before," Everett added.

"Thine own magic proved false enough," Avery shot back.

"Hey, we were ready to take you back to our world last year!"

"Be silent, squire!"

"I'm not your squire anymore, and anyway, I was *Everett's*."

A burst of orange flame shot up through the roof of the cottage, sending little cinders of thatch floating to the floor. Everyone stopped talking and stared at Holly, who gave Áedán a little pat before letting him crawl back onto her shoulder.

"*I* want to see the nautical maps." She looked pointedly at Everett, fearing the answer. "You do have them, right?"

Everett's satchel was sopping wet, but at least it was mostly waterproof. The sheets of parchment were just a little damp. Holly unrolled them and spread them out on Almaric's low table.

"That be no sea chart," said Morgan in a low voice, glancing at Holly.

He was right. The first in the stack was a land map of Anglielle, and many of the rest were dull: Some showed tenant farmers' borders, the locations of prime water sources, and surveys of hunting lands. But finally, in the middle of the stack, Morgan put a grimy webbed index finger on the parchment. "Drown and sink me if *that* not be a proper sea chart."

The map, yellowed with age, showed Anglielle as a roughly triangular island with a broad sea off its western coast. To the north, a few lonely islands were scattered here and there, and to the south, a lumpy-looking coastline, unfinished.

"That must be Europe," Everett said, pointing to it. "Or . . . whatever it's called. But the Channel is far too wide. And where's Ireland?"

Everett was right: the Channel looked as wide as the Mediterranean Sea. And scrawled across the undefined coast was the word PESTILENCE, with a drawing of a skull and crossbones.

"They haven't mapped very much," Holly said.

"My father doth not employ seafarers." Avery nudged Ben out of the way to get a better look. "His court hath ne'er been to sea."

"This has naught to do with yer father, lad." Morgan

pointed to a corner of the map, where a notation read:

Drawn by the Royal Cartographer Étain
by Order of His Royal Majesty King Lancet II

"This map is too old. It was drawn before Reynard's time," Holly said.

"Long before." Jade startled everyone by leaping onto the table. "This map was commissioned by Lancet the Second. The king who preceded Reynard was Lancet the Fourth." Jade wrinkled his nose at Avery as if he smelled bad. "Your Highness's grandfather."

Avery blushed.

The other maps weren't much better. Some later ones showed a few more islands dotted here and there, but none were labeled with anything like what they'd hoped. Instead they had strange names like Isle of the Forgotten and Land of a Thousand Eyes. And still that wide, empty sea stretched away to the west.

"This is no good," Holly said. "We need a map showing us where the Adepts were exiled to."

Morgan pushed back from the table. His black eyes searched each face. "So it's the Adepts ye're after? And ye think my crew can—or *want*—to help ye find 'em?"

Almaric smiled in a kind of frozen grimace. "Er . . .

that would be correct, Captain. Who knows the seas better than yourself? And, if I'm not mistaken, you are no friend to the king these days."

"These days?" Ben asked. "When *were* you his friend?"

"Never," Avery said at once. "The king does not consort with brigands."

"I think ye'll find there's more'n one thing ye don't know about yer father, lad," said Morgan.

Áedán crawled over to Holly's left shoulder. He was restless when nervous, and Holly didn't blame him. "So which is it?" She did her best to look the captain in the eye. "Whose side are you on?"

"I'm on the side of the *Sea Witch* and her crew. We answer to no one."

Which was exactly what Holly would expect a pirate to say.

"At one time," Almaric added, "the captain did have a—well—agreement with His Majesty. Am I not correct?"

"Any accord we had was good only till the job were done." Morgan grunted at his empty mug, then looked at the prince. "Where d'ye think ye get yer sugar, lad? And yer cinnamon? And wolfroot, lamb's-hip tea, and all the rest? Only *my* crew were willin' to brave those waters to the west and bring the kingdom such delicacies. And we were well paid fer it. Until . . ."

"Until?" Holly prompted.

"Something's been afoot the last twelvemonth or more," said the captain. "The king wants more from us, fer less money. He asks us to go farther and farther to sea, to uncharted waters, dangerous islands. And now it's not payment he's offerin', but *threats.*"

"But why?" Ben asked. "Does he want you to find gold or something?"

"Aye," said Morgan darkly. "Or something."

"What?" everyone asked together.

"Same as ye all want," said Morgan, sitting back in his chair. "He wants the Adepts."

CLAIRE M. CATERER

Chapter 26

To Sea

"That doesn't make any sense," said Everett. "He was the one who exiled them. I thought he knew where they were." He appealed to Almaric. "Right?"

"Perhaps the Sorcerer enchanted them," said the magician. "No doubt he hid them so completely that even he does not know where they are—like dropping a pebble into the sea."

"However it happened, the king wants 'em found," said Morgan. "Or someone else does."

"Raethius of the Source," Holly said. The others looked at her, and she could tell that they all felt the way she did at the mention of the Sorcerer's name—that, despite the cozy fire, something had sucked all the light and warmth from the room. The captain raised his eyebrows in assent.

"But I don't see why he wants you to find them," Holly went on. "They'll just join together and bring down his power. Isn't that why *we* want to find them?"

"Ye want them all, lass. The king only wants one."

"You mean he wants you to kidnap one." Somehow this sounded a lot worse. "But what does he want one Adept *for*?"

Morgan's dark eyes looked Holly up and down, and his voice softened to a whisper. "Ye're one of them. You'd do, wouldn't ye?"

Holly swallowed.

Almaric sprang out of his seat, his face very red. "See here, Captain! Just what are you threatening?"

Morgan only smiled and waved his hand dismissively. "Just a jest, o'course," he said, but Holly wasn't so sure. The king wanted an Adept—and now he knew she was in Anglielle.

Almaric sat down again. "Yes, well . . . not terribly amusing, if I may say. But I think we're overlooking a rather good source of information." He turned his attention to the prince. "His Highness must know something about the Sorcerer and his designs."

All eyes turned to Avery, who threw up his hands. "I know naught of what you speak. My father hath no commerce with sorcerers. He does not even believe in magic. I would swear to it."

The pirate snorted.

"The king's advisor, then," Almaric amended. "Raethius. Surely you know of him?"

"He is but an elderly man from whom my father seeketh counsel," Avery said. "And he is rarely at the castle. He travels far and wide on his own errands. It hath naught to do with the kingdom."

The captain spat on the floor in the general direction of the prince's shoes. "This boy don't know what goes on under his own nose. I'd throw him in the brig for the night."

"Coming back to the point," Almaric said, "the king and Raethius have been searching for an Adept this twelvemoon. The question is why."

"That I know not," the pirate admitted. "I've severed any accords with the crown since Iona went missing."

"Who's Iona?" Holly asked.

"Me first mate. Never was there a finer sailor nor a better friend. His Majesty warned us if we couldn't find the island that one of the crew would be taken. After our last voyage, Iona disappeared. If not in the king's dungeon, I daresay my mate's swimmin' in Davy Jones's locker."

"There was no one left in the dungeon except Loverian," said Everett quietly. "We set everyone else free."

"As I thought." Morgan fell silent for a full minute, during which no one felt right about saying anything either, and then added, in a stronger voice: "So I'm not doin' any favors for the king, whatever his design might be."

"That's exactly why you should help us," Holly said. "I don't know why he wants an Adept, but if we bring them all back, that would finish him. Raethius, too. Right, Almaric?"

The magician nodded. "It is what we have hoped for, but I confess I am at a loss. If you don't know how to find them, Captain, and the king's maps are no help—"

"Hang on a tick," said Morgan, giving a devious grin. "I *know* how to find 'em. I just ha'n't done it yet."

"Why not?" Holly asked.

"Because, lassie"—the captain gave her a broad wink—"I ha'n't had you."

The next day Holly awoke to the sound of rain lashing at the shutters, and a feeble gray autumn light struggling through the beetling clouds. She was cold and stiff, and Áedán had a dull gray cast about him. But he leaped into the hearth and lit a fire that he nestled in for a full five minutes, which restored his golden color and bright eyes. Holly picked him up and left Jade snoozing by the fire. She ran through the drizzling rain to see Ranulf, who was recuperating in Almaric's garden shed.

She was afraid she would find him weak, maybe

even unconscious, but she was surprised to see him finishing up a hot mash that Almaric had given him. Though still bruised, the centaur had trimmed his beard and brown curls. Was it possible he was even less thin? Ranulf looked up from his breakfast with bright eyes and inclined his head. "My Lady Adept," he said. "I owe you my life."

It was perhaps more proper, in such a serious moment, to return the bow, but Holly stepped around a hay bale and gave him a hug instead. "Ranulf, you look so much better," she said, then turned to the magician. "Almaric, how did you—"

"The Mounted are quick healers," said Almaric, beaming modestly. "But I do have a few tonics up my sleeve that speed the process. I trust you slept well, Lady Holly?"

"I'm okay," she said, though the events of the previous night before were catching up to her. It felt like she hadn't slept at all. "The captain said they were sailing at dawn," she remembered suddenly.

"So Almaric has told me," Ranulf said. "We had best ready ourselves."

"So . . ." Holly had hoped Ranulf would have some wisdom to impart. "You think we should go with them?"

"Lady Holly," said Almaric gently, "if you don't sail

with the *Sea Witch*, there's no hope of finding the Adepts."

"But *I* don't know where they are. How can I help?"

"I cannot say. But Morgan believes that having you aboard will make all the difference."

"I—I don't exactly trust this . . ." Holly started to say *pirate*, then out of politeness, substituted *captain*.

"Once, many such crews plied the seas," said Ranulf, "but today only a very few remain. Perhaps Morgan's crew alone. There be none else to trust."

Holly left Ranulf to finish his breakfast and went to seek her own. The dawning sun had broken through the thinning cloud cover, lighting it in brilliant streaks of orange and pink. The sunbeams shot through the trees and lit up the hull of the *Sea Witch* as she came upon it. Holly halted in her tracks, spellbound.

The ship was magnificent, for all that it sat wedged among the ruined trees. Its two masts stretched twenty feet into the canopy, the square-rigged sails rolled neatly up, and all manner of complicated rigging stretched to the deck in a spiderweb array. Two long ropes like ladders reached up to the crow's nest, where one of the men stood peering over the treetops with a spyglass. The shallow keel was sunk into the fertile woodland soil, where it had carved a track. On the deck above—which curved above Holly's head and was too high to see properly—the crew scampered about, readying the ship for sailing.

But even this formidable sight was not the most surprising.

At the stern of the ship a figure emerged from a cabin. The sun glinted off a riot of black curls, and Holly knew it was the captain. The full beam of the sunrise hit Morgan's slight shoulders, smooth face, and lithe, webbed fingers. He stretched, pulled the hat from his head, and raked one hand through his hair.

No, Holly realized with a shock. Through *her* hair.

Holly blushed. Quickly, her memory rewound, and she recalled how Morgan had appeared in the moon-light, and then in the dim firelight of Almaric's cottage; how she had bellowed for ale, and strode so purpose-fully through the room; how she *was* tall, after all, at least six feet, and broad-shouldered for a girl. And her face was lean and darkened by the sun, and her brows as black as her hair, and still . . .

"Wow," someone said breathlessly behind her, and she turned to find both of the boys staring up on deck, realizing their mistake just as she had.

"Um," Ben said uncomfortably, "do you guys see what I'm seeing?"

"Well, what's the big deal?" Holly said, finding her

voice at last. "A pirate can't be a girl?"

"That's not just a girl," Everett said softly.

At that, the captain noticed them in the glade and gave them a broad wink before hollering to her crew.

"Oggler! Down to the deck, yeh bilge rat. All hands, fore and aft! To shore, and feed yer faces afore we sail!"

"Come on, quit staring," Holly muttered, and pulled both of them toward the cottage.

Once Morgan and her dozen crew members had eaten their fill—Holly and the boys hardly had time to take a bite before they descended and cleaned out Almaric's larder—they prepared to set sail. Morgan and the crew climbed nimbly up a rope ladder that dangled from the deck down to the forest floor, and the captain bellowed, "Rowan! Throw down the stair!"

At that, a folding staircase descended like an accordion, and Holly and the boys followed Almaric and Ranulf aboard. Avery had already been taken aboard the night before and stowed in the brig, at the captain's insistence. From the main deck, Holly saw how the ship had cut a neat path through the wood and felled at least six large beech trees.

Holly craned her neck up to the sails, one hand on the rigging. The mast in the center of the deck flew a small square sail and a large, trapezoid-shaped sheet that stretched over the stern; the second mast, forward of the first, held two square sails; and the long bowsprit, which extended like a swordfish's nose off the bow, had two jib sails that Oggler and another crew member were busy unfurling. Above it all flew a black flag with a skull and crossbones.

"All hands below for descent," called the pirate captain, and the men scurried to finish their duties before shoving past the others to open a hatch in the center of the deck.

"What're we doing?" Ben asked.

A red-haired crew member—another girl—noticed him. "We're puttin' to sea, lad. Now get below, Captain's orders."

The passengers followed the crew down the hatch through a narrow passage that opened into a large open area crowded with barrels and lit by swinging lanterns. Holly found a porthole, and the boys crowded around her to watch what happened next.

With a great creaking and groaning, the *Sea Witch* began to sink.

The forest floor grew closer as Holly watched. The low shrubs rose to the level of the porthole. Then the grass split apart and they sank into the mud. Darkness enveloped the ship, and the only thing that broke it was the dim light of the lantern that swung from the ceiling.

"Uh . . . where are we going?" Ben asked. His face looked a bit green.

"To sea, I guess," Everett said, though he sounded worried too.

"Where's the captain?" Holly asked the red-haired pirate.

"Morgan goes down with the ship," she replied, as if that answered the question. Holly imagined Morgan standing at the wheel, the cavern opening beneath her, the dirt closing up over her like a grave.

"I can't breathe," Ben said, coughing.

"Yes you can," said Holly, though she too felt odd, as if a giant foot were standing on her chest. It was her imagination, she told herself. She knew they were underground, where there was no air, but Morgan had done this before, and the rest of the crew were all right; so they would be too. Ben's breath came in hitching little coughs, and he pawed through his jacket pockets for his inhaler.

All around her the hull moaned and creaked, and above she could hear cracking noises, as if the masts were breaking in half. Even the crew huddled together. From somewhere in the shadows a soft clucking told Holly there were chickens on board.

And then, just as the weight on her chest became unbearable, she felt a tiny bit lighter.

She took a tentative breath. And another.

"Look!" cried Everett, his face pressed to the porthole.

There appeared a faint greenish light, which brightened the longer they gazed at it. A moment later a fish swam by.

"We're . . . we're underwater," Ben said. Holly could tell this was not an improvement in circumstances, as far as he was concerned.

"It's okay," she said, striving to be calm. "The captain knows what he's—what *she's*—doing."

And suddenly her stomach dropped, just as it did when she was in a rising elevator. A few more fish flew by the porthole, and then stands of seaweed and small creatures. The light became brighter still, until with a *whoosh* they broke the surface, and the crew gave a rousing cheer.

"On deck, on deck!" called Rowan, and the crew scrambled to the ladders.

Holly couldn't see how it had happened. The masts were perfectly straight and sound, glistening with seawater, which sluiced off the decks over the gunwale and dripped from the bowsprit. Yet somehow the sails themselves flapped dry in a brisk wind. And at the helm, looking damp as if from a brief shower, stood the captain, smiling at last, the salty spray on her face.

Holly and Everett ran to the railing and gazed out to sea. The land was nowhere to be seen. Ben nudged up between them.

"I just hope they have lifeboats on board," he said.

Chapter 27

What His Highness Brought on Board

For their first few days at sea, Everett and Ben and Holly spent a lot of time getting to know the ship. The *Sea Witch* was a brigantine, which for all its grandeur was a relatively small and speedy sailing craft. Amidships, it was about twenty feet wide, with all manner of rigging and coiled ropes and stowed casks and barrels and hatches in between. The deck, made of gleaming mahogany planks, ran about eighty feet end to end, with a raised poop deck in the stern, and a quarterdeck and forecastle in the bow. Everett thought it might feel like a rather large ship if there weren't crew running all over it most of the time, climbing into the rigging, yanking on the braces to turn the square sails, and swabbing the decks.

The crew, as many women as men, were tall, muscular people with rough, scarred hands. The women—girls, really, in their late teens—had webbed fingers like the captain. They worked quickly and chatted rarely. Rowan, the first mate, was a thin, ropy girl with kinky red hair and a sharp voice; she was always barking out orders. Kailani, the boatswain, was the friendliest. She climbed the rigging in her bare feet, her straight black hair falling down her back, and often grinned at Everett, crinkling up her dark, almond-shaped eyes.

Among the lesser crew were Innes and Quinn, two younger girls who despite their slight forms could crank the windlass as well as anyone; and Darcie, the cabin girl. The rest of the crew were men, about a dozen hands in all.

Everett and Ben shared a cramped cabin below-decks with the skinny cook, who walked with a pronounced limp, and Oggler, the burly man who had pulled the boys out of the castle moat. Holly's cabin, which she shared with Kailani and Rowan, was a bit nicer; she even slept in a proper bunk instead of a hammock. The captain had the finest cabin, a roundhouse that curved out over the water beneath the poop deck. Everett reckoned he'd never see the inside of it.

The morning after they'd set sail, Everett came out on deck to find the old magician breathing in the salt air. Everett stood next to him against the gunwale,

CLAIRE M. CATERER

trying to get used to the rise and fall of the ship. Almaric seemed to have gained his sea legs in a hurry.

"It has been too long since I have sailed," he said at last, opening his eyes.

"Gawks!" Rowan hollered. "The spanker to leeward, and with a will."

An old scowling sailor only nodded, adding, "To leeward, aye," and pulled the sail into the wind.

"They don't cause any trouble, do they?" Everett whispered. "I mean, taking orders from—well, a girl."

"I should say not," said Almaric. "Punishment is swift on Morgan's crew, I've heard."

"It's just, you don't see it much, do you? Women captains."

Almaric raised his eyebrows. "I daresay I'm no expert on the subject, but I have never heard tell of any other type. 'Tis rare to see so many men on a ship like the *Sea Witch*. Sailing is quite sophisticated work, you know."

Everett knew that, though he didn't have much experience on boats. Still, he and Ben offered to help out where they could. The captain, wanting to be mostly shut of them, said they could join the two-hour dogwatch in the late afternoons alongside Gawks and Frigg. Rowan and Kailani, who alternated as officers of the watch, assigned the boys duties like swabbing the

decks or repairing the ship's lines. The helmsman—
or helmswoman—often hollered for sails to be furled or
loosed, as need be; and then someone would clamber up
the rigging and fight to tame the flapping spanker or
topsail. Ben said he was glad that wasn't their job.

Oggler, despite his gruff manner, showed them
how to yank on the braces to turn the sails. He and his
friend Quelch told them seafaring tales, and Oggler
even gave Ben a spyglass to use while on board.

When he wasn't learning what he could from Oggler,
Ben liked hanging around the galley to scrounge
whatever food there might be. The second day at sea,
he and Everett found Cook frantically pushing aside
the boxes and jars in his tiny galley.

"How'm I supposed to make the captain's chicory?"
he said in a trembly voice. "Or anything else she wants?"
His goggling eyes opened even wider than usual.

"What's the matter?" Ben asked.

"The tinderbox. I can't find it noplace, nor me extra
one. She'll hang me from the yardarm if they're gone!"

For the first time since they'd left the castle, the
gold locket trembled against Everett's skin beneath
his shirt. He pulled it out.

"What's a tinderbox?" Ben was asking.

"Little metal box for lighting the cook fire. About so
big." Cook held his fingers out in a three-inch spread.

The locket vibrated again, and a shape glowed on its surface. The teardrop.

"That's the fire symbol," Ben said, suddenly interested. "Why's it doing that?"

"I haven't any idea," said Everett. "But it's done it before, outside the Chamber of Maps." He held tight to the locket. Now that he knew it was something special, he didn't want Ben to take it. The chain tugged at his neck, straining toward the floor as if magnetized.

"What're you doing?"

"The locket's pulling me." It yanked so hard that Everett dropped to his knees.

"Whatever it is, can you do it outside my galley?" Cook said. "I got to find the—"

"Tinderbox?" Everett held up the little metal box containing the charred cotton and flint. He had plucked it from the edge of the galley door, where it had gotten wedged.

As soon as he laid his fingers on it, the locket went dark. The uncomfortable pulling sensation stopped.

Cook nearly shook his arm off in gratitude. He said the boys were welcome to the choicest bits of whatever he made, puddings and what all, and clapped Everett on the back so hard Everett wished he hadn't found the tinderbox at all.

And, he realized, he hadn't. The locket had.

In all the excitement of putting to sea, and learning the pitch and roll of the ship and how not to stumble across the deck, and reassuring Ben that the creaks of the wood and the rigging were not evidence of poor seaworthiness, it was a full twenty-four hours later before Everett even thought about Avery, the crowned prince heir of Anglielle, who huddled in the brig somewhere belowdecks. In fact, if he hadn't seen Darcie carrying a tray of food up from one of the lower holds, he mightn't have remembered him at all. He felt a stab of guilt as he stopped Darcie on her way to the galley.

"Is that for the prince?"

"Was, you mean," said the cabin girl, tossing back her single black braid. "He ain't touched a crumb since yesterday. Puttin' on airs and all. Well, I ain't forcin' it down his gullet, am I?" She grinned. "More fer me, I reckon. D'ye like some yerself?"

"No, thanks." Everett let her pass, then slipped down into the hold.

He had to descend another level below their quarters to find the brig. He passed through several rooms filled with barrels of drinking water and rum, wine casks and dried beans, and wood stored up for Cook's fire. Another room held stores of arrows and

CLAIRE M. CATERER

crossbows, cutlasses, and other weapons. But tucked off in a corner, he found something he had never expected to see.

It was a barrel like the rest, but instead of food or water, it was filled with black powder. Next to it was a satchel containing twisted bits of paper. He had seen the like before, somewhere, and when he shined his lantern into the dark corner, he remembered. For there, set up in a wooden rack, were half a dozen Brown Bess muskets.

Where on earth, Everett wondered, would Angliellans get *guns*?

A hacking cough startled him. Avery. Everett left the gunpowder and muskets and crawled through the main hold. Finally, just when he thought he must be beneath the bow of the ship, he came upon three damp-looking cells. Only one was occupied.

Avery sat on the floor, his head hanging between his knees, shielding his blue eyes with his arms. His blond hair was dirtier and more unkempt than Everett had ever seen, and his fine clothes were muddied and torn. The cell reeked of filth, and nearby Everett could hear the bilgewater sloshing about and rats squeaking.

"Avery," said Everett. He felt the need to whisper, though he couldn't say why. "How's it going?"

Avery's pale face jerked up at once, then fell when

he saw who it was. His cheeks were dirty and streaked as if he'd been crying. "Who art thou to ask such a thing of me?"

"I just wanted to see if you were all right," Everett said. "Getting enough to eat and all."

"Prisoners do not get the choicest cuts from the table."

"Not if they don't eat them."

Avery dropped his head again. "It matters not. I am to die here, or be strung from the yardarm."

"No, you're not." Everett didn't like to think about the captain stringing up anyone. "I reckon you'll be ransomed, won't you? A prince and all."

"Aye." Avery gave a short, cheerless laugh. "His Majesty values me so highly." He shielded his face, and it looked as if he were toying with something Everett couldn't see. "I dare not hope for ransom. 'Tis my life in exchange for Iona's, the captain's missing first mate."

A faint glow came from the dim cell, illuminating Avery's face for a moment.

"What's that you've got?" Everett asked, peering through the bars.

"Leave me in peace, Sir Everett, I beg thee."

"Come on, show us." The glow on Avery's face changed color from white to blue.

When Avery didn't answer, Everett kicked at the

CLAIRE M. CATERER

cell bars, which hurt his toes quite a lot. He was tired of everyone second-guessing him. Holly was helping find the Adepts, Ben spent most of his time with Oggler, and no one else on this boat needed him. Avery had no right to act all stuck-up at this point. "I'm trying to help you, though I can't see why, seeing as you nearly *killed* my friends and me. *Twice.*"

"I did not betray you to my father," Avery shot back, standing up. Something clattered to the floor behind him.

"You led us straight to him!"

"I thought him abed!"

"And what about last year? Was that just a mistake too, setting the whole wood on fire? I don't know why I bother." And just then, Everett *couldn't* see why he bothered, except that for some reason, he still sort of liked Avery. All the same, he gave the cell bars another (gentler) kick for good measure and turned around to head back to his cabin.

"Wait!" Avery called. Everett wouldn't have stopped if the prince's voice hadn't broken in the middle of that one lonely, fragile word. But he took his time walking back.

"What is it?"

"I—I did not mean to harm thee afore. Nor the squire."

"*Ben.*"

"Aye. Ben. Not even the Adept—"

"*Holly.*"

"The Lady Holly. Quite."

Everett hadn't said *lady*, and he didn't see why Avery needed to add it. But he said nothing.

"I was of more tender years then," Avery added. "And my father is a man of great power. He said you wouldst betray me, and I believed him. It was—foolish of me."

It was the closest the prince had ever come to an apology, in Everett's experience.

"I will show you what I have," Avery went on eagerly. He turned around and brandished something. "See here, Sir Everett!"

Avery held up a long, thin wooden stick.

Everett's wand.

CLAIRE M. CATERER

Chapter 28

The Other Wand

Everett gazed at the tapered mahogany stick, at the dragon faces and tails curling around it. "What . . ." he spluttered. "But how?"

"I didst find it in the moat! The captain searched me for weapons, but I hid it well within my cloak." Avery grinned at his success. The wand was still wrapped around with the scrap of red silk, which looked dirty and bedraggled.

"And you still have the scarf—the lady's favor."

"I cannot do much," the prince admitted. "But I do set small bits of paper ablaze, for warmth."

"I can't believe it still works," Everett said, as if the wand were an old motorcar shut up in someone's garage. He knew that, as a stolen wand, its talents were erratic at best, unless imbued with the power granted to it by the lady's favor. And Sol, the fiery little fairy who had granted that power, was long gone, back to the Realm of the Good Folk. "It just seems odd."

"Odd or nay, 'tis something thou and I couldst master together." Avery's voice fell to a whisper. "Only think on it, Everett. Mayhap we could learn to conjure great beasts, or rule the oceans with such a tool!"

"I don't know about that." The thought made Everett's stomach queasy. He'd done wondrous things with the wand before, but they weren't the sort of things that made him feel all warm and fuzzy. Still, who knew what they were sailing into now? Anything could be out there. This wasn't his world.

"We must be able to defend ourselves," Avery said. "We sail with a savage captain, after all. She is comely, but she is no sweet damsel. Nor are her crew."

He had a point there.

"I will share this wand with thee, Sir Everett. It would be just for the twain of us. Together shall we come to know its powers."

"But what about Ben? And Holly?" It wouldn't do to forget them. They were also sailing with a pirate captain.

"They have the Adept's own wand, nay?" Avery pressed his face close to the bars. "And if we tell them of it, would not the Adept surely take it for her own? Perhaps give it to her allies?"

"But . . . her allies *are* our allies. Or mine, anyway. I can't tell whose side you're on."

"Thine, as ever, Sir Everett," Avery assured him. "But the Adept wishes to gather all the magicks to herself, and is mayhap blinded to the good others could do. Is it not so?"

Everett couldn't deny that Holly was awfully keen to hoard the magic. She never let anyone else even touch her wand, let alone give it a go. And if Avery wasn't being up-front with him, what difference did it make? He couldn't go anywhere. He was locked up, and they were at sea.

"Show me what you can do with it," Everett said finally.

Avery grinned, forgetting his haughty persona for a moment, and grasped the dirty red scarf around the wand's shaft. "I have essayed fire a few times," he said. A small spark glowed at the tip, and when Avery waved it in the air, it left a golden afterimage.

"Are you mental?" Everett cried. "We're on a boat made of *wood*. You'll set the place on fire."

"I have control of it," said Avery loftily. "I have only lit flames inside the chamber pot." He crossed the cell to pick up a large urn.

"Ew, that's okay—I believe you. Pour that out, why don't you?" He pointed to a large jug of fresh water that Darcie had left in the cell.

Avery did as he asked, then set the jug on the floor.

He and Everett sat down in front of it, the cell bars between them.

"It be but a wee spark," Avery said nervously, holding the wand over the jug.

"Just show me."

Avery took a deep breath, then turned the wand counterclockwise in a circle no wider than the mouth of the jug. The blue spark glowed from the tip, then turned indigo, and floated down into the jug. It was almost like fire and water combined. It glowed there briefly, beautifully, then hissed and disappeared.

Everett released his breath. "How did you do it?"

"I know not," Avery said. "I made several turns with the wand, holding the scarf always, and all at once did I feel a sort of power grow within, and this beauty issued forth."

"It *is* pretty cool," Everett acknowledged. Then suddenly his chest felt quite hot, as if the skin were burning. He pulled the chain from inside his shirt. It was the locket. It glowed now, the water symbol pulsing with a blue light very like the one Avery had just conjured.

"Whence came this?" whispered the prince.

"I found it in the wood." The gold cooled in Everett's palm to a pleasant warmth that soothed them in the dark hold. "It reacted to the wand. I think they're connected somehow."

"The locket is magic as well," said Avery. "Perhaps it has found its brother. Canst open it?"

"I've tried. It's stuck somehow." Everett pulled at the catch with his thumbnail, but the locket held fast.

"Mayhap the wand can open it, as the Adept has done." Avery circled the wand over the locket. The water symbol glowed blue again, but nothing else happened. "There was an incantation the Adept uttered in the king's dungeon—if I can only recall it—"

Everett remembered it, though it gave him a cold feeling in his chest when he thought about telling Avery. But so what? Holly didn't own the magic. And anyway, Avery probably couldn't even do the spell. Still, when he uttered the word, he whispered. *"Osclaígí."*

Avery nodded, then touched the wand to the locket. *"Osclaígí!"* he repeated. The word sounded different in his mouth, as if it belonged there.

The locket's catch sprang open.

It was a large brass compass with a lid, like a pocket watch. But unlike the compass on Holly's watch, which she used so faithfully whenever they entered the woods, this one had so many markings and such tiny writing that Everett could hardly read it. The needle spun around madly. "It must be faulty," Everett said. "It's meant to settle on a direction."

Avery took it in his hands. "Only look at the workings, Everett."

The longer they stared at them, the more legible they became. When Everett squinted at them and brought the locket to his eye, suddenly he could see all sorts of things, as if he were looking through a microscope. One direction pointed to a sandy beach; another to an island whose coastline was ringed with impossibly high cliffs. Around the dial to the east, he even spied the king's castle. And something *moving* in front of the castle.

"Let me," Avery said, and took the compass from him. He did the same thing Everett did, holding it to his eye like a spyglass. "Look here! I see Sir Pagett pacing before the gatehouse! But how can it be?"

Everett ran his fingers over the locket's gold face. It was warm, almost breathing. He glanced at Avery's hand, where he still held the wand tightly. He could see it trembling. "I think the wand is helping it, letting us see what's usually hidden." He took the locket and peered at it again. Away to the southwest, something dark loomed on an open sea. An enormous ship with black sails. Rising from the ship were tendrils of black smoke, like Everett had seen in the wood. He pulled back and closed the lid of the compass.

"Can you not tarry a bit longer? I would see more of this instrument," Avery said, looking sulky.

"We have to be careful. We don't know what we're dealing with." *And we should let Almaric and Holly know,* he thought. *Before something bad happens.*

"These two objects act in concert, Everett, and only we know how they work. We can learn more about them together, but only if we keep them secret. Are we in accord?"

Everett considered the black ship. He only saw it, he reasoned; he didn't create it. Besides, all sorts of ships must be roaming these seas. And the smoke was just some odd feature of the compass. Holly didn't own rights to all the magic in this world, and anyway, it wasn't like before, when an evil fairy creature was brainwashing him. "Right then, here's the deal," he said at last. "I'll stay mum about the wand, but we'll learn how it works *together*. And Holly doesn't get hurt, clear?"

"I have no quarrel with Lady Holly. I only wish to know her better, to learn from her as well—in time." Avery shifted his feet and looked down at them as if there was something to learn from the dank floor. "She does not favor me, I gather."

Everett snorted. "I'd say that's a fair guess. If you want to be friends with her, with any of us, you can't be allied with the king."

Avery looked up. "Then consider me a friend. For I swear the king to be my greatest enemy."

Chapter 29

Captain's Orders

A few mornings after they'd set sail, Holly stood on the deck of the *Sea Witch*, proud of her calm stomach and steady sea legs. She stood beneath the main staysail and gazed up at Kailani, who stood in the crow's nest with a spyglass to one eye. Holly thought she'd love to be like Kai, as she was called, at home on the sea, inspecting the sails and hull, giving orders to the crew. More than one of them stopped to watch her when she scrambled up the ratlines in her bare feet, her long black hair swinging down her back, but if she caught them staring, they busied themselves with swabbing or pulling on the braces. Holly leaned on the ratlines and nearly stumbled over Ben, sitting cross-legged in the middle of the ship's waist.

"Oggler taught me this trick," said Ben. "Keep a low center of gravity. And keep an eye on the horizon. It's helping with the—you know. My stomach."

"Which one's Oggler?"

"The guy with the eye patch. He's helping Pike at the steering wheel—I mean, the helm." Ben pointed astern. Holly remembered Oggler. Pike was no more than seventeen, with short, curly brown hair. She double-checked his face for stubble to make sure she'd judged his gender right.

Kai waved at Holly from the crow's nest. "Come up, if ye've a mind to," she called down.

"Do you think it wise?" asked Jade, who shadowed Holly's every move.

"I'll be okay." Holly put her foot into the ropes.

She was used to climbing. At home she had topped every rock wall in town, even the forty-foot one at the giant sporting-goods store. Still, it was dizzying to see the deck shrinking the higher she went. Jade became a small black dot amidships as the wind puffed out the flapping spanker sail to her left. And even when Holly reached the crow's nest, she wasn't at the very top, where she spied another crew member hanging above the topsail.

"Too high for ye?" Kailani asked, grinning.

"I'm fine. It's beautiful up here." Holly steadied herself against the ratlines. The stiff breeze blew back her hair, and tiny salt crystals peppered her glasses. "I can't believe how far we've come."

"It's the sea portal. Only the captain knows where to open one. They're connected, one t'other, like tunnels. One portal will seek out another. Here, have a look." Kai handed Holly her spyglass.

The sea stretched on forever. The masts creaked in the stiff breeze, the deck below looking not quite big enough to land on if she were blown off into the air. Holly wrapped one arm around the mast, feeling foolish as Kai stood holding on to nothing, and she scanned the horizon. It wasn't much to look at; only a straight line of unending blue, topped with whitecaps and leaping fish and—

"There!" she cried. On the southwestern horizon she spied a bump with little sticks poking out of it. They looked like trees. "I see land!"

Kailani's eyes widened and she took the spyglass from Holly. Her face went white beneath her tan. "That ain't land. That's a ship. Get below, Lady Holly. At once." She cupped her hands and hollered down to the deck. "A sail, Captain! A sail!"

"But who is it?" Holly asked.

"Now, milady," said Kai, and there was no disobeying her.

Holly backed down the ratlines, wondering who it was Kai could've seen. Below, the sailors ran to the rails, hollering about a ship. She kept her eyes fixed on her hands and the spanker sail until she felt the sun-warmed deck beneath her feet.

Ben stood peering out to sea. "Everybody's yelling about a ship. Could you see it? What'd it look like?"

"I could hardly see a thing," Holly said. The ship pitched suddenly, and Holly lost her footing, bowling into the captain, who was striding across the deck.

Morgan nudged her aside. "Pike!" she hollered to the bridge. "Helm quarter to port! Hands aloft to loosen topsails. To the north, Kailani!" She jerked her head at Holly. "And you lot—down below. Now."

Holly, Jade, and Ben followed the captain down the hatch and to the ship's mess, which was like the dining room. The rest of the new passengers had gathered around the small table.

"Is this about the ship we saw?" Holly asked. "Who is it?"

"Let's just say it's a party best avoided," said Morgan grimly. "So we're stepping up our itinerary. That's where you come in, Lady Adept."

"You propose to use Her Ladyship as a tool for navigation?" Ranulf asked.

Morgan glanced up sharply. "I've been sailin' for months lookin' for this island, to no avail. But I've since learnt of a legend: The Adepts can be found only by one o' their own."

"It still seems strange," said Holly, "that the king—or the Sorcerer—wants to find one of the Adepts that he sent away in the first place. They must have some kind of plan. What if we end up helping them?"

"Setting a horde of spell casters free won't give 'em any help, that's sure," the pirate said, swigging a stein of rum. "And if he ever wants to see his own flesh and blood again, he'll pay handsome, as well."

"You're gonna ransom the prince?" Ben asked, his eyes wide.

"What did you think?" Holly asked, trying to look like she knew exactly how a pirate's mind worked. "He's not here to join the crew."

"True enough." Morgan stared straight into Holly's eyes. "And he's takin' up rations as it is."

Holly didn't quite know what to say to this.

"Have you contacted His Majesty?" Almaric asked.

"Aye, Crews was sent just afore we set sail."

"Who's that?" Everett asked. "A page or something?"

Morgan snorted. "Ye'll meet him when he returns."

Holly wondered how anyone could find them, especially if they were changing course, but at the captain's dark look she closed her mouth.

CLAIRE M. CATERER

"Now then," Morgan went on. "Adept navigation's got to be done at the right time. Kailani will wake ye tonight, at the end of first watch." The captain pushed back from the table.

"But—" Holly started. She had no idea what Morgan meant.

Jade spoke up. "Captain, is Her Ladyship to steer the ship?"

"By the sea demon, she'll not be at *my* helm." Morgan scowled. "Ye're there for the navigation, as I say. *Lady.*"

"But . . ." Holly looked at Almaric, who shook his head. "*How* am I supposed to navigate?"

"Ye'll do what the crew tells ye," the captain said. "And see that ye steer us true. If ye don't fancy feeding the fishes, that be." She left the mess hall, slamming the hatch behind her.

"Well!" Almaric said. "I never! The cheek!"

Jade pressed a warm paw to Holly's face, which had gone suddenly cold. "Are you quite well, Lady Holly?"

She tried to smile. "I guess so." The truth was that a chill fingered down her back and through her toes, despite the stuffy mess hall, and her stomach heaved a little with the gentle pitch of the brigantine. The hull groaned.

"*I'm* not well," Ben said. "It sounds like they're just

going to point Holly out at the horizon, and if they don't find this island, they'll dump her overboard. In fact, it doesn't look good for any of us." He paused. "Am I the only one who thinks we're more like prisoners than passengers on this boat?"

"But we conjured the ship, not the other way round," Everett said. "Doesn't that put us in control?"

"No one controls the captain of the *Sea Witch*," said Almaric. "We may have netted ourselves a bigger fish than we can stomach."

Jade raised his whiskered eyebrows.

"Yes, all right. I realize I pushed the idea." Almaric looked so upset that Holly patted his shoulder. "But we're here now. All we can hope is that our own desires will marry happily with the captain's."

Chapter 30

Midnight Watch

Holly went to bed long after dark, but she couldn't sleep.

She sat in her bunk, swaying with the waves, a tiny lantern just above her head. She finally put it out after Kailani suggested it with a silent kick from the lower bunk. She counted the ship's bells as they rang every half hour through the night. A bleak loneliness wove its way around her like mist.

She was only dozing when Kai nudged her awake. Her black hair gleamed in the light from the lantern she carried. "Come on then," she urged. "Yer up for middle watch, and Pike don't like laggards."

Holly groaned. Her movement roused Jade, who stretched and followed her up out of the hatch into the damp midnight air.

"And there she be, before two bells yet," said Pike as she made her way to the bridge. "Hope ye had a good lie-in, yer Ladyship."

"I got here as quick as I could," Holly snapped,

rubbing her eyes. "It's not like I'm used to getting up at midnight."

"More like slumbering all the day long." Pike sniffed and adjusted his cap. His long, ropy arms were darkened by the sun, and his curly hair ruffled in the breeze. As he grasped the wheel, Holly noticed his fingers weren't webbed like some of the other crew members'. She wanted to ask about it, but it hardly seemed polite.

"So," Holly said to him, "what exactly am I supposed to do, if I can't take the helm?"

"Stand here." Pike backed up to allow Holly between him and the wheel. He glanced down at the cat. "That beast blows an ill will, I'll be bound. 'Tis bad luck on a ship."

"Then you know naught of an Adept's familiar," Jade observed. He leaped onto a nearby barrel and folded his paws beneath his chest.

"He stays with me," Holly said, trying to muster a voice that couldn't be argued with.

Pike muttered under his breath. He pulled a bit of charcoal and paper from a satchel, and set a large brass compass on top of the wheelhouse.

"What are you doing?" Holly asked.

"Takin' a reading, what d'ye think? Now hold still. The captain said to put yer right hand on the top spoke

CLAIRE M. CATERER

of the helm. Just the *top*, mind." Pike's eyes were wide and tense as he stood poised with his charcoal.

Holly wrapped her palm around the wooden spoke. "Like this?"

"How should I know? I haven't done this afore, have I? Bleedin' Adepts on a ship . . ." He continued to mutter as he watched the compass. "Now, don't try to hold 'er steady. She'll turn on ye, that's as what's wanted."

Sure enough, after a moment, the wood warmed in her hand, not unlike the wand. Gradually the sensation grew that the ship was changing, as if it were a whale awakening from a long sleep. Holly felt it stretch its rigging; it took deep breaths from its hold, blubbering a sigh through the bilgewater.

Jade's fur bristled along his spine. "What is that?"

"Fiend's name," whispered Pike. "What're ye doin' to the *Sea Witch*?"

Holly should have been frightened, but in fact she felt warm and right, as if she were wrapped up in her quilt with a good book. The boat creaked and dipped, as if nodding to her. Her braids whipped back from her face, and the chill breeze turned warm, enfolding her. The helm pulled to the south. The spanker sail luffed, sounding like applause.

"Lady Holly," Jade said above the wind. "What manner of magic is this?"

"I don't know. I'm just following it." She let the helm pull as it would, gently turning through her fingers. "It's—it's just the wind changing, right?"

"Nay, it's our *course* changing," Pike said hoarsely. He looked like he was going to be sick. Finally he remembered the charcoal and scribbled down numbers as he read them off the compass. "The captain said this'd happen—but I never saw the like . . ."

"Do you see the Adepts?" Jade said.

She didn't ask what he meant. She just closed her eyes and gripped her wand in its scabbard. In her mind she saw a rocky beach, where waves rolled and crashed at the foot of a cliff. A young woman sat on a boulder that jutted out to sea. She held something thin—a wand!—in her hand. She pointed it vaguely at the surf. Holly felt a jolt, as if something had punched her in the chest, and at the same moment, the lonely woman raised her chin with a jerk. She turned her gaze directly at Holly—or where Holly would be standing, if she'd been hiding in the copse beyond the beach. Their eyes locked. A lump rose in Holly's throat, as if she were coming home after a very long time away.

Suddenly a wave surged over the *Sea Witch*'s starboard side, drenching Holly head to foot. Her eyes sprang open, and the ship's wheel turned hard starboard. The sea, as if obeying some force, rocked and tossed the ship. A moment later, all was becalmed.

"Wet from Samhain to Yule. One might stay indoors the entire season." Jade shook his thick black fur.

"Rip me jib, that's seven points south," Pike mumbled. "We've turned a full seven points. D'ye think I should rouse the captain?"

Holly shook her head.

"And look who I'm askin'! Go on, then. Ye still have the watch till two bells, but ye won't go near the helm again."

"I was just doing what you told me," Holly shot back, her face growing hot.

"Her Ladyship," came a voice from a dark corner of the deck, "is a full Adept and worthy of your respect, seaman."

"As if I—" Pike broke off as Ranulf walked into the moonlight. "That is, sure enough. Apologies, milady."

Before Holly could respond, another massive wave broke over the gunwale, this time from the port side.

Pike gripped the helm. "What in blazes is it now?"

"What is happening?" Ranulf asked sharply.

"You lot and yer magic! I can't hold 'er steady!" Pike staggered, and the helm spun out of his grasp.

Áedán's sticky feet clung to Holly's damp neck as another wave swelled beneath the ship. A glint of light caught her eye. "Ranulf, look at the compass!"

The brass compass sitting on the wheelhouse was spinning madly, and a white-blue glow issued from it, as if the moon were shining on its face.

"Take the helm," said Ranulf. He pulled Pike's fingers from the wheel. "There is other magic afoot. Something is interfering with your navigation."

Jade leaped on top of the wheelhouse, placing one paw on the helm. "Together," he said, and Holly placed a tentative hand on the spokes.

"Leave it go, ye unholy witch!" Pike lunged for her, but Ranulf's strong arms held him back.

Holly ignored him. Something was pulling the *Sea Witch* in another direction. She grasped the helm lightly, as before, and closed her eyes, calling to mind the lonely girl on the rocks.

Again the wheel spun through her fingers, and the sea suddenly calmed.

Heavy footsteps came running down the deck, and Holly's eyes flew open. Kai's black hair shone in the lamplight. "Leave her be, Pike! You, there"—this to Ranulf—"loose him."

"Only if it be safe for Her Ladyship," said the centaur.

"Is anyone takin' the readings, then?" Kai picked up the charcoal Pike had dropped, and made notations off the compass. "Pike, go pump the bilge for the rest of the watch."

CLAIRE M. CATERER

Ranulf let him go, and Pike broke away with a curse. He gave Holly a black look before retreating down the hatch.

Holly and Jade followed Ranulf to the main deck. She took a small seat set against the gunwale. "Thanks," she said. Her knees were shaking now.

"It went well, Lady Holly," said Ranulf.

"I hope I really did point us to the Adepts' island. I saw someone. She looked lost. She had a wand; she must have been one of them." Now that it was over, Holly couldn't quite believe she'd changed the ship's course.

"It is one soul calling to another," Ranulf said. "The closer you ally with this land, Lady Holly, the more you feel them, even across many leagues."

"But what happened after that? You said some other magic was interfering."

"I cannot say."

"At first, when I saw the Adept, the ship kind of fell into alignment. Like it was meant to go there. But then something else was pulling it away. Like a magnet." Holly shuddered, and Áedán trembled too.

"I felt it as well," said Jade. "Mayhap Pike is not eager to find the Adepts and has magic of his own."

"I don't think so. He seems pretty scared of all magic."

"He is mortalfolk, not a Seafarer Elemental," said

Ranulf. "It is rare to see him on a ship like this one."

"He means us no good," Jade said. "Elemental or no. The magic, whatever it was, felt misused, uncontrolled, to me."

They fell silent. Another thought occurred to Holly, one that made her chest feel hollow. She took out her wand, comforted by its warmth. "Ranulf, when they come back—the Adepts, I mean—I won't . . ." She paused, not liking the way she was voicing the thought.

"You wonder what need we shall have of you," Jade supplied. He had finished his bath and was curled up on a coil of rope.

"That's selfish, isn't it?" She couldn't explain to them how much she loved it here, and how, if she weren't needed, if she never returned, how bleak everything would seem. She gazed out at the black sea, which glinted here and there in the starlight. "You need all the help you can get, and all I can do is point the way to this island. Almaric said it too. I need to be trained if I'm going to be any good at this stuff."

"Your reason for coming to us is not yet clear," Ranulf said, inclining his head to the skies. Holly winced; he was still too thin, his bruises not quite healed. "It is not just to find the Adepts. You have a special purpose of your own."

"And the training?"

"There must be a way. We will keep searching for it. Perhaps you will apprentice with one of these Adepts we seek."

Her heart lifted a little. "That *would* be cool." On her shoulder, the little Salamander shifted his sticky feet and warmed her skin. The desire to stay here in this world, with Jade and the others, suddenly overwhelmed her. "Do the stars say how long I'll stay?"

Ranulf smiled. "They do not predict exact movements, but they predicted your coming. The final outcome is a more cloudy matter."

"That figures."

"Do not let it trouble you. None of us knows his or her true purpose. Only that we have one."

"To pass between worlds is an unusual feat," Jade added. "That alone says much about your need to be here, beyond serving as a pirate's compass."

A warm gust of wind ruffled the main staysail above her head. Their course was true and steady now. She gazed out to sea again and thought she saw, in the blackness of the horizon, a tiny bump. The waves swelled. The *Sea Witch* pitched astern, then down again into the well. The spray hid anything further from sight. But she thought, if only for a second, that she had spotted land.

Chapter 31

What the Compass Did

Everett crept after Avery back down the hatch, the compass clutched in his hand. His face felt very hot and his chest fluttery and shaky. He had hoped that the compass would help Holly, not hurt her.

"I told you this was a bad idea," he whispered fiercely to the prince.

Avery stowed the wand as they made their way back to the brig. "It seems the ship is doing what it must, whatever we have done."

"We nearly mucked up the whole thing. And why's the locket acting this way? That's what was pulling the ship. I know it was."

"Only think of its power." Avery didn't sound nearly as worried as he ought to, Everett thought. "We were able to move an entire ship, Everett!"

Yes, Everett had felt that too. The question was, ought they have done it at all? He knew in his gut he should've told Holly and the others about Avery's plan, though it seemed harmless enough at the time.

Watch the Adept take her bearings, Avery had said. He had wanted to see the magic.

Avery caught him staring at him. "You do not trust me."

"Should I? Why were you so keen on sneaking up there?"

"I wish to study magic, Everett. You yourself have said the lady does not favor me. How else am I to learn, if not in secret?" They approached his cell.

Or, Everett thought, he'd wanted to sabotage Holly's navigation.

Everett closed the door on him. Avery immediately turned away and drew out the wand, making little glowing lights dance around the cell. Just beyond, he could hear Pike working the pumps to rid the ship of bilgewater.

Everett walked away from the brig's smell and settled in another corner of the hold. He pulled out the locked compass. He didn't want to rely on Avery's wand—*his* wand, as it originally was—to explore its properties. But it scared him a bit as well. It *wanted* something. It didn't just point the way—it *pulled*, directing the ship just as Holly's wand had.

Could Avery have known that would happen? Or did he just want to study magic, as he said?

Everett pushed his thumb against the catch. Now that Avery had unlocked it with the wand, it came open easily. The needle spun crazily in its housing, and Everett held the compass up to one eye.

Even in the dim light, he could see the castle to the northeast, and through the forest, Almaric's little cottage. Away to the north of Anglielle, moors rose out of the dun-colored earth, and farther north still, something dark was moving. A horde of creatures. Though he couldn't make out what they were, they had to be enormous—one of them crawled over a mountain like it was a hillock, turned, and opened a gaping mouth of fangs in his direction.

Everett slammed the locket shut, and the ship rolled, throwing him into a corner near the rack of muskets.

The ship righted itself. It yawed in the other direction—toward the southwest, where Holly had directed it. Everett stood. He had nearly dropped his lantern.

The flame flickered, and a stream of black smoke flowed out of it, as if the wick had been wetted. The tendril wafted from the lantern up to his nose, then around his head. For a moment, he thought he heard a hissing right inside his ears.

Open me.

Startled, he opened his hand. The locket hadn't spoken—*couldn't* have spoken.

CLAIRE M. CATERER

"Everett?"

He startled. Ben was standing at the other end of the hold. "I thought I saw a light down here. Did you feel the boat going back and forth? I was afraid it was a storm."

"Um, yeah, that was weird," Everett said, stowing the locket. "I was just . . . checking something. For the captain. Stores and stuff. Looks like we've got plenty of . . . stores." He was glad it was dark, because his face felt very hot.

"Riiiiiight," said Ben slowly. "Well, I'm going back to bed."

Everett followed, ignoring Ben's chatter. He no longer heard the whispers. But somehow he knew they still lingered in the dark.

Chapter 32

The Gale

Later that morning Holly found Ben and Everett up on deck, braced against the gunwale, enjoying the stiff breeze that urged the brigantine ever westward.

"Wow, that was a big one." Ben lurched against the railing. "We went right down into a big water-trench thing."

"It's choppy this morning." Holly's stomach tightened. She hoped she wasn't suddenly getting seasick.

Everett nodded. He looked a little green too. "How did your navigation go?"

"Kind of weird, but I think the ship is moving in the direction I pointed it to. The helm moved on its own. All I did was stand there." The sun hit a glint of gold in Everett's hand. "Is that the locket you found?"

"It's not just a locket," Everett said with some pride. "Look, I finally got it open."

He handed it to Holly, though she noticed he didn't take the chain from around his neck. What had looked like a pocket watch was an intricate compass with hundreds of point markings around the dial. Too many, it seemed. And yet it did look like a watch as well. She could see tiny gears revolving behind the needle, which spun with the pitch of the waves. And she thought she saw—

She turned the compass over and snapped the lid shut.

"Hey, don't lock it again!" Ben said.

"I'm not." She hoped. She wanted to see the symbols on the lid, the wave and the swirl and the earth and the flame. She was sure she had seen something glow on the surface, but now the symbols looked quite ordinary. Jade leaped onto the railing beside her and peered at it.

The wind calmed, and the ship settled into the water.

She turned the locket over. "Are you sure it's all right? It almost feels . . ." *Alive,* she thought *Like the wand.* Was that another thread of smoke uncurling from the hinges? A wave of nausea washed over Holly. "You should show it to Almaric. Make sure it's nothing dangerous."

"Oh, come off it," said Everett, taking it from her. "You just don't like that I found something cool before you did."

"Don't be stupid. Keep it if you want, what do I care?"

She couldn't see why Everett insisted on taking things she said the wrong way, but there *was* something odd about the compass. Jade frowned at her the way he did when he was guessing her thoughts. She gazed back at the horizon, which was finally level. "Hey, what's that?"

She pointed at a red spot in the sky to the east. It grew steadily bigger. Áedán tensed on her shoulder. Jade lifted his nose to the air. "I cannot tell. The wind is against us."

The spot flashed, changing color from red to blue, and it wobbled, moving irregularly. "Maybe it's a UFO," Ben suggested. Holly gave him a look.

"What? It's an *O*, and it's *F*. And it's definitely *U*. So technically—"

"It's a parrot!" Everett cried as it landed on the mainsail yard.

It wasn't just a parrot. A bit larger than a crow, it was covered with scarlet plumage, except under its wings, which were a deep indigo—in fact, it was exactly like the bird Holly had seen in the Hawkesbury forest, the one that had showed her the bridge across the stream. But how was that possible? The bird glided down to the poop deck, where it flapped importantly and raised a high crest from its forehead. "Captain!" it squawked.

Morgan emerged from her cabin. "Has Crews

arrived?" She smiled warmly when she saw the parrot. The bird lighted on her hand.

"*That's* Crews?" Ben whispered.

The captain and parrot cooed at each other until Morgan realized the crew was staring at them. Then she cleared her throat and said gruffly, "Well then, Crewso, what news have you?"

"What news, what news?" cackled the bird. "The king has been told of his son's ransom. He is willing to pay, Captain! Most handsomely. He awaits your return, he does!"

"Very good," said Morgan. "Aught else, friend?"

"Aye, Captain! Seven leagues to the northwest, the black schooner sails in our direction." Crewso fluffed his feathers and nibbled on one wing. "That is all."

A sudden gust of wind toppled the bird from the captain's hand. Morgan scooped him off the deck and shielded him in her coat. With a groan, the *Sea Witch* reared like a stallion and the bow popped out of the water, then fell with a crash. Holly stumbled backward, then scrambled up again. "Jade!" she called, her heart sick.

"Here, Lady," said the cat at her feet. Somehow he had not been swept off the railing to sea. Holly's stomach heaved, and a cold sweat spread across her face and shoulders. Áedán made a kind of *urggh* noise as if he wasn't feeling too good either. The ship reared again. It was like having the flu. Her breakfast gurgled, threatening to resurface.

Holly dropped to the deck again, with Ben and Jade beside her, as the deck pitched. "It can't be a storm," she said weakly. "There aren't any clouds."

She pulled herself up to find the captain beside her. Morgan clapped a glass to her eye and swore. "It can't be! How'd the devil find us?"

"How did who find us?" Ben asked.

"Who d'ye think?" Morgan muttered, then called up to the poop deck. "Rowan! He's closing fast, but likely he's not espied us yet. Let this gale take its toll. Spanker to windward, and topsails, too!" She curled her lip at Holly and Ben. "And you lot, get below. This'll get worse, I reckon."

"Come on." Holly crawled along the deck to the railing. "Where did Everett go?"

"He just went below. He said something about looking at his compass again."

Holly took Ben's spyglass and peered over the gunwale. "Who do you think that ship belongs to?" She could see the black schooner for herself now, a three-masted ship quite a bit bigger than the *Sea Witch*.

"I don't know, but look up there."

Ben pointed at the clouds. How had they gathered

so fast? Holly squinted. She thought she could see fingers of black smoke roiling out of them, but it must have been a trick of the light as the clouds changed shape. Morgan and Rowan shouted as the breeze whipped the sails. The waves and wind were pushing them closer to the other ship, which bobbed calmly on the waves. The sky darkened. The next moment the wind turned cold, and fat raindrops began to fall.

"All hands on deck! Aloft to furl the sails!" shouted Morgan, and suddenly everyone was very busy. Quelch nudged by Holly and Ben to ring the ship's bell. The crew poured from the hold and the forecastle. Rowan stayed at the wheel as the others clambered up the ratlines to furl the topsails, spanker, and foresails. It was wretched to watch the crew clinging to the masts as the ship rolled and pitched. But they scurried down to the deck unharmed as the wind cranked up several notches. Holly threw open the main hatch and followed Ben belowdecks.

The gale blew all that day. Two of the crew—usually Morgan and Rowan—hauled on the ship's wheel at any one time, while the rest of them tended the sails or bailed water. Three different times, Morgan called Holly on deck and had her touch the wand to the ship's broad compass. The moment she did so, it was like the *Sea Witch* suddenly remembered where it was supposed to be going, and it bucked against the storm to pull back to the proper direction. Holly only stayed on deck long enough to reestablish the direction; it was all her stomach could take. The deck pitched like a big amusement-park glider, its stern heaving up one minute, its bow the next, and Holly heard the most awful crackings and groanings, as if the ship were an old soldier trying to hold itself together. At one point the bowsprit snapped in half, and the jib sails fluttered free; but Morgan managed to keep them from capsizing.

Meanwhile, life belowdecks was dull and punctuated all too often by someone retching into a bucket or moaning, holding his or her stomach with both hands. The passengers stayed together in the open room between cabins for the most part. Holly tried to make up games for her and Ben and Everett to play, but at times they felt too ill even for that. Everett, Holly noticed, continually toyed with his locket, gazing at it, opening and shutting it, sometimes holding it right in front of one eye. She couldn't help thinking that the storm had hit right after he'd shown it to her.

She noticed he still hadn't shown the compass to Almaric, who was oddly unaffected by the storm. Jade, and even Ranulf, who was obliged to sit with his horses' hooves tucked beneath him, didn't seem too bad off. The galley fire had been put out at once when the wind had started, so there was no tea or soup, only hardtack and some kind of chewy dried beef that Holly wisely avoided.

It was on the second day that, as the group sat morosely in their usual spots (everyone had found a particular place to hold on to something heavy as the ship rolled and pitched), a face appeared from the bow end of the hold—a face as green as Holly's and Ben's. It belonged to the prince.

"What are *you* doing here?" Holly demanded, then turned on Everett. "Did you let him out?"

"What if I did?" Everett said. "Have you seen where they're keeping him? It's horrid."

"Then maybe he shouldn't have come aboard in the first place," Holly shot back, though she felt a twinge of guilt. The prince was filthy, his clothes muddied, his hair matted with something. Clearly, he'd been sick too, and looked like he soon would be again. Was he thinner since they'd set sail? She didn't even know if he'd been fed.

"Are you okay, Avery?" asked Ben, who looked about as far from okay as anyone could get.

"The stench." Avery's voice sounded croaky. "I could bear it no longer." He stumbled forward, and the rest of the group backed away. He did smell foul. He collapsed in the middle of the floor, gasping big gulps of air. "Is there water?"

"Oh, here, I'll get you some," Holly said crossly, heading to the barrel. "Don't sit on anything of mine."

"His Highness has not been treated well," said Ranulf from the corner. His jaw was hard, and Holly remembered he had lately been a prisoner himself. "He could be granted fresh air, at least. He cannot escape."

"The captain does not mean to keep me alive for long. She has no cause to bother with me." Avery grasped the ladle Holly brought him and downed the water before she could pour it into a cup. "My thanks, Lady."

"But she doesn't mean to kill you, surely?" Almaric said.

The prince shrugged.

Holly remembered what Morgan had said about the rations. She wondered if the captain would keep Avery alive, ransom or no. "Well," she said, unable to keep from sounding irritated, "it's not like we'd let her kill you. Give us a little credit."

"How would we prevent it?" said Jade. "As captain, Morgan's word is as good as a king's aboard ship. And she is not above stealing into the night and slitting His Highness's throat."

"Okay, cut it out," said Ben. "This is sounding creepy.

The crew isn't like that. Oggler, for example—"

"He may teach you to sail, and seem amiable enough," said Ranulf, switching his tail, "but he has killed before. They all have."

"Then we stand up to her," Holly said. She couldn't quite believe she was talking about sticking up for Avery, who had tried to kill her own brother. But Avery's thin face and racking cough made her stomach even more queasy. The wand trembled and shifted in its scabbard, as if it, too, was unhappy.

"What's that mean, exactly?" asked Everett. Ben turned an even ghastlier shade of green.

"It means we protect him," said Holly. "I'll try to convince the captain to let him out of his cell once in a while. He may not be my best friend, but—well, just *look* at him."

The rest of them looked at the prince's tattered clothes and greasy hair. Avery widened his blue eyes and cast his gaze down like a whipped puppy.

"Okay," Holly said. "Don't overdo it." She crawled back to her place against the barrel, but not before she saw the prince give Everett a satisfied smirk.

Chapter 33

The Prince on Deck

The storm passed after another two days, and when everyone staggered out of the hold, it looked to Everett like someone had thrown a wild party. The deck was strewn with seaweed, and some of the planks were splintered; the bowsprit was a jagged stub; the main staysail had a gaping hole; the railing around the forecastle was broken through, its pieces scattered. Some supplies had been washed overboard, and the mainmast yard had cracked. But all in all the ship was still seaworthy. The weary crew busied itself making the necessary repairs. Kailani was in charge of this duty, and she seemed to be everywhere at once, bellowing at Darcie to count the grain stores, enlisting Innes and Quinn to repair the sail, and getting Oggler and Quelch to sand down the upper deck.

Morgan kept a constant lookout for land through her spyglass. "If this is the Adept magic we all hear so much tell of, ye can throw it to the sharks," she muttered one morning. "We need to land and make repairs. Ye'd best make yerself useful, Lady. And soon."

"Useful and soon, useful and soon," squawked Crewso the parrot, who shadowed Morgan's every step.

Morgan had already granted Holly one victory, and it seemed she would be made to suffer for it. The two of them had spent a long time talking in the ship's mess right after the storm let up, and afterward all Holly could say was, "She says Avery can come out." But Holly looked shaken.

The prince wasted no time in making himself useful. He bathed, and one of the crew even loaned him some clothes, since his finery was beyond saving. In fact, he managed to look and smell better than anyone else on board. He was up on deck almost all the time now, and even got Darcie to string up a hammock for him there. He wanted to know all about the *Sea Witch*, and listened eagerly as Everett took him around to the helm and the forecastle, and showed him how the sails were trimmed. He stood with the rest of the crew to haul the braces in to turn the topsails, and beamed when he saw the wind catch them, puffing them up like parachutes.

"I should like to go aloft as well," he said to Ben and Everett a week after the storm had passed. They were watching Holly clamber up the rigging to the crow's nest.

"You'd have to get Holly or Kai to take you," said Ben. "That's not gonna happen anytime soon."

"I cannot see why," Avery said, sulking. When Holly came down, he approached her at once.

"That's just what they want," Holly said. "You'd fall into the sea, and they'd leave you there."

"Not if I had your better skill to guide me." Avery flashed what Everett supposed he meant to be a shy grin.

Holly was headed to the foremast's crow's nest now. Avery trailed behind, wheedling her. "If it please thee, my lady, I couldst grasp thy comely foot to keep from falling."

"Oh *brother*," Ben whispered to Everett.

Anyone who had seen Holly's feet might call them large, a bit brown from all her climbing, callused maybe, but not *comely*.

"Stay here," she ordered. "Don't you have someone else to bother?"

"She will agree," Avery said with confidence as Holly heaved herself up into the ratlines. "Ladies are to a one charmed by me. And soon enough, she will train me in her magic."

Everett eyed Holly as she scowled through the spyglass under the bottom edge of the topsail. "I wouldn't bet on that, mate."

Suddenly Avery stumbled into him, and Everett knocked Ben over in turn. When they looked up, Pike was walking by, whistling. He glanced back. "Best get yer sea legs, lads," he said, grinning.

"That was a-purpose," Avery said hotly, righting himself. "He put his hands upon me, I am certain."

Pike turned around. "Did ye say somethin', Yer Highness?"

He was at least three years older than Avery and a good thirty pounds heavier. He towered over him, blocking the sun. The prince swallowed hard but stood his ground. "I believe you pushed me aside, sir," he said.

"It was just an accident, Avery," said Ben. He coughed to keep his voice from squeaking.

"My pardons, Yer Grace." Pike bowed so low that his forehead nearly brushed the deck. "Lemme make it up to ye. I'll help ye climb the ratlines, if ye like. Impress that fair maiden." He cocked his eye up at Holly.

"You have my thanks, seaman," said Avery grandly. "I wouldst take your aid."

"Avery, no!" Everett said. At Pike's scowl he added, "You were going below to help me with—with—"

"Our royal manners," Ben cut in. "He's giving us lessons."

But Avery didn't catch on. "Another time, squire. As for now, this noble seaman will help me aloft."

The prince put a foot onto the ratlines and hoisted himself up a few feet. Pike grabbed on behind him. "No!" Everett said, pulling on Pike's arm. "He's not going!"

Pike jumped back onto the deck. "Ye didn't just put yer hands on me, lad, did ye?" He pushed his face so close to Everett's that his foul breath warmed Everett's cheeks. He gave Everett's arm a wrench. "I say he *is* goin' aloft. So leave it be, unless ye're wantin' to go up as well."

"Land! Land!" Kailani hollered.

Pike shoved Everett away from him as Avery scrambled back down the rigging, asking, "Is it the island? Are we to meet the Adepts at last?" He was so excited, he had forgotten he would be better able to see from the crow's nest.

"So it would seem, Your Highness," said Ranulf, who had come up behind them.

The Island of the Adepts was finally in view.

Chapter 34

The Island

"I must say, it's very exciting," said Almaric as the crew shared a quick supper of fish chowder. "We shall be there in the morning, I presume, Captain?"

"Midday, I reckon." Morgan tore a piece of bread with her teeth. "Mind, I don't know how many of them we can take at once. Perhaps fifty at most. We'll have to load more rations."

"I don't understand how we got here so fast," Holly said.

"It was that first bit, when we went underwater," Everett said. "Wasn't it, Captain? We're not anywhere near Anglielle."

Like going through a wormhole in outer space, Holly thought. She had read about wormholes in a book Mr. Gallaway had given her.

"The *Sea Witch* is a ship like none other," said Morgan. "Once we captured her, we were forced to make . . . modifications, ye might say."

"You *captured* her?" Ben stopped chewing, his eyes round.

"Aye, on a voyage we made many ages past. She was laden with goods. We boarded her, then took her for our own."

"A pretty prize she was, pretty, pretty," Crewso added. He sat on his own perch in front of a mess of nuts and pulped fruit.

"What about . . ." Holly hesitated.

"The crew? What d'ye think?"

"Did you make them walk the plank?" Ben asked eagerly.

"Ben, there were *people* on this boat." Holly raised her chin at Morgan. "So? What did you do with them?"

The captain, unruffled, ladled out more chowder for herself. "Don't be boilin' yer blood at me. Pike there, on the dogwatch, was one of 'em. And Cook. T'others had no use for the life of a privateer. We locked 'em in the brig and put 'em to harbor at first sight of land, afore we deserted that accursed place."

"What sort of place was it? Was it far from here?" Everett asked.

"A fair piece." The captain winked. "The *Sea Witch* goes where none else does."

Holly thought back to the bird in the forest in Hawkesbury. "And Crewso? Does he go where none else does?" she asked, but at the captain's look, she swallowed the question. Instead she turned to the magician. "What will we do, Almaric? When we find the Adepts?"

"I think it best that Ranulf, you, and I make up an emissary party," he answered. "Jade, too, naturally. Some of the Adepts I knew personally will still be among the living, and Ranulf's presence will assure them we are not friends of the king. And they will know one of their own, of that I am certain."

"They'll be surprised to see me." *And hopefully happy about it,* Holly added to herself.

"As were we all," said Jade, who sat beside her, chewing on a piece of fish. "Perhaps the Adepts will have knowledge of the land whence you came, Lady Holly."

"If you don't mind, Captain," said Almaric, smiling and twisting his napkin, "I think it may be best if you and your crew hang back for a bit. So as not to alarm anyone."

"I sleep on the *Sea Witch* in any case. We'll come ashore to replenish our rations and make repairs, nothing more."

"Excellent. Then prepare to meet your Anglielle cousins, Lady Holly." Almaric beamed, but Holly had the feeling she wouldn't be sleeping well tonight.

The ship made amazing speed all through the night. When Holly emerged onto the deck at dawn, she could see a small bay that faced a rocky beach. A few brown mountains shrugged out of the land in the distance, and the beach they approached was ringed with trees and a steep dune-covered slope. By noon the ship was anchored, and Holly and the others rowed to the shore by longboat.

"It does not look to be a large island," Jade observed.

"It seems . . . deserted." Holly stepped onto the beach. Off to one side, a low cliff tumbled to the water, and a boulder jutted into the bay. Wasn't that where she'd seen the Adept girl?

Despite Morgan shouting orders to her hunting party and the sailors gathering supplies, an oppressive silence hung over the place. Holly gazed up past the dunes to the forest. A sudden loneliness bloomed in her chest. The tree branches drooped; the leaves were cracked and brown. On her shoulder, Áedán hunkered down onto his belly.

"This place feels . . . dead, Almaric. I don't think the Adepts are here. Or if they were, they're not anymore."

The magician sucked in a gasp. "You don't mean someone's killed them?"

CLAIRE M. CATERER

"I don't know. It's just that . . ." She appealed to Jade and Ranulf. "Don't you feel it?"

"It is weird," Ben said, shuddering.

"But you saw them at the helm," Almaric pressed. "They exist somewhere."

Holly sat down on the cool sand, pulling her knees up to her chin. A breeze flicked her braids around her face. "I'm sure I saw them here. But they're gone now. I'm sorry."

Morgan's tall figure blocked the sun. "Crewso will find out for certain if this island be inhabited," she said. "If not, we sail on. In the meantime, we'll replenish our stores and make repairs to the *Sea Witch*." She nodded to the parrot, who flew off into the brown trees.

Almaric patted Holly's shoulder. "The captain is right. Perhaps the Adepts' island is a bit farther on. Let us enjoy our time on land, if we may."

It didn't look like a place that invited enjoyment. Holly wanted nothing more than to sail away from it. She couldn't say why, but the thinning trees and burned, brown plants worried her. "If the crew is going hunting, we can at least look for water or maybe berries to eat." She stood up and gazed into the dense copse where Crewso had vanished. "I'm going for a walk."

Chapter 35

The Silent Meadow

For a few minutes there was a lot of tedious argument. Almaric objected to Holly wandering off; Ranulf insisted he should go along as protection; and Everett said he was going with her whether she liked it or not. The captain was displeased to be losing so many hands that could be used for other work, and Ben said even if Everett wasn't staying to help, *he* would. In the midst of this discussion, Crewso returned and confirmed that the island was uninhabited. So in the end, Holly grudgingly let Everett and Ranulf come along because she couldn't stop them. Jade followed her everywhere anyway. So what she had hoped would be a bit of solitude turned into something rather else.

And yet, as their small party climbed the hill off the beach and wound their way through the desiccated trees, Holly's annoyance lightened. The sense of abandonment she'd felt was keener now that the sailors' voices had faded behind them. Every once in a while she had to look down to make sure Jade was still at her feet, and that Everett and Ranulf were still following behind.

It was an odd sensation; she could see everyone, but they were like films or holograms, not real living beings. A minute ago she'd wanted a little quiet more than anything, but now suddenly she wanted to talk, if only to reassure herself that her companions were real.

"So," she said to Everett, "you've been hanging out with the prince?"

He blushed. "Well, yeah."

"I wish we could just send him back where he came from."

"He's decent," said Everett. "He did all right by us in the castle. He could've sided with the king."

"You make it sound like he's joined us, when really he's just running away from home. *If* he's not spying on us."

"I agree with Her Ladyship," said Jade.

"Wow, big surprise."

"His Highness may know a trick or two you are not aware of," said the cat. "And you do not know this land."

"Nor does Holly."

"I think Jade just means that we have to be careful who we trust," said Holly.

"Talking of trust, I'm not all that keen on this crew,"

Everett said in a lower voice. "The captain seems in it for herself, and I think Pike would throw Avery overboard if we gave him half a chance."

Holly stopped. They had come out of the brush and into a broad meadow crackling with brown grass. A copse of trees lay at the far end, spilling yellow leaves around their roots. She had just noticed something.

"What is it, Your Ladyship?" Ranulf asked in a low voice. His sword was drawn, and Holly took out her wand.

"Don't you hear it?" she asked, and everyone was still.

"The birds," Jade said after a moment. "There are none."

"No birds, no anything," said Holly. The silence weighed on them like a heavy blanket. She strained to hear the chittering of a squirrel or the rustling of a snake or rabbit, but even the brown grasses waved in the wind without making a sound.

"It's like . . . it's just dead," Everett said softly. "All of it."

Holly knelt and parted the grass. There was not an ant, not a beetle. The soil had great, yawning cracks in it. She waved her wand, stirring the dust, but still nothing skittered out of the holes. "I don't understand." She looked up at Ranulf.

"Something is very wrong here." The centaur moved

CLAIRE M. CATERER

in a circle, twitching his tail, though no horseflies plagued him. "We must go back and find the others. Sail at once if we can."

"But we need to find water. A lot of our casks were washed overboard."

"There can be no water here," said Jade. "Even these trees should be dead."

It was then that Holly caught something on the breeze. The faintest of sounds. "There! Did you hear something?"

The others froze for a moment, then shook their heads.

"It came from . . ." Holly peered across the meadow, at another stand of near-dead trees. "Over there. It was like . . ." She heard it again. "Like a trickle. A stream."

She saw the look Jade gave Ranulf, and she stood up. "Well, I'm going to see what it is, anyway."

"I advise against it," Ranulf said sharply.

Holly walked into the meadow. "I know. But I've got my wand. And Áedán." Although she noted that, despite the arid place, the Salamander felt sluggish and not as warm as usual on her shoulder.

"You shall not go alone." The centaur started forward, and the others followed.

But then a curious thing happened. The others

were only a few paces behind Holly, and she heard the grasses rustling as they walked, but a moment later they had fallen at least twenty yards behind her. It was as if the meadow had grown, stretching behind her a good ways, although the grassland before her looked the same.

Holly frowned. "Hurry up, if you're coming," she called, but her voice sounded oddly flat, as if she were inside a closet instead of the open air. She turned around. Everett and the others kept moving their legs, but they weren't making any headway.

"Ranulf!" Holly called. "Are you guys okay?"

She started back, but no matter how far she walked, she never got any closer to them. Her feet flattened the tall grasses in front of her, but the path behind her hadn't lengthened at all; and the others looked to be walking on a treadmill.

Jade tried to leap over the tall grass, and Ranulf slashed at the meadow with his sword. Everett cupped his hands and seemed to be calling to her; but it was like they were behind glass. Once again the world had gone silent.

She peered again at the copse of trees on the far side of the meadow, then back at the others. Holly raised her wand at the tall grasses and whispered:

Clear the way.

At once the shaft warmed in her hand, and the familiar current zoomed up her arm to her heart and back again. A jolt of power shot from the wand, but almost at once a backblast knocked her off her feet, as if the spell had rebounded off a stone wall. She stood up, unharmed, and scrabbled around to find Áedán, who crawled onto her palm and then up to her shoulder.

Holly picked up the wand, which trembled, hummed, and bent like a divining rod. It pulled her toward the copse of trees.

There was nothing for it. She couldn't go back, and the wand was calling her on. "It looks like it's just the two of us, Áedán," she whispered to the Salamander. She pointed the wand in front of her, much as Ranulf wielded his sword, and turned her back on the others.

Chapter 36

The Well

Áedán and a steady, cooling breeze were Holly's only companions. Not even a grasshopper crossed her path. Within twenty steps, she reached the copse of trees and stepped between them.

She stood at the foot of a rocky mountain, which had somehow not been visible before. It rose straight up, but there were plenty of handholds and a clear path. She started to climb.

The wind stilled. The incline was steep, sometimes obliging her to crawl on all fours. The wind had carved juttings of sparkling granite into the slope and polished them like a rock tumbler. After about ten minutes Holly reached the broad peak. But it was not at all what she'd expected.

She had arrived on a plateau that stretched for miles. She stepped onto a carpet of deep green grass. Riots of flowers spread at her feet—corn cockles and oxeye daisies and buttercups and red campion. She waded through them until she reached a semicircle of hazel trees clustered around a well.

Its blocks of roughly hewn limestone formed a low arched wall affixed to a dry basin. A carved dolphin leaped over the top of it. Holly ran her fingers along the wall's sharp edges and peered into the basin drain. How deep did it go? Feeling around in the dirt for a pebble, she found instead a brass coin. Etched onto its face was a tiny profile of a lady with long hair and a pensive expression. Holly wanted to keep it, but before she could stop herself, she tossed the coin into the basin and listened. Several seconds later, a soft *plop* echoed from the bottom.

At once a stream of water gurgled out of the stone dolphin's mouth. Holly skipped back as it overflowed the well basin. In a moment it had become a brook that cascaded over the mountainside.

A dragonfly flitted above the well, then settled on its dusty edge. "My, what a nice job you've done!" it said brightly, and then with a loud *pop*, it changed into a hare and hopped off the basin's rim.

Holly's mouth fell open. "I know you," she said. "The changeling! Do you remember me? Holly—I met you last year."

The hare looked up at her and chewed a few blades of grass. "Oh, I remember! Of course I do. The Adept.

You nearly got us all killed." Despite the accusation, the changeling sounded quite cheerful.

"I'm . . . yeah. Sorry about that."

"No worries." The hare sat up on its considerable haunches and cocked one shiny brown eye at her. "As you can see, I'm perfectly fine. I turned into a beetle and scurried out of the way when things got dodgy."

Holly had a sudden vision of the mayhem on that day—the tournament pitch erupting in dust and smoke, Ranulf and the other centaurs besieging the king's knights, the Dvergar falling . . .

"But where did you go?" Holly asked. "Almaric has been looking for you. Everyone's so scattered, the Dvergar, Fleetwing, the Mounted—"

"Can you blame us?" The hare nibbled on a clump of clover. "It's all very well for you, to anger the king and send the Sorcerer into a rage, and then nip off to some other world. I went back to my colony, told them it all looked a bit pointless. How were we to know you'd come back?"

"I didn't know you had a colony."

"Hmph." The hare sniffed, then morphed into a bob-cat, which turned its back to her. "Not that you asked, either."

A gnawing guilt rose in Holly's stomach. "I really am sorry. But I came back to help. We're sailing to find the

Island of the Adepts—Almaric and Ranulf and Jade, and Ben and Everett and me. When we bring them back, we'll have a real chance of defeating Raethius."

The bobcat stalked toward her. Its shoulders rolled under its skin. A flicker of fear passed through Holly's belly, but the bobcat settled nearby. "What makes you think you can bring them back?"

"Well, I . . . because I'm one too. I can navigate the ship and all. . . . I saw them here, on this island. I know the king exiled them, but—"

"But you know nothing." The bobcat bared its teeth. "They can't be *found*. They aren't *lost*."

Holly's heart sputtered. "What . . . what do you mean? Sure they are. The king sent them away."

"Don't speak of things you are ignorant of. I was there." The bobcat shrank before her eyes and sprouted wings, becoming a sparrow. "The night of the massacre, I was in the trees. I saw it all. The knights stole over the cliffs into the initiates' caves. They rode the silent steeds, rendering themselves invisible, undetectable. Even the guardians couldn't see them. They took the children first, before their teachers even woke." The sparrow bowed its head, then with a crackle, it became a skunk. "Sorry. I can't always control it."

Holly reached out a tentative hand and stroked the

silky black fur. "And . . . what happened then?"

"What do you think? A slaughter."

"But . . . they weren't *all* killed?"

"No. They had plans ready. Some were left to hold the knights at bay while the rest sailed into the night. No one's heard of them since. Well, almost no one."

The skunk snuffled in the dirt. Holly thought it might be crying. Then it shuddered along its white-striped spine and turned into a red-tailed hawk.

"Almost no one? Do you know where they went?"

"I followed them," said the changeling. "I hid on the boats as a ladybug, then swam alongside as a porpoise. But they discovered me once we reached the island. They could have killed me, but instead they sent me back to spread the king's tale, that they'd been bested by his knights and exiled by his decree. But they weren't exiled, Lady. They *escaped*." The hawk cocked an eye at her. "Unless they're ready to return, until they *want* to be found, you'll never locate them. They have abandoned this land for good."

"That can't be right," Holly said. "Don't they want to see Raethius defeated?"

"Of course. But they left in the first place because things looked so hopeless. The Good Folk retreated to their Realm; the Mounted battled in the forest; the beasts squabbled among themselves. Without a united

CLAIRE M. CATERER

force, the Adepts could see which way the tide had turned."

"So that's it, then?" A swell of anger bubbled up in Holly's chest. Why had she bothered coming to Anglielle at all? Everyone cowered in their corners while Raethius eliminated them one by one. "The Adepts are just fine with Raethius terrorizing the whole kingdom? What kind of heroes are they?"

"They're not heroes," the changeling said. Its feathers smoothed into fur, and it became the hare again. "They never have been. When they lived in Anglielle, they kept to themselves and studied their magic. Why do you think the magicfolk were so happy to see you? You were different—an Adept who rallied them, who wanted to harness magic to defeat the king. Or at least, to rescue your brother."

Holly gazed at the bubbling well. "What if things were different? If I *was* able to rally everyone, bring them together? Do you think the Adepts would come back?"

"It's possible." The hare nibbled a daisy, then gave her a sidelong look. "I can't say for certain."

The wildflowers waved in the breeze. Beyond them, below the plateau, Holly recalled the dead meadow and the girl she had seen. "I did see them—or one of them—on this island. Were they here?"

"They move constantly. But yes. They were here, only days ago."

Holly looked at him very hard for a moment. "You're in contact with them. You know where they are right now, don't you?"

"Don't be silly. Of course not. They cover their tracks very well, but . . ." The hare hesitated, and scratched a flea.

"But *what*?"

"They do leave traces. Can't you sense that magic has been done here? Can't you smell it?"

It was what she had been sensing ever since their landing, Holly realized. Magic *had* been done here, and then the place was abandoned. That was the loneliness she felt. If only the *Sea Witch* had been quicker. They had come so close. . . .

"This well is a sacred place," the hare went on. "Do you recognize it, Lady Adept?"

Of course she didn't. She didn't know much of anything about this world.

"It's a shrine to Coventina, the water goddess." The hare sat up on its hind legs, leaped into the basin of water, and transformed into a golden carp. Its head poked out of the water. "Coventina never comes to land, but she does grant boons. That's why the Adepts came here—to alter the time stones."

"Time stones?"

The carp leaped from the water, grew legs, and became a golden frog. It splayed its sticky fingers over the stone wall behind the basin. "Raise your wand; you'll see them."

Holly did as the changeling asked, and then she did see them—three small, hazelnut-shaped stones embedded in the wall above the basin. "What are they for?"

"Oooh, they're quite powerful. They grant the owner magic to tear the veil of time."

Tear the veil of time. "Can I use them, changeling?" Holly asked, breathless.

The frog bobbed his head. "Only an Adept can extract them from the well. And only for a price."

"What is it?"

"It is steep," the frog cautioned.

"Yes, okay, but what is it?" *How bad could it be?* Holly thought. Anything would be worth mastering time. She could travel to the past, change things if she wanted. . . .

"As I understand it," the frog said carefully, "you must give three days of your life as payment—one for each stone."

"That's all?" But that was easy. Three days was nothing.

"I don't think you quite understand. You don't choose the days. The stones choose them. The day taken from your past, for instance, might be a very happy one. Or a day you learnt something important."

"Or the day I got the wand," Holly murmured, gazing down at it.

"No, you're lucky there," said the changeling. "The stone cannot take a day that has direct impact on your coming to this point. But still, you don't know what it *will* take—"

"I don't care," Holly broke in. "How do I do it?"

"Lady Holly, think of what you're giving up. The days, once given, can never be retrieved," the frog said anxiously.

Holly raised her wand. The frog skittered out of the way with a squeaky croak. She touched the wand to the stones and closed her eyes. "I agree," she said. The wand trembled. "I agree to give three days of my life to retrieve the time stones."

The wand jerked in her hand toward the well, and Holly's eyes flew open. The stones fell into the basin with a plinking sound, and she scooped them into her palm. But the wall looked unchanged.

"Did it work?" she asked the frog. "They're still embedded in the stone."

"Any Adept may claim a set of time stones," said the frog. A tear fell from one of his bulbous eyes. "Do you know which day has been lost, Lady?"

CLAIRE M. CATERER

A day from her past. Holly thought back. How would she know if it was gone? At once a wave of panic rushed through her, causing Áedán to sit up in alarm. What if she'd erased the day of Ben's birth? She scanned her memories. No, she *remembered* Ben. Her mother and father were both fine too. But . . .

Something *was* missing. A small wound, a tear, opened in her heart. Something had been taken. Tears welled behind her eyes; but how could she cry for what she couldn't miss? What *was* it? What had she lost?

"Oh," she said softly. She turned to the changeling.

But it had disappeared. She sank onto the grass, lost in thought, heartbroken.

Wondering.

Chapter 37

The Time Stones

Holly was startled to see that it was getting dark by the time she and Áedán made their way back down the mountain. The stream from Coventina's well had turned the island lush and green. She wasn't surprised that the others had returned to the beach. She found them gathered around a campfire, conferring with Almaric.

They all crowded around her in great relief. Ben gave her a big hug, and Everett tried to explain that they never would have left her there, they were just trying to regroup.

"I'm all right," Holly said, pulling the stones out of her pocket. "I found these. And I saw the changeling."

Holly sat down at the fire with the others and told them what had happened, and what the changeling had said about the Adepts. "We conjured the *Sea Witch* for nothing. There's no way we can sail to the Adepts' island."

CLAIRE M. CATERER

The circle was quiet for a long moment after she finished. "Maybe it's a trick," Everett said finally. "Can we trust this changeling? Maybe it doesn't want us to find the Adepts for some reason."

Ben nodded, but Almaric and Ranulf shook their heads. "There have been similar rumors for years," said the magician. "And the changelings have always been loyal to the Exiles." He paused, thinking. "Let me see the stones," said Almaric. "Jade, are they genuine?"

The cat stepped forward and sniffed them in Almaric's palm. "They are. Therein lies the key, to be sure."

"The key to what?" Ben asked.

Almaric held the three stones close to the firelight. "The changeling was correct. Time stones are quite powerful, and rare. The fluorite—that's the blue one, Lady Holly—represents the past. The obsidian, the black stone, is the future. But look at the crystal. It rules the present. Usually, it is clear, but see how this one is cloudy? I believe that's what the changeling meant when it said the Adepts altered the stones. They have clouded the crystal to hide themselves. When it clears, the Adepts will be ready to come home."

"But, Almaric, how do they work? What can I learn from them?"

The old man smiled at her, his blue eyes sparkling. "A great deal, Lady Holly."

While Morgan's crew elected to sleep on board the *Sea Witch*, Holly and the other passengers camped on the beach. The next morning the captain sent Cook and Darcie along the beach to gather crabs and fish, and Quinn and Innes hiked off in another direction to hunt game and fill the water casks. Kailani and Rowan took charge of making repairs to the bowsprit and the sails.

In the meantime Almaric took Holly over the dunes, out of the way of the others. The dead burned trees had turned into a lush jungle that crowded close to the sand. She sat down in a clearing with Almaric and Jade, and took the three stones from her pocket. Áedán crawled out from under her collar and perched on her shoulder to watch.

"So what exactly do time stones do, Almaric?" she asked. "Can I actually travel in time?" It was something she had always wanted to do, particularly during her math fundamentals class.

"Not exactly. The stones are used to call people to you—*they* become the time travelers."

"Oh." Well, that was still pretty interesting.

"Each stone calls people from a different time," Almaric went on. "With the fluorite"—Almaric held up the slate-blue stone—"you will be able to call on those from the past to come to you. But beware: They cannot come to your aid if you are in any danger. If the stone perceives danger, it cannot work, because the traveler might be killed and vanish from his own past, which could alter the caller's future."

"Like if my great-grandfather got killed," Holly suggested. "Then I wouldn't even be alive to call him in the first place."

"Just so."

"But what if I called my great-grandfather just when he was about to meet his wife? I could still change his history, right?"

"I believe not," Jade put in. "I have seen these stones work before. The traveler moves outside of his own time. It is as if the events of his time are frozen until he returns."

"So no one even knows he's gone," said Holly.

"Correct."

Holly's mind spun with the possibilities. She could talk to *anyone*—Lewis and Clark, or President Lincoln, or—

"Or the Adepts. I can call *them!*"

Almaric smiled. "Exactly."

"But what about the other stones?" Holly asked.

Almaric picked up the crystal. "The crystal, as I

said, represents the present. This stone calls people from your own time across distances. But it affords no protection to the traveler like the fluorite."

"So that means I can use the black one to call people from the future," Holly guessed.

"I would presume so," Almaric said. He held the stone up to his eye, but not even the sunlight reflected off its surface. "I have never seen the obsidian used. You will not need it, in any case." He laid it next to the others and looked at her kindly. "What did you sacrifice, Lady Holly?"

She blushed, as if she'd committed a crime. "Three days, Almaric. I hope it wasn't the wrong thing to do. I don't know which day in the past I gave up, but I feel like part of me is missing now." She felt a ridiculous urge to cry again.

The magician was quiet, and Jade stole up next to her, warming her skin. "A day in your present will disappear as well," he said. "You will not see it coming, but at some moment it will disappear in front of you."

Holly sniffed. "What about the future?"

"That too has already vanished," said Almaric. "You will someday realize what has been lost. It is potential. I hope the loss will not be severe."

She had been reckless. She'd wanted the time stones

CLAIRE M. CATERER

so badly, she hadn't thought of what the price could mean.

"All novices make mistakes," said Jade softly.

"Yes," said Almaric, and then more brightly, "but we press on. The good news is, you have a way to further your training now. I suggest you make use of it."

Holly sat back and crossed her legs. So the Adepts could help her, could teach her magic, if she were able to call them. What would she say to them? What would they think of her, she who couldn't even fight off a few knights? Her cheeks burned as she remembered the scene with Grandor and the others.

She took out her wand.

Áedán tensed on her shoulder.

"You won't need the wand, Lady Holly," said Almaric. "Just as with your work with the captain's compass. You need only the stones."

"But who do I call, Almaric? I don't know anyone's name."

"Try a general call. Something like, 'Adepts of the past, I call for your wisdom and teaching.' Whoever is open to mentoring a novice will be receptive to the call."

Holly sat up straight, and Almaric placed the fluorite stone in her hand.

At once she felt it respond. Instead of warming her like the wand, it felt cold, and got only colder. It was like holding a piece of ice. Holly closed her eyes, and a sudden chill breeze gusted around her face, whipping her braids behind her head. Áedán huddled close. *It's safe,* she told herself. *It has to be safe; Almaric and Jade are right here.* But she didn't open her eyes to check. Instead she took a breath and uttered the words Almaric had instructed her.

"Adepts of the past, I call for your wisdom and teaching."

The wind blew stronger. It hurt to hold the fluorite; she felt the prickling along her palm that meant she was in danger of frostbite. She said the words again:

"Adepts of the past, I call for your wisdom and teaching."

Her heartbeat slowed; her limbs grew heavy. She couldn't be freezing to death, with Áedán so close, but he didn't move. What if she was hurting him? But she felt Jade's soft paw on her knee, urging her on, and she called once more to the Adepts.

"Well?" said an impatient voice. "You called and I came. What is it you want?"

Chapter 38

Ailith

Holly's eyes flew open.

Standing before her was a slight, dark-haired girl of about fifteen, dressed in a linen tunic over loose trousers. Something about her—the tilt of her eyes, which were large and brown—was familiar, but Holly couldn't quite place it. She sat speechless; Jade and Almaric were as silent as she was.

"Will someone tell me what I'm doing here?" the girl asked, her dark brows coming together.

"Sorry," Holly hastened to say, and stumbled to her feet. Almaric and Jade bowed their heads. "I'm Holly Shepard—um—I'm an Adept too." She held out her hand, hoping her beating pulse wasn't too obvious.

"No kidding." The girl frowned at the hand as if not knowing what to do with it. "I am Ailith."

Almaric raised his eyes. His face was quite red, and he kept twisting the hem of his robe in his fingers. It reminded Holly of when he had first met her, and she felt a pang of jealousy. "I am Almaric of the Elm, Your Ladyship, and this is Jade, Lady Holly's familiar."

Ailith sat down cross-legged and beckoned Holly to join her. "I am an Adept mentor and guide. Where is this place, and what have you called me for? I assume someone is in need of training."

"I . . . well . . ." Holly hardly knew how to begin.

"Allow me, Lady Ailith," Almaric cut in, and then explained quickly that Holly had come from another world, though he said nothing about the king or the Sorcerer or the Adepts being exiled.

"I've never heard of such a thing," said Ailith. She frowned again at Holly. "Another world. How can you be an Adept, then?"

Holly rubbed the stone in her hand. She had wondered the same thing more times than she could count. Then she remembered the wand, and drew it out.

Ailith cocked an eyebrow. "Your wand is lovely. You forged it yourself? Have you been presented at King Lancet's court?"

"Well—"

"Your Ladyship," Jade interrupted, "you have traveled into the future. We cannot reveal details of our time. Those are the rules by which the time stones are used."

Ailith rolled her eyes. "Yes, fine. I'm here to render

service, no questions asked. You're stuck on an island in the middle of nowhere and you need to train. I suppose I don't need any more information than that. What can you do, Adept?"

"I—I can do *osclaígí.*"

"Easy enough. Is that all?"

"And the Vanishment."

Ailith nodded. "The Vanishment is advanced. You've got some talent. Maybe you're not a complete waste of my time."

"I hope you're not a waste of mine," Holly shot back before Jade could stop her. He and Almaric exchanged looks.

"I think *I'm* doing the favor here, Adept."

"It's *Holly.*"

"*Holly.* Let's start with . . . Oh, I don't know. Your training so far is all over the place." Ailith sniffed the air, then examined a few of the plants nearby. "It's the season of water? Let's start there. Manipulation of the Elements. Water should be easy, since we're in season, and you've got plenty of the stuff to practice with. Besides, it's a good idea to start with the opposite of your native Element. You're obviously a fire person." She shuddered. "Anyway. Let's begin. Raise your wand."

Ailith was not the sort of mentor Holly had hoped for. She was bossy and impatient and, Holly thought, too self-important for someone who was hardly older than Holly herself. Still, Ailith said she had been in training for several years, and she had already mentored several younger Adepts. Compared to Holly, whose movements felt jerky and overdone, Ailith moved with liquid grace. One movement spilled effortlessly into the next as she spun waves out in the distant sea, raised them into whitecaps, and slammed them into the rocks. But after working for an hour, Holly only succeeded in creating ripples in the current that might have occurred naturally anyway.

"This shouldn't be that hard for you," Ailith said. "Ocean waves are easy—they already have volume and movement. You're just directing them, not creating them out of thin air. Believe me, *that's* tricky."

"I'm *trying*." Holly's hair was damp with sweat, her muscles shaking.

"You're fighting the water. Get underneath the wave's energy, then give it a boost. Watch again." Ailith raised her wand to the outer bay, flicked it, and uttered the spell, *"Tugaigí uisce."* The waves in the distance rolled and crested, dancing with one another.

"Lady Holly," said Jade quietly. "The Salamander."

Of course! Holly had forgotten about him, crouched

CLAIRE M. CATERER

against her neck as he always was. Holly plucked him gently from her shoulder and nestled him in the sand.

"You've been holding a Salamander all this time?" Ailith rolled her eyes. "No wonder. You know you can't mix fire and water magic, don't you?"

"But he helps me. Isn't there a way to combine the fire and water magic? Maybe it would—"

"Maybe it would be helpful if you took instruction instead of giving it," said Ailith shortly.

Holly glared at her, then took a deep breath. *"Tugaigí uisce!"*

The gentle tide where she'd pointed the wand shot in the air twenty feet and bubbled over like a saltwater fountain.

"I did it!" Holly cried, laughing. Even Jade didn't seem to mind getting wet.

Ailith shook her head. "If I'd known you had a Golden Salamander, this whole thing would've been easier. That's not bad. Let's try again."

By the end of the day Holly was exhausted. Almaric built a campfire apart from the crew and fried up the shellfish they had found along the beach. She tried to listen to the boys, who had spent their day repairing sails, filling barrels with water, and loading the longboats. Everett described how the women on the *Sea Witch*'s crew swam beneath the boat at anchor, plugging holes in the hull. "They can hold their breath forever, like whales," he said, and though Holly found this interesting, her mind kept wandering as she gazed into the firelight.

Ailith had already returned to her own time. She said Holly could call on her again, or rather, "You'll need a lot more work," as she put it.

"You did very well today, Lady Holly," Almaric remarked as he cleared away the dinner remains. "Once Áedán was out of the way."

Holly unfolded her bedroll beside the campfire. "I still think I should be able to work with fire and water together. I like to keep Áedán with me."

"On rare occasions one can harness opposing elements," said the magician, "but ordinarily, no, especially not for a novice. Even fire and air, though they complement each other, can be dangerous. The Adept must be very skilled."

"Now that I can call Ailith, I can train just like the other Adepts, can't I?"

"For a time." Almaric sat down and stretched his short legs with a groan. "I'm afraid you cannot call her indefinitely. If you pull her from her timeline too often, she will fall out of synch with it. You must practice as much as you can without Ailith's help, and use your lesson time wisely."

And what could she do for Anglielle in the meanwhile? Their mission had failed, but she wasn't ready to go home. She smiled at Ranulf, dozing just beyond the campfire. He and the Mounted would devise a battle plan, she guessed. Her job would be to bring the scattered Exiles together, as the changeling had said. She would continue to train, and eventually she'd be so powerful, it wouldn't matter if the Adepts never came home. She would learn to defeat the Sorcerer all on her own.

Chapter 39

The Captain's Promise

It was near dawn when a loud screech wakened her. She leaped up from her sandy blanket to find the red parrot flapping his wings from the palm tree above her. "Wake up, Adept! The captain sends for you in the longboat! To the *Sea Witch*!" Crewso flew off with another loud squawk.

"An infernal noise for this time of morning," Jade said with a low growl as he stretched each limb. "But I suppose we must obey the summons." Together they walked down the beach to Oggler, who stood ready with the longboat.

Crewso had flown ahead of them, and when Holly climbed aboard the *Sea Witch*, he was waiting on the poop-deck railing. "Inside the captain's cabin, Lady! Haste, haste, haste!" he called.

Having only seen it from the outside, Holly was unprepared for the cabin's luxury. The ceiling was high enough that Morgan could stand up quite straight and not hit her head, and there were windows all along the poop deck and portholes out to sea. Brass lanterns hung here and there, and a real bed draped with gold curtains sat in one corner. Morgan nodded at one of the leather chairs facing an oak table, and Holly sat down. Jade settled into the other.

"So," the captain began, "I hear tell ye've been talking to Adepts and changelings on this island, Lady. When were ye goin' to tell me what ye've learnt?"

Holly took a deep breath, inhaling the sharp scents of tobacco and salt. Morgan's dark eyes were fixed on her. "I was waiting for . . . the right moment, Captain."

Morgan drew out her dagger, letting it play between her webbed fingers. "Ye're in luck," she said softly. "The right moment's come."

Holly swallowed, watching the lamplight glint off the dagger's blade. "I'm sorry," she said desperately. "I didn't know. None of us did. But I guess—or at least, the changeling said—that the Adepts have hidden themselves. You can't sail to their island until they want to come home."

Morgan's brow darkened like the clouds before a gale while Holly talked. Then she allowed for at least two full minutes of silence before saying in a low voice: "The *Sea Witch* was badly damaged this voyage. And I've lost cargo."

"I know," Holly said anxiously. Clearly, Morgan thought it was her fault. "I'm really sorry—we did our best—"

"This ship, Lady Adept, is all I've got. If the schooner finds us again, she'll finish us." She stood and pulled a sea chart onto the table. She squinted at it, mumbling.

"But what is the schooner? Is it another"—she hesitated, hoping not to offend—"ship like yours? Like a competitor?"

But Morgan was absorbed in her sea chart. "The devil take me if I know *how* they find us. The *Sea Witch* stays hidden from most vessels at sea."

Holly shifted uneasily in her chair. "I don't suppose . . ."

The captain looked up. "Suppose what? D'ye know something about it?"

"It's probably nothing," Holly said. "But Everett found this gold compass in the Northern Wood, and it's . . . strange."

"'Tis more than that," said Jade. "A compass with odd markings, and a thousand different directions. When the lad opens it, storms appear. As does the schooner."

"We don't know that for sure," Holly protested. "It might be a coincidence."

CLAIRE M. CATERER

Morgan pulled a piece of parchment from her desk along with a quill pen that she hastily dipped in ink. "Tell me. This compass—does it have markings like these on its cover?" She sketched out the Elemental symbols.

A line of goose pimples danced across Holly's shoulders. "Yes, but those are just the elements. They could mean anything, right?"

"Anything but good. Curse it! I ought to have searched the lot of ye. That compass *belongs* to the schooner. O' course it leads her right to us!"

"But what is the schooner? Whose ship is it?"

Morgan smiled bitterly. "Do ye not know, lassie? I thought by now ye'd be acquainted with him. Raethius of the Source."

The warm breeze chilled Holly. Even her shoulder, where Áedán nestled, went cold, and her stomach clenched.

Morgan leaned forward. "He's got weapons beyond our powers. He could kill us all. But he wants you, and you only. What would you do in my place?"

Jade leaped onto the arm of his chair and hissed. "Whatever you might do, Captain, it is foolish to threaten an Adept."

Morgan stood her ground. "A captain's first duty is to her crew. Second, to her ship. Third—and last—to any stray passengers that prove to be more trouble than they're worth. Looks like only two of ye'll bring me any ransom from the king."

Holly's fear drained away. Her wand vibrated in its scabbard, and she drew it out in front of her. Jade's green eyes grew round, and even as Morgan's hand sought her sword hilt, she backed away. Holly stepped around the oak table, pressing her advantage. "Is that all we're worth to you?" she said. "Is it just about ransom now? The Adepts *will* come back someday, and I'm the one who will call them. But they'll never return unless there's something to come back *for*. We have to stand together. If everyone scatters, taking care of their own, Raethius will just pick us off one by one. This is bigger than you, can't you see that? And all you care about is this boat!"

Morgan sat back, fingering the dagger, and took a breath. "Ye've got it right at last. This boat *is* what I care about. And if he comes for ye—"

Suddenly a cry came from high in the crow's nest, echoed by Innes, who was at the helm on the poop deck: "Captain, a sail! A sail astern!"

Morgan lurched out of her chair and threw open the cabin door, with Holly at her heels. She seized the spyglass from her belt and held it to her eye, scanning the horizon. But she needed no glass; Holly saw it too:

CLAIRE M. CATERER

the black-sailed, three-masted schooner, small as a toy but clear on the horizon.

Morgan jerked the glass from her face. "Innes, the longboat! Back to shore at once, and gather all hands!" she shouted. "No more repairs; we can't wait. Bring the sails and give orders to hoist them at once. We sail in an hour." She pushed past Holly, then turned back to her. "Here's yer chance, Adept. Show yer worth, and we'll keep ye on and get ye home. But fail us, and we'll not shelter ye. That's a promise."

Chapter 40

The Prince Tips His Hand

"I don't see why we can't talk to Morgan too," Ben said, pouting. He sat next to Everett with a large woven basket between them. Not long after Holly left, Rowan had loaned Ben a sword and sent them into the jungle to pick the gourdlike yellow melons that had sprouted there since Holly's visit to the mountain.

"I'm not surprised," Everett said now. He and Ben sawed on the tough melon vines with their swords. "She learns magic and chats with the captain while we're swabbing decks and picking melon things."

"At least we got to come ashore," Ben said. "I bet they've got Avery pumping the bilge." They'd hacked up all the melon vines in their general vicinity. Ben wiped his forehead. "I don't see any more. And the basket's not even half full. I guess we'd better keep looking."

They stood up and moved farther into the jungle, using their swords to slash at the foliage. "I hope

Crews was right about there not being any people here," Everett said, his voice dropping to a whisper.

"I notice he didn't say anything about wild animals." Ben smacked at a mosquito on his neck. "And who knows what diseases these things are carrying. That's all I need, something new to be allergic to."

They walked on for a few minutes until Ben said, "Try your compass. Maybe it can find the melons like it found Cook's tinderbox."

Everett pulled the chain out of his shirt and grasped the locket, trying to envision the fruit. A weak pressure tugged at the chain and the locket trembled. "This way."

They started down a vine-covered path and soon came upon another grove of melons.

"That thing is cool." Ben squatted down to cut the vines. "I could use one of those at home."

But Everett was thinking about what Ben had said before. "The tinderbox," he muttered. "That was odd, wasn't it?"

"What *isn't* odd here?"

"No, I mean the fact that Cook even *has* a tinderbox. Ones like his weren't invented until, I don't know, the eighteenth century?"

"I guess. You're the one who knows that kind of stuff. Hey, did you hear that?"

Everett listened, but all he heard was a rustling in

the underbrush. "It's just some animal. Anyway, Ben, think about it. In Anglielle it's still the Middle Ages, right? So where did this ship come from? The *Sea Witch* is a brigantine like they had in the seventeen hundreds. The navigation, the sail construction—it's a proper pirate ship."

"Except there's no cannons," Ben pointed out. The rustling grew louder. Everett stopped to listen. Whatever it was, it was big and clumsy. Maybe a wolf or a bear or some creature they'd never seen before. He stood up with his sword raised. Ben raised his, too, darting behind Everett. "What if it's a wild boar?" he whispered.

"I am *not*," Avery panted as he tumbled through the broken foliage, "a wild boar."

"How the heck did *you* get here?" Ben asked.

"Pike took me ashore in the longboat," said Avery, beaming. "I believe you have misjudged his intent. He even bowed as I came aboard."

That sounded very unlike Pike to Everett. He could tell from Ben's face that he didn't believe it either. Everett thought the crew would be just as happy if Avery stayed on the island.

"What is it you harvest here?" Avery asked. "Are they not sunfruit? I have never seen them grown before."

CLAIRE M. CATERER

"All I know is, they're really hard to cut off the vine," Ben said. He started sawing on the plant again.

"Stand back, squire," said Avery. "Perhaps I can aid you in this endeavor." And before Everett could stop him, Avery pulled out the wand wrapped in the red scarf and uttered triumphantly, *"Osclaígí!"*

The vine collapsed in pieces, but so did the sunfruits. They exploded in a pulpy yellow mess, spattering the boys with their sweet pink juice.

No one said anything for a few moments. Ben sat back goggle-eyed; Avery gave that infuriating superior grin he was so good at; and Everett's stomach turned uncomfortably as he realized what would happen next. Finally it came from Ben:

"*Where* did you get that? I thought Everett lost it in the moat!"

"'Tis my own now, brave squire," said Avery. "And I have learnt one of the Adept's spells!"

Ben turned on Everett, who he must've realized didn't look exactly surprised. "And you knew about it?"

"It's not what you think," Everett said. "I was just helping him with it."

"Keeping it a secret from everyone else?"

"Well . . . yeah."

"Then it's what I think," said Ben. "Why don't you ever tell me what's going on? Did you even wonder *why* he's messing around with a wand? Ever think maybe we should take it away from him?"

"But I only want to learn magic as the rest of you," said Avery.

"And then what?" Ben asked. "Take over the ship? Turn us all in?"

"Why will you not accept that I mean no harm?" Avery demanded, looking angry now.

"Oh, I don't know, maybe the fact that you tried to kill us before has something to do with it!"

"That was my father!"

"He didn't set that forest fire, you did!"

"But I am a different man now!"

"And you're still a *boy*, Avery."

"I believe you mean 'Your Highness.'"

"I believe I mean 'You Turncoat'!"

"Shut it, you lot!" Everett shouted above them. Both Avery's and Ben's faces were very red, and they stood close together, Ben's sword raised against Avery's wand. But Everett was more interested in the locket. It rose on its chain, hovering above Everett's chest. Avery's spell had opened it. The water symbol on its lid glowed with its strange white-blue light, and inside, the needle spun in a dizzying circle.

"What did you do?" Ben whispered.

"It's the wand. It—interacts with the compass."

CLAIRE M. CATERER

Avery waved the wand over the top of the compass. "Look ye here, Ben. The wand and the locket, they are stronger together."

Even without holding it, Everett could see some of the directions magnified by the compass. He held out his hand, and the locket settled onto his palm. He gave it to Ben. "Put it up to your eye, like the spyglass."

Ben did as he asked, then gasped. "Cool!" He forgot all about his fight with Avery. "I can see all kinds of stuff! There's a place with weird rocks on the moor—like Stonehenge, maybe—and here's a mountain lake—and over here—"

He dropped the locket into the grass. He had stopped breathing for a moment.

"What?" Everett demanded. "What did you see?"

"It was—it was—"

But before he could finish, they heard the cry from the beach: "A sail! A sail! It's the *Black Dragon*!"

Chapter 41

The Black Dragon

Everett leaped up as soon as they heard the call. The boys bolted through the jungle and back to the beach. "Look," Everett said, pointing at the *Sea Witch*. "What's going on over there?"

Ben pulled the collapsing spyglass from the pouch on his belt. He peered through it. "They're lowering the longboat."

"Let me see." Everett took the spyglass and scanned the horizon. He couldn't see much from their sheltered beach, for the trees crowded in on either side; but he could see Morgan running down the deck, gesturing at the crow's nest and shouting at Oggler. Then Morgan turned to Holly, who was behind her, and shouted something else. "Morgan and Holly are yelling at each other—blimey, it looks like a big row. And Jade's hissing and all. Uh-oh—Holly's got the wand out—"

Avery nudged over Everett's shoulder, suddenly interested. "Does she call the Adept?"

"Excuse me, that's mine." Ben snatched back the spyglass. "It doesn't look like it. She uses those stones for that, anyway. No, she's waving it, like she's going to put the whammy on Morgan . . . she's . . . *Wow!*"

"What?" cried Everett and the prince.

But no one needed to be told. Holly had leaned over the railing of the *Sea Witch,* waving the wand in circles above the water where Oggler had climbed into the longboat. A wake opened beneath it as Holly spun the wand faster, and the boat churned toward shore as if a motor were attached. In minutes the longboat had arrived.

Avery's eyes were shining. "How is the lady Holly able to do such a thing?"

"You know as much as I do," Everett said.

Avery held up his own wand—Everett's wand, really—and gazed at it.

But there was no time to think about whatever spell he had in his head. The sailors were frantically loading up the longboats; one had already cast off. Ranulf galloped up to the boys. "We must hasten back to the *Sea Witch.* Morgan will try to outrun the schooner."

They bolted for the remaining longboat and found Pike and Innes loading the last of the barrels. Innes grabbed Ben's hand. "Come, we've no time to lose!"

"We've no room for the lot of them," said Pike. "Let's

make another run. Here, lad, you"—he gestured to Ben—"and the old man. Into the boat." He wrinkled his nose at Ranulf. "Ye'll swim yerself, I trust. Best get to it."

"But there be space to spare, by my eye," said Avery. "We must all go at once."

"He's right," Everett said. The boat looked half empty.

Pike shoved past Ben and stuck a pudgy, scarred finger in Everett's face. "And *I* say this longboat's too heavy as it is, with those barrels. Stay put till I come back for ye."

"But you won't," said a quiet voice. Pike whirled around to find Innes standing in front of the longboat as the tide lapped at its hull. "Stand aside, Pike, and let the lads board."

Pike strode up to her. "And ye'll do what, exactly, if I don't?"

Innes waved a hand behind her. The quiet tide suddenly reared up like an animal, engulfed Pike's legs, and threw him to the sand. He sputtered, struggling to his feet.

"Why you . . ." He spat a mouthful of sand at her feet. "You lot—yer magic and yer webbed hands, like fish, ain't ye? Ye might've cowed my captain once, but ye won't do it to me." He gave her shoulder a hard shove, and Everett winced, waiting for her to tumble onto the sand.

But he couldn't budge her. Her strawberry hair blew back in the stiff breeze. "Do not try me, Pike. You'll find yourself in the brig afore long."

"Is that right? But yer just a *girl* after all, ain't ye?" And now he sprung at Innes in earnest, both hands on her, and brought her to the ground, grasping for her throat. Ranulf bounded forward, raising his sword, but before he had reached the pair, Pike bellowed in pain. Innes had disengaged him, kicking him in a very unfortunate part of his anatomy. Ben leaned out of the longboat, grinning. "Wow! How did you—"

"Not now, lad," said Innes grimly as Pike doubled over, groaning on the beach. "'Tis time we go."

Ranulf trussed Pike like a Christmas goose and pushed him into the longboat. Avery was all for marooning him there on the island, but Ranulf said it wouldn't be honorable, and even Innes said the captain wouldn't like it. Everett, peering at the brigantine, could make out Holly, who waved her wand toward them. The longboat sped over the water, its bow tipping up out of the spray. When they reached the *Sea Witch*, the boys clambered up the ropes, then turned back and helped bring up the barrels and sails.

There was no time to talk once everyone was aboard. Morgan barked that she needed all hands, whatever Pike had done, and sent him aloft to help the crew affix the mended sails to the yards. The boys got behind Quelch and Oggler, and yanked on the halyards to lower the topsail to its full length, and then turned it as the captain ordered. Holly and Ranulf stood at the foremast with Pike and Quinn, doing the same duty for the foresail and jib. The crew then leaped to the windlass and walked in a groaning circle to haul up the anchor. The ship heaved; the *Sea Witch* was under sail.

Ben joined Everett and Cook at the gunwale. "That's the *Black Dragon*? Why's everybody so panicked? We can outrun her in a minute if we do that submarine move." He muttered in a lower voice, "But I really hope we don't."

"There be no sea portals here, and we can't outrun her," Cook said as if trying to steady his voice. "We'll have to stand and fight."

Everett looked around the clear deck. "But what'll you fight *with*?"

"If ye're lookin' fer cannon, lad, ye'll find none," Cook said. He took his eyes from the schooner at last. "This lot don't need guns."

Morgan appeared above the poop deck and bellowed from her perch. "Officers on deck! And you"—she gestured to Holly—"Lady Adept, you as well. Crewmen, hands to braces! Passengers, below!"

It hardly seemed possible, but the schooner was already closer. A lot closer. If Everett hadn't known better, he'd have said she was driven by a motor. The *Sea Witch* was clear of the lagoon now, and headed in the *Black Dragon*'s general direction.

"Best get below, lads, as the captain says," Oggler said, and pushed past them to take his post near the foresail.

Ben nodded, but neither he nor Everett moved. "I don't suppose they'll notice if we stay?" Everett whispered.

"Not if we get out of the way," Ben said. "I want to see what they expect Holly to do."

"Under here!" Everett darted to the port side of the ship and huddled beneath the forecastle, sheltered from the wind. Ben followed. The crewmen gathered around the sails to haul them in as directed. But the girls—women—took up posts around the ship: Kailani clambered up to the mainmast crow's nest; Rowan took the bow; Quinn and Innes stood amidships, one on each side; and the captain stayed at the helm, with Holly beside her. Morgan held a small trumpetlike device that she used to amplify her voice as she gave orders. Then, out of nowhere, the wind hurled a huge wave at them, rocking the ship dangerously.

The foremast creaked above their heads. Everett peeked over the gunwale at the *Black Dragon*. They were heading straight for it, and it was shooting across the water all the faster.

"Everett," Ben said, poking him, "what if the *Black Dragon* has cannons?"

"They can't have," said Everett. "This part of the world didn't even have gunpowder back then—er, now."

"But you said they didn't have schooners and brigantines, either," Ben said. "I just don't get it. How did they—"

He was cut off when a wave broke over the side, drenching them. The *Sea Witch* lurched, dove into the sea, then righted again. Everett wiped the saltwater from his eyes.

"Low waves, portside!" hollered Morgan.

Innes, who was only a few feet from them, responded by extending her webbed fingers. She brought them up at right angles, as if she were getting ready to push a door open. She gently scooped her hands into the air, then rolled them outward; and just as she did so, the ship listed to port, and a gentle swell rose below them and rolled toward the schooner.

"That's it! Keep to!" called Morgan.

Kai shouted down from the crow's nest. "Ten leagues, Captain!"

Ben and Everett gasped as another rogue gust rocked the mainmast. Kai grabbed for the ratlines to keep from falling.

As the schooner closed in on them, the weather got worse. The wind whipped through the sails, and Morgan bellowed orders to turn them leeward, now lower them, and the men on deck sweated as they hauled the lines this way and that. It was far worse than the recent storm, but the skies were clear and bright. Besides that, the waves didn't match the wind; the air came in strange rolling microbursts, but the waves seemed to fight each one, kicking up huge sprays and geysers that fountained over the open sea and onto the deck. The other officers mimicked Innes, extending their webbed hands and sketching elaborate patterns in the air. Everett realized that they were sculpting the waves, fighting the wind with them. Innes's taut brown arms strained against the breeze. Her feet were planted firmly on the deck, keeping her balance even as breakers crashed over her and the wind flew her strawberry hair like a crazy flag behind her head.

"What's Holly doing?" Ben shouted.

Everett peered up at the captain. Holly stood with her at the helm, wand in hand, making stirring motions at the sea. She too was churning up waves and sending them toward the schooner. He explained all this to Ben, who craned his neck around Everett to see.

And still the *Black Dragon* came on.

Somehow it had the wind behind it, though the *Sea Witch*'s sails were full, and the *Dragon* approached almost square to starboard. It was as if two opposing gales were driving the vessels together. But Morgan's crew had no control over the winds. Their talent was manipulating the water, which crashed against the wind currents as if smacking brick walls. Sometimes they broke through, but like a relentless tide, the wind pushed them back and back and back.

The ship pitched and rolled crazily between the opposing forces. The top of the foremast gave a mighty crack and tumbled into the sea, ripping the topsail away with it. The bow lurched at least twenty feet into the air and then dropped straight into a trench of gray water that opened in front of it. The hull rolled danger-ously, and Kai, above in the crow's nest, clung to the mainmast with both hands. She disappeared into the rigging, trying to climb back to the decks, but a few of the lines snapped free and she was flung over the side of the boat, floating on the air current over the sea.

Morgan saw this as soon as it happened, and poked Holly. Everett could see even from his position how very white Holly's face was, how hard she gripped the wand, but she pointed it at the water below Kai and turned the wand in a spiral. Small spouts of water, as if from a lawn sprinkler, shot from her wand and then into the sea, where they gathered into a small wave. The wave caught Kai as she sank, and it threw her back onto the deck. Holly winced, mouthing *I'm sorry*—the wind was screaming too loud to hear her properly—but Kailani only grinned and righted herself, then joined Quinn on the starboard side, sending larger swells to break through the wall of wind and capsize the *Black Dragon*.

The ships were only a few hundred feet apart now. Everett swallowed, his throat dry despite the constant drenching. The schooner was massive, its hull twice the height of the *Sea Witch*. Its three masts carried eight square-rigged sails from topsail to mainsail, and three wide jibs as well as a huge spanker in the stern. The *Sea Witch* looked like a toy beside it.

Everett could see at least three dozen crew members running all over the deck of the *Black Dragon*. But though they looked like men at first, he soon saw they were only wisps of black smoke, appearing and then vanishing just as he got a good look at them. They had very long arms, or armlike extensions, which swirled several feet into the air and spun like Catherine wheels; a few moments later a whirlwind like a steel ball headed straight for the *Sea Witch*. The first one punched a hole through the main staysail. The second broke off the tip of the mainmast.

"They must be, like, air Elementals or something," said Ben. "They're shooting *air* at us!"

They were the same creatures Everett had seen every time he'd opened the locket.

The problem was, they controlled the water, too. Though the boys couldn't see any web-fingered women, someone was hurling waves at them. Innes and Quinn raised huge balls of water to break over the *Black Dragon*'s bow, but others just as powerful whizzed back at them, borne by the ferocious wind, and exploded over their heads in a salty shower. Morgan answered by congealing her water, rolling it into icy balls that broke through the wind and knocked the *Black Dragon*'s rigging askew. Its foremast creaked ominously.

"Good hit!" Ben cried.

Holly apparently couldn't freeze her water missiles, but she hurled as many as she could. Still, the wind was on the side of the *Black Dragon*, and no matter how furiously the *Sea Witch* fired, the schooner's superior numbers won out. Half the crew were charged with deflecting Morgan's ice missiles; the other half fired missiles of their own, devastating the little brigantine. The foremast was in splinters; the staysail was tattered. They couldn't keep going much longer. Morgan was going to have to retreat, however she could.

"We need to do something to help!" Ben said.

"Like what?" As Everett spoke, a wind-driven ice ball the size of a school desk punched a hole through the deck planking in front of them. "We need to get below; we'll get killed up here!"

"We can't leave Holly up there by herself! She's got nothing to fight with!"

Then a thought dawned on Everett that seemed, at the time, very brave and quite brilliant. "Then let's give her something," he said, and darted to the main hatch, pulling Ben along with him.

Belowdecks, Almaric was huddled low against one bunk next to the prince, who looked quite green, and Ranulf was pacing. "Have they boarded us yet?" he demanded as soon as Everett showed his face.

"No, and don't bother going on deck. You'll only get in the way."

"If they try to board us, they will pay," he said tightly. He had drawn Claeve-Bryna, which gleamed and sparked impatiently. "'Tis folly to sit here doing nothing, no matter the captain's orders."

"I've got something that will help." Everett threaded his way along the narrow passageway and down another level. "I saw them back here."

"Everett, whither goest?" Avery asked. He stood up, weaving, and then was promptly sick at Almaric's feet.

"Your Highness, do sit down!" Everett heard Almaric say. But then Avery's footsteps came up behind him.

He joined them as Everett stopped in the dark corner just short of the brig. In front of them was the barrel of gunpowder.

"What the . . ." Ben didn't bother to finish his sentence. The barrel spoke for itself. "How can they have *this*?"

"The *Sea Witch* isn't from this world," Everett said. He was only now realizing it. "And neither is the *Black Dragon*. They were stolen from our world, like the crew—like Pike and Cook."

"What nonsense do you speak?"

"It's true," Everett said to Avery. "It must be. These ships are from our world, and so's the gunpowder. Remember? Morgan said Pike and Cook were picked up somewhere else? I'm thinking Morgan can some-how sail to our world. She took the ship from there, or someplace like it. She must've left the cannons and such because she didn't know what to do with them. And this gunpowder's just been sitting here. They must've forgotten about it. But look what else is still here." He pulled aside the sacks of rice and flour to reveal the muskets.

"What be these?" Avery asked. "Magic sticks?"

"Magic sticks?" Ben scoffed. "Those are *guns*."

"Brown Bess muskets," Everett explained. "They're

primitive, but they could help. The *Black Dragon* won't have them."

"But how do you know?" Ben asked. "If that ship's from our world too, it could have a whole load of weapons."

"It doesn't. Otherwise they'd have used them by now. They're trying to destroy us, so why hold off if they've got cannons? Look, here's the charges."

Everett picked up the hip satchel filled with little rolls of paper.

"What're these for?" Ben asked, pulling one out.

"It's what you load the muskets with," said Everett.

"You know how to load a musket?"

"It's not hard. I've seen demonstrations."

Avery stepped forward. "Give me one of the sticks, Everett. I shall defend the *Sea Witch* and Her Ladyship, the both!"

"One each," Everett said, handing a musket to Ben and another to Avery.

"Just hold up, use your head a second," said Ben. The ship lurched and they all stumbled toward the brig. "We don't know how old these things are, how they work—"

"*I* do," Everett said with confidence. He grabbed the satchel full of charges. "Now, are we helping or not?"

Chapter 42

Aloft

Holly had never felt so cold. Under the tropical sun, the wind and even the seawater should have been warm, but the winds that assailed them came from some different place. Their northern bite cut through her thin shirt, and though the crew hurled waves and ice as quickly as they could, only five of them had that ability. Now that the ships were nearly alongside each other, the men could only manipulate the sails to keep the *Sea Witch* from crashing broadside into the schooner.

Holly shivered, gripping the base of the wand as tightly as she dared, for fear that some breaking wave or whirlwind would wrench it from her grasp. Her fingertips were turning blue; her legs shook beneath her. One minute she was following Morgan's barking orders—"swell off the starboard; now one astern; send that one clear over their bow! Harder now!"—and the next she was standing stock-still, having forgotten the last several minutes. How had the foremast broken? Were there *holes* in the deck? Water was pouring over them from every corner. She could only hope Ben and the others were all right, but there was no time to worry about them now.

She shook her head. She'd thought Kai was up in the crow's nest, but the crow's nest was in pieces, and there was Kai on the starboard side, shouting and flinging shards of ice at the schooner, which suddenly loomed within a hundred feet of the *Sea Witch*. And still, along the decks, Holly couldn't quite see the *Dragon*'s crew; they seemed to fade into mist as she followed them, dozens of people, and yet not *solid*, somehow. A shrouded, inky figure, thin and towering, stood at the schooner's helm. Holly tried to make out who it was, but an icy blast of wind and water assaulted her. She swayed at Morgan's side.

Jade was close at her heels, concentrating, boosting her powers with his own. His black fur was slicked against his head, making his green eyes more huge and brilliant. She glanced down at him and realized suddenly that he had been calling her name for a couple of minutes now.

"You are tired, you must get belowdecks, my lady!" he was saying.

"She's not goin' nowhere, not when there's battle to

be waged," Morgan growled. "What's wrong with ye? I said whitecaps astern!"

"She cannot go on, no matter how you browbeat her," Jade said.

"Don't think ye're takin' the coward's way!" Morgan yanked Holly's wand arm, and she cried out. It was *so* sore. Jade reared back, hissing; Holly swayed, so dazed she didn't know which way to run. Vaguely she felt Áedán scamper up her pant leg to her shoulder, then remembered she had tucked him in a corner beneath the gunwale when she'd needed to summon the waves. She warmed for a moment beneath his touch but then staggered again. Her eyes fluttered closed, then open, and the sky turned dark, then light, then clouded with stars . . . but no it hadn't, that was *her*, that was the inside of her eyelids. . . .

She couldn't tell if she was asleep or awake. She felt scuffling at her feet, and in a sudden burst of awareness, saw Jade sink his teeth into the captain's ankle. Morgan bellowed and shoved Holly away from her. Holly wavered and then, with the next roll of the ship, tumbled down the steps of the poop deck. In a moment Jade was after her, leaping onto her chest, breathing into her face.

"I'm okay, Jade. . . . I'm . . . " What was the word? She couldn't remember it now. She was very, very cold. If

CLAIRE M. CATERER

she could just find someplace out of the wind and rain. How could it be raining, when the sky was so clear? She curled up on the deck, which was slick from the shards of ice that had broken around them.

"Belowdecks," Jade kept saying in her ear, tugging on her shirtsleeve. If only he would be quiet and let her sleep. "You will freeze here . . . Rowan, Her Ladyship needs aid. . . ."

But Rowan had no time to help her. Holly stretched her fingers forward, trying to crawl. The slivers of ice bored into her temples now; she could barely concentrate through the pain. The deck tipped, listing nearly perpendicular to the sea, and Holly slid like a sack of flour along the planks. Someone trampled her outstretched fingers, and she thought dully how lucky it was that her wand had not broken. Then she realized Jade had it clenched between his teeth.

On her shoulder, Áedán felt like a cold, wet lump. Could he live through so much ice? She touched him lightly, but he didn't move. "Áedán . . ."

"The water has weakened him," said Jade. "Come, the hatch is just a bit farther. I shall call Ranulf to come help you." The cat darted away, and she heard anxious voices below. The deck shuddered; Ranulf was somewhere nearby.

The hatch was thrown open with a boom, and Holly

raised her head, hoping to find Ranulf's strong arms reaching out to her. But instead, all three of the boys scrambled up onto the deck, each holding something long and thin. Her mind was so fuzzy; those couldn't be . . .

Another splash of water revived her a little, and her eyes grew wide when she saw Everett shoulder what looked like a hunting rifle in one hand, while chewing a wad of paper that he'd stuffed in his mouth. She couldn't make sense of it. Where were Ranulf and Jade? The boys were going to be hurt, the missiles . . .

Something cold and very wet, yet solid and pressing like fingers, gathered beneath her. Had someone come to help at last? Her mind *must* be going; she heard Everett saying ridiculous things: "No, don't swallow it; *bite* it, I said! Now pour a little bit in here . . . just enough to fill it . . . and close it. Ben, yours isn't shut all the way, here, let me . . ."

The cold fingers lifted her.

"Now pull that rod thing off—see it underneath? Turn it round . . . no, *around* . . . yeah. No, this way, Avery . . ."

Her fingers closed over Áedán. She didn't want him to fall off. They were rising; it must be Ranulf, helping her to the hatch. But she couldn't move.

"Stick it back on there, you don't want to leave it in the barrel. . . . Now cock it. Pull it all the way back—

CLAIRE M. CATERER

that's only halfway. Yes, Ben, that's got it. Up to your shoulder . . . rather like a bow, Avery . . . good . . ."

Then Holly's stomach dropped the same way it did when she'd looked down from the crow's nest, but Ranulf couldn't be lifting her that high. She was so very wet; she was floating in water. She opened her eyes, calling for Ranulf and for Jade, but they couldn't hear her; she was so far above them.

Above them?

Her mind cleared for one crystal moment, suspended, and she saw what had happened: She was floating far above the *Sea Witch*. On the tiny deck below the boys raised the rifles to their shoulders, and she heard a feeble shout: "Fire!" There was a satisfying explosion and a huge puff of smoke as Everett cheered; but the next moment Kailani screamed and fell onto the deck. Everett darted forward. Avery fired his weapon, aiming for the schooner, but instead lit one of the *Sea Witch*'s last remaining sails aflame; Ben peered up into the sky—to *her*—and she saw him through a wavy mirror—no, through a wall of water—and he called out to her.

He shoved Everett out of the way and started yelling at Avery, who pulled something red from his pockets.

Was it Everett's wand? The one wrapped in the red scarf?

Holly looked around. Where *was* she?

She was *sitting* on water.

A tender wave cradled her in what seemed to be a hand, but it was so cold, she had gone numb. She held Áedán tight, waiting to be flung into the sea. Instead the wave suspended them in the air, high above the melee. Avery stepped forward and thrust his right arm into the sky. How small, how fragile the wand looked, with its red scarf fluttering off one end. Where was *her* wand? She scrambled to find it, but then remembered Jade, with the wand in his teeth.

She was a prisoner of the wave.

It had started to move now, bearing her away from the brigantine, toward the higher mast and black sails of the schooner. Avery was doing something—she wasn't sure what—but she felt a tugging back toward the *Sea Witch*. The wave resisted, and the tension was horrible, like she was a fish on a line, but she moved closer to the boys and dipped lower in the sky. *If it drops me now,* she thought, *I'll still land on the deck. Or they can pull me out of the sea.*

She felt a sharp *pop.* Avery's spell snapped like an overstretched rubber band. The wave broke free, bearing her aloft. She could just see Avery cursing, waving the wand in futility, Everett grabbing it from him and trying to ape his movements, but she was out

CLAIRE M. CATERER

of their range now, if there was such a thing as range. She could feel it: the defeat.

She was descending—no, falling—now, through the fountain of water. The masts rushed up to meet her, the rigging of the *Black Dragon* threatening to slice her in two. She heard a final gunshot echo off the bow, and she landed on the deck.

Everything—the world—went dark.

Chapter 43

Nursing Wounds

"How could they be gone? Where did they go?" Ben babbled to Everett, who heard him as so much static on a radio. All Everett could do was gaze at the empty sea. The *Black Dragon* had vanished.

And Holly with it.

Everett stood staring at the sky, the wand limp in his hand. Nothing he had tried had done any good. A horrible, airless feeling overcame him, like being slugged hard in the stomach. Near the stern, Kailani was moaning. Quelch bent over her. He ripped the sleeve off his shirt and wrapped it around her shoulder where Everett's musket ball had nicked her. She was lucky to be alive. Avery's shot had set a sail ablaze, though a wave had broken over the side the next moment and dampened it. And then the impossible: A huge, watery hand had scooped Holly right off the deck and into the sky. Ranulf, who had just arrived at the hatch, clutched at her hand but just missed it;

Almaric cried out behind him. Jade made a mighty leap—Everett had never seen a cat jump like that—but was tossed back to the deck like a wet rag.

That's when Ben went mad and shoved Everett out of the way and yelled at Avery—what was wrong with him, why wasn't he using the stupid wand to save her? And Avery, for once, didn't question him but yanked the wand out of his pocket and tried. He did try.

At first it seemed to be working. His eyes were fixed on the giant water hand, and he muttered something low, making a pulling motion with his wand hand. Holly floated closer to them, and Everett held his breath. It might work; she'd be dropped and might be hurt, but she'd be all right. . . .

Avery's jaw clenched. He panted between his teeth; his knees shook. It was like a tug of war. Then with a gasp, he fell backward to the deck, and Everett seized the wand.

But whatever Avery had been doing, it didn't work for Everett. Holly had floated away on a geyser of water, all the way to the deck of the *Black Dragon*. A moment later, a great whirlpool had opened in the sea like a crater, and the schooner had disappeared into it as if down an enormous drain.

The sea was calm. The air was warm.

Ben collapsed onto the deck, crying. Almaric

crawled out of the hatch and tried to comfort him. Jade looked utterly defeated. He dropped Holly's wand with a light clatter.

Only Morgan acted like nothing was wrong. She walked the length of the deck, inspecting the tattered sails and broken masts. She checked on Kailani and praised Quelch for his quick thinking. Eventually she made her way to the fore hatch, where the rest of them were assembled in a shell-shocked heap.

She didn't even mention Holly. Instead she reached out a webbed hand and grasped Everett around his shirt collar, hauling him to his feet. "Mutinous dog, shew me yer weaponry!" Then, eyeing the muskets lying on the deck, she shoved Everett aside and picked one up.

"We did essay to aid the *Sea Witch* in battle," said Avery, standing up rather bravely to face her. "'Twas not against you, Captain."

She grunted, seeming to realize this. "Are ye an Elemental, that ye spew fire such as this?" she asked, peering down the barrel. It made Everett nervous, even though the musket wasn't loaded.

"It came from the hold, Captain," he said. "It was down near the brig. Left over from . . . wherever you got this ship."

Her eyes narrowed, then gazed off as she tried to recall having seen them before.

CLAIRE M. CATERER

"Who *cares* about the muskets?" Ben cried. "We have to get Holly back! Do your submarine thing and follow that ship!"

"Do ye dare to command me?"

"Yeah, I do! We need to get my sister back now!" Ben stood up and glared at Morgan, breathing hard.

The captain brought her hand back as if to strike Ben, but Ranulf suddenly appeared and drew his sword. "The time has come to show some honor, Captain. The Lady Adept fought well alongside you. Perhaps she even saved your ship. Now you must return the favor."

"Put yer cutlass away," growled Morgan. "D'ye not think I'd follow if I could? 'Tis not a matter of opening a portal wherever one wishes. I cannot follow in the wake of the *Black Dragon*. I know not whither she sails."

Everett bent his head. Suddenly he was so very tired. Idly, he pulled the locket from inside his shirt and worried his thumb over the raised symbols. He heard a gasp and looked up. The captain was gazing hungrily at the compass.

"I cannot trace the path of the *Black Dragon*," she said softly, then crouched on one knee and took the locket gently from Everett's hand. "But you, laddie— *you* can."

But the *Sea Witch* wasn't going anywhere soon. Large holes were punched in the brigantine's hull and decking, the railings broken, the masts in stumps, its sails in pieces. The ship limped back to the island's lagoon, and the crew quietly set about repairing the damage.

They were a sober lot. Frigg and Gawks, who had been manning the foresails, had been swept overboard during the attack. Oggler, who'd been near the stern, had caught one leg in the rigging, which had snapped it in more than one place. Quelch tried to set it, but he muttered privately that the leg would have to come off at the knee as soon as they located the hacksaw. Kailani's wound ought to have been minor, Everett thought desperately, since the lead ball had only grazed her. But the musket, Innes explained, shot fire, and Kai was a Water Elemental. The wound was deep and painful, and though Innes thought she would recover, it would take some time.

Everett and the other passengers sat around a bleak campfire on the beach as night fell.

"It isn't perhaps as bad as we fear," Almaric said at last. "The *Sea Witch* is no ordinary vessel. Morgan has formidable magic at her command."

Oggler's moaning floated across the beach.

Everett felt sick in his stomach.

"The longer we wait, the harder it will be to find

Holly," he said in a low voice. "That's right, isn't it?"

"Your compass will find the *Black Dragon* wherever she may be," said Jade. "If a sea portal can be opened, why . . ." He trailed off, as if too drained of hope to continue.

"'Tis how he was following us all along," Ranulf said, completely unnecessarily, Everett thought. "It must have been the Sorcerer's plan for you to find the compass in the wood, near your portal."

"I cannot think what you mean," said Avery dismissively. "I tell you, we have no sorcerer in the king's employ. His Majesty despises magic. It hath always been thus."

"Open your eyes, boy!" said Almaric, and everyone fell quiet; Everett had never seen him so angry. "Raethius of the Source has controlled the throne since long before your time. He raised your father from infancy. It is he who rules Anglielle, not Reynard." Almaric scowled at the fire. "You were brought up in ignorance, Your Highness. It is time you grew up and realized the sort of man your father is, and his so-called advisor. They are murderers, the both of them."

Avery's face turned red. He opened his mouth as if to argue the point, but then shut it again. Everett thought he saw tears in his eyes. Avery stood up, kicked a log into the flames, and stalked off toward the jungle. Everett wanted to go after him, but Ranulf put a firm hand on his shoulder.

"Leave him be," he said. "His Highness is only being told what he knows in his heart to be true. Let him come to it in his own time. Meanwhile, we must wait until our vessel is seaworthy. Then we will go and rescue Her Ladyship."

"Yeah, but *when*?" Ben asked. "We could be here for days, and that—that guy has Holly. What's he going to do to her?"

No one wished to conjecture on that point.

Chapter 44

Raethius

It was a long time before Holly came to with the sort of headache that needles you behind the eyes and makes you sick to your stomach. She had been so cold for so long that it took a moment to realize that she was warm and dry now, lying on a rough surface. With a jolt, she recalled everything that had happened, and sat up abruptly.

She was sitting on a black tapestried rug embroidered with silver symbols. Beneath it were rough flagstones. Above her yawned tall stone columns and an arched ceiling. Altogether, the place was like an ancient chapel. How had she gotten off the *Black Dragon*?

Then the floor pitched, and she recognized the motion of a ship at sea. She *was* on the *Black Dragon*. But how could such a room be on a schooner?

Her hand went to her shoulder, and Áedán crawled into her palm, blinking his bulbous golden eyes at her. She wondered if he was warm enough, and she breathed on him as she would a dying fire. His scales flushed a warm gold. She placed him back on her shoulder, where he nestled beneath her collar against her neck.

Through the tall arched windows along one wall, a calm sea stretched in every direction, although the ship's railing and the long black line of the spanker sail cut across her view. She was in the stern, then, beneath the poop deck. But the ceiling arched thirty feet above her head. It didn't make sense.

The chapel was empty except for a pair of tall pedestals at the far end flanking a kind of altar. She could see no door, but maybe she could break the windows.

She felt around her waist for the wand scabbard and opened it.

The scabbard was empty.

Suddenly the chapel went dark as if a black curtain had fallen over the leaded windows. Along the walls, several bracketed torches cast a gloomy, flickering light. Beneath her feet, the floor pitched and rolled.

The first torch went out.

She was reminded of her dark walk through the king's castle, the safe feeling of having allies around her. No one was with her now, except Áedán. Even Jade was gone.

A second torch went out.

"Who's there?" Holly called sharply.

A rustling sound came from the far end of the room.

The third torch went out.

"I know what you're doing," Holly said, trying to steady her voice. "I'm not scared of the dark."

A thousand whispers answered her, a susurrus like the rustle of silk: "Only of what comes out of the dark."

Áedán stirred on her shoulder, gathering his energy. He would protect her, but he was all she had in the way of weapons, and she didn't want to expose him too soon. "Wait, Áedán," she whispered to him. "Not till I say."

The final torch went out. The chapel was plunged into a darkness so complete Holly could almost touch it. The whispers gathered around her, a hundred voices speaking so softly she couldn't make out what they were saying. They crept up her legs, crawling into her ears, tangling in her braids, winding around the wire frames of her glasses. She felt them tickling up her sleeves and inside her shoes. But they were just *voices*, weren't they?

She tried to slap them away, but her fingers couldn't grasp them. Goose bumps shivered along her arms, and the hairs on the back of her neck prickled in response. An acrid, smoky smell circled her body, swirling around her head.

Áedán stirred. Silently, Holly shook her head. Her heart was pounding now as the whispers grew louder; the smoke filled her throat. She covered her ears and found she had locked the whispers inside her head, where they circled and laughed. "Get away from me!" she cried out.

A burst of light. A single candle on the altar had lit.

"Where are you?" Holly asked, moving toward the candle. She tried to keep the tears from her voice. "I'm not afraid of you, whatever you are."

The whispers ceased. In the dim light something dark and thin flew before her eyes, but it was gone the next instant. As she moved forward, a black shadow began to grow behind the candle like an expanding balloon. She halted, afraid to go farther.

"Expecting someone?"

The voice came from behind as an icy puff of air tickled the nape of her neck. She spun around.

A few feet away stood a figure.

Too thin to be human, he was a humanoid figure at least eight feet tall, with grotesquely long, pencil-thin arms that ended in only slightly wider hands. The fingers were more like talons, multijointed and in almost constant motion, like a spider's legs. The creature was covered in a silky black cloak that it wore like a second skin, with sleeves that were feathered like

CLAIRE M. CATERER

wings. But the most awful thing to Holly was its pale, birdlike head, which glowed with a sick light of its own beneath a loose hood. The white skin was puckered like a plucked chicken. Its black, lashless eyes, hunched close together under a jutting brow, rarely blinked, and its mouth moved in a jerky, exaggerated motion, as if unused to talking.

Holly's breath coughed out in horrid little puffs, hardly filling her lungs. Her muscles froze. A smoky stench floated off the creature in waves.

"You. Were. Expecting. Someone," it said. The hissing voice flew to her ears, shot through them, and then faded.

Her knees weakened. She backed up. "Who are you?" she managed to ask, though she knew.

"Raethius," hissed the creature. It threw up its great winged sleeves, and as it did so, grew like the shadow she had seen. In one movement it flew to the ceiling, then collapsed in on itself again. "Raethius of the Source." He extended a taloned hand to her. "Sit, Adept."

Holly fell backward onto the stone floor without meaning to, her legs turning to mush beneath her.

The smoky air stung her nostrils. The voice spoke only inches from her ear. "It is not control. Only persuasion."

Holly pulled herself up off the ground. The Sorcerer perched on a large stone chair that had materialized out of nowhere. On either side of this throne stood two tall blazing candles that cast sharp, flickering shadows all around them; on the other branches of the candelabras sat several large, bloodred birds.

"It wasn't Crewso I saw in Hawkesbury," Holly said. She forced herself to look into the Sorcerer's horrible face. "It was one of these birds."

His neck stretched out impossibly long, like taffy, and his beaklike face darted forward into hers. "I speak. *I* speak!" he hissed. "You are but dust."

Raethius retracted his neck and swept his winglike arm across the room. "These are the Elements of the earth: stone. Dust. Iron. See how I command them."

The flagstones rumbled beneath her. A crack split the floor at the far end of the room and opened into a chasm. Holly scrambled out of the way, but the fissure chased her until she fell through it. Her fingers grasped the jagged edge of the abyss, from whence a cold, fetid breeze blew. Her hands began to slip.

Just as she let go, the earth rushed up under her feet and threw her back onto the stone floor. Her heart rattled in her chest, her back drenched in a cold sweat despite the icy air. Through it all, the Sorcerer's black eyes stared straight ahead.

CLAIRE M. CATERER

"These are the Elements of the water: the sea, the rain, the rivers." He pointed to the windows. The sea rose up, then crashed inside. Holly barely had time to scramble to her feet before the water engulfed her. Seawater filled her lungs. A moment later she fell, warm and dry, onto the flagstones.

Holly panted. *It's not real,* she told herself. She thought it again, like a mantra: *It's not real. It's just a show. It's not real. It's just . . .*

"These are the Elements of the air: the wind, the smoke, the storm."

By now she knew what was coming. From nowhere an icy breeze blew back her hair and gathered itself into a cyclone. It picked her up and flung her toward the leaded windows. But as unreal as she knew it was, she couldn't help but shield her face, and the wind died.

"These are the Elements of fire," the Sorcerer said. "The heat, the flame, the destruction."

A sphere of fire bloomed at the far end of the chapel and rolled like a great cannonball toward her, gaining speed. But this was *her* Element; Holly stood her ground. At the last moment, she whispered to Áedán. He threw up his curtain of flame just as the fireball engulfed her. She felt warm and safe behind the orange wall, but she hoped Raethius couldn't tell Áedán's magic apart from his own.

Áedán pulled back the fire curtain with a jolt as the Sorcerer's fireball vanished. Holly sat on the stone floor in front of the Sorcerer's throne, unharmed.

"You do see, Adept," he said. "I create you. I destroy you. Most important, I contain you." Raethius stood and walked in a broad circle around Holly. "Do not for a moment doubt that it is at my whim that you breathe the air and walk the earth. *Because I allow it.*" He stopped in front of her, towering over her, his clawlike feet just inches from her own. His neck stretched down and thrust itself in front of her. "Do you understand?"

Holly licked her lips, trying to revive her dry throat. "I . . ." She took a breath. "I understand that you . . . you need me."

Áedán winced and he crouched lower on her shoulder. Raethius's black eyes blazed back at her, but she could tell she'd struck a nerve. Why else would he capture her, if he had all the power?

"You do *not* understand." The Sorcerer threw out a hand, and a gust of wind hurled Holly against the stone wall. With another gust he yanked her back. "You are a piece of the puzzle I construct. A part of the power that I amass. But you are not *needed.*"

His strange, birdlike mouth curled in disgust. "The wand. Where is it?"

Holly's heart warmed only briefly. She was all too aware that her greatest weapon was gone, but at least Raethius couldn't take it from her. She tried one pathetic tack: "I—I don't know what you're talking about."

"Don't be a fool." The Sorcerer folded his winglike arms. "I know it exists. My emissaries have seen it. But I wonder: How did you forge it?"

Holly closed her eyes. She pictured Almaric and Ranulf, the forest, the Elm. She pictured Ben and Everett. She repeated to herself again: *I will not tell. I will not tell. I will not tell.*

But his voice crawled into her ears like a wriggling insect, chewing its way through her ear canal and into her brain, where it bounced off every neuron. She found she could think of nothing else, even when she tried to picture her home, her father and mother; every person, every scene, had the Sorcerer's face on it, asking, *How? How? How?* until she knew she would soon go mad.

"What difference does it make?" she screeched. "It's mine!"

"But you do not come from this world." Raethius glided to the wall beneath the tall windows, then back again. "It appears the Wandwright still lives, though I have not seen her for many an age. How are you, who do not come from this place, one of us?"

"I'm not one of *you*," Holly said. "I don't know what you are."

Inside her head, her mother's voice said, *Stop it! You'll only make him angry*. But alongside it she heard another, newer voice: *But he needs me alive*.

"I am the Fire and the Water, the Earth and the Air," said Raethius. "I am above and beyond your kind."

The wind gathered underneath Holly once again and swept her up to the chapel's lofty ceiling; then, abruptly, the wind died and she fell onto the hard flags. She landed on her ankle as it twisted the wrong way. She screamed.

"Before you are insolent to me again, Adept, remember that I do not need you whole. Only alive. And only for a brief time. My mercy will last no longer than my patience."

Holly cradled the ankle, which was already swelling. It was broken. She tried very hard not to cry, but a few tears escaped her. Áedán paced; his feet felt sticky and hot on her shoulder. Raethius approached her.

Before she could stop him, Áedán emerged and threw a bolt of power from his tiny foreleg. The curtain of fire sprung up around them. As warm and comforting as it was, it frightened her more than the Sorcerer himself. *Now he knows.*

Bring the water, said the new voice in her head. *That's the power—fire plus water.*

But even if she could manage it, she had no wand.

Through the orange flames, Raethius smiled and waved one hand.

Áedán's flames froze in place. They faded to a pale blue, hardening, until they fell in icy shards all around her.

"Your little Elemental friend is impetuous," said the Sorcerer casually. "One of three Salamanders, am I right? The weakest of the three, if I make my guess." One of the pasty-white claws extended. "Give him to me."

"You can't have him." Holly stumbled away, one hand over her shoulder, where Áedán huddled. She knew she had nowhere to run, that Raethius would take Áedán if it pleased him, but she would not hand him over. The Salamander crawled into her sleeve.

A tiny, powerful cyclone whirled around Holly, pulling the Salamander out of her grasp. His sticky feet clung to her, but she didn't dare hold on to him, for fear of tearing him apart. For a moment he hung suspended in midair between Holly and Raethius, his golden fingers splayed out. He looked to Holly, his eyes full of tears; and then the wind shot him to the far end of the chapel, where the red birds waited. They descended.

Holly covered her eyes. She couldn't help the tears now; they poured through her fingers, her chest heaving. The Sorcerer had once been only a horrible creature, but now he was something she could hate. A throbbing ache opened inside her, a black place. Her eyes were swollen, her cheeks streaked with tears. She said in a thick, awful voice: "I will never help you. *Never.*"

Raethius weaved his spidery fingers through the air. Something off to his left clanged, like pipes being dragged across the stone floor; a moment later several pieces of iron assembled themselves over her head and around her body to form the bars of a small cell.

"We commence on the morrow," said Raethius. "You, who are so in tune with this world that you earned the loyalty of an Elemental Salamander, will be affixed to the bow of the *Black Dragon*. You will guide this vessel to the Isle of the Adepts. And then you will surrender the wand to me."

She would not look at him now. Her hate was so overwhelming, she thought she might tear her own body in half just to push through the bars and murder him.

His neck elongated, stretching to meet her gaze. He whispered in her ear. "You will not refuse me, Adept. There are others you cherish. They will be reduced to dust like your Elemental ally. Do not think on it."

CLAIRE M. CATERER

He stood and raised both arms wide, the sleeves becoming black, glossy wings. "On the morrow, when the moon is full," he said. The cloak enveloped the Sorcerer as the beating of a thousand wings filled the air. Then a thin column of very black smoke shot up from the floor, and he vanished.

Holly was alone.

Chapter 45

Chasing the Dragon

"I don't favor this idea at all," said Almaric firmly. "However talented His Highness appears to be with the wand, the magic is borrowed, and therefore unreliable. Not to mention that the spell itself is highly advanced."

He sat at the table in the ship's mess with Everett, Ben, and Avery. Jade and Ranulf stood nearby. Only half a day had passed since Holly had disappeared, and miraculously, they were at sea again. Kailani and Rowan had spent hours underwater fixing holes in the ship's hull, and Almaric and Morgan had repaired the sails with patchwork magic. They wouldn't hold forever, but they would do for now.

The boys hadn't even argued about revealing Avery's wand to Almaric and the others. It was the only tool they had left besides the locket, which Morgan had strapped to the ship's compass. It would lead them to Raethius.

"But it be possible," Avery was saying. "Lady Holly performed this trick before, and didst transport many of us at once."

"The Vanishment," said Almaric icily, "is not a *trick*. It is an advanced spell. Lady Holly used a wand of her own forging, she trained for some time, and she is an *Adept*, you forget. I beg Your Highness's pardon, but you are mortalfolk. It would be foolish to try. One leg would end up in a shark's mouth whilst another in the crow's nest, and an elbow in another kingdom altogether. No. I shall not allow it."

"But he can already do *osclaígí*," Everett put in. "That's an Adept spell, isn't it?"

"A much simpler one, my boy," said Almaric. "It does not involve transporting *people*."

"But how else are we going to get onto this Sorcerer guy's boat?" Ben asked. He had been quiet since Holly had disappeared, and his voice sounded small. "He kicked our butts before. We can't just meet him in open battle."

Everett eyed the muskets, which were stacked in a corner. "If we could just get a good shot at him—"

"*No,*" several voices chorused at once.

"The firewands are even less reliable than His Highness's stolen magic," Jade said. The fur along his spine bristled, and it took him a moment to smooth it down. "They were designed to use against mortals, not magicfolk."

"We must use stealth," said Ranulf. "If we stay submerged until just the right moment, Raethius will not know of our presence. Then may we storm the bridge."

"His control of the Elements is formidable," Almaric said. He twisted the hem of his long tunic. "I have not seen the like since the days of the Adepts themselves."

"Perhaps there is another spell the wand could be used for," Avery said. "If the Lord Magician would aid me—"

"Perhaps, Your Highness," Almaric said wearily. "But for now I suggest we all get some rest. Let me think on it. We cannot do a thing until we are in sight of the *Black Dragon* in any case. That will be a few hours, according to the captain."

Everett lay in his hammock, swaying with the steady chugging of the ship. Morgan and the exhausted crew took shifts to augment the becalmed sea with their own water power. At least his compass could be of some use now. So far Ben hadn't mentioned how Everett oughtn't have kept the wand a secret; in fact, Ben was hardly speaking to him.

And then Everett had gone and fired the muskets, which had seemed like such a good idea at the time, though only Avery had been able to do anything to help Holly. He still couldn't quite believe it, but they had all seen it: Avery standing alone on deck, making complicated patterns in the air with the raised wand. How had he even known to do that? Ben didn't blame *him*, Everett noticed; in fact, Ben had patted him on the back and said, "That was a really good try." No one had patted Everett for coming up with the idea of using real guns.

"You're turning over every ten seconds," came Ben's voice from below, sounding flat and annoyed.

"Sorry. I can't sleep."

"Me either."

Everett hung his head over the upper hammock to look at Ben. "How do you reckon Avery does it? How's he working that wand so ruddy well?"

Ben lay on his back, looking morose. "Maybe he didn't steal it."

Everett rolled back into his hammock with a huff. Avery *did* steal the wand, he started to say; he'd stolen it from Everett himself. But that wasn't what Ben was talking about. That voice that had been niggling him for days, even weeks, nudged at him again. Finally he climbed out of the hammock and knelt next to Ben.

"All right, listen. If I tell you something, can you swear not to tell Holly? Or Avery either?"

"And when do you think I'll be seeing Holly again?" Ben shot back.

"Okay, fair do's." Everett took a deep breath and gritted his teeth. "I . . . I *did* nick that wand from Gallaway's house last year."

Ben rolled over and faced him. "No kidding."

"I *know* what I kept saying. I'm sorry, I was younger, all right? I just couldn't see why Gallaway straight-away gave Holly the coolest present *ever*. And those keys were just sitting there—"

"You don't have to explain it," Ben said. "I might've taken one too if I'd had the chance. I mean, I *doubt* it. But I can see how someone could."

"There's more," Everett said. "That red scarf wrapped round the wand? I didn't just find it. One of those Elemental fairy things gave it to me to boost the wand's magic, but she was evil. I know that now. Maybe—I don't know—maybe us having the red scarf is helping that Raethius git." He hung his head miserably.

Ben lay there, quiet, making it worse. His big eyes blinked. Finally he said, "Geez, Everett, I don't think so. Unless Raethius found it in the castle and put the whammy on it. Unless you think *Avery's* working for him—"

"I really don't think he is. He tried to get Holly back and all."

"So what if you got a magic doohickey from some wicked fairy?" Ben went on. "We're all new here. It's easy to make mistakes. Holly isn't perfect either, even though she acts like she is."

Everett laughed. It wasn't much of a joke, but it made him feel better. The knot in his stomach dissolved like honey. He'd finally said it. And Ben understood.

"I feel ruddy awful about what happened to Holly. I know you think I don't care. But I want to get her back."

Ben struggled out of his hammock to a sitting position. "Then maybe we should just do it instead of waiting for the grown-ups to make a move. We're not worthless, are we?"

Before Everett could answer, Avery appeared from around the corner. He twirled the wand in his hand. "Exactly as I say."

Everett picked up a lantern, and the three of them slipped out past Cook and Oggler, then through to the little room just astern of the brig. The prince shifted some barrels of pickled meats aside to give them space.

"I am quite sure I can do this Vanishment, whatever the magician may say," Avery began. "I recall the Adept's words—"

"Incantation," Ben corrected him.

"Aye. With the magic imbued by this lady's favor, I

believe we can transport ourselves to the blackguard's vessel."

Everett thought Avery was assuming quite a bit, but he kept quiet for the moment.

"But Almaric said you could send our elbows and kneecaps to different places," Ben said. "Are you sure you know what you're doing?"

"I thought we weren't going to bother with Almaric and the others," Everett said.

"Everett speaks true. If we wait, the Adept could disappear forever. Or die." Avery drew himself up in his cross-legged position. "'Tis a matter of honor."

"But we can't even see the *Black Dragon* yet," Ben pointed out. "Holly said that to do the Vanishment, you've got to at least know where you're pointing us."

Avery waved away his comment. "That is the Adept's way, perhaps. But I am able to do things with this wand that even she cannot do."

Ben raised his eyebrows as if he'd not seen evidence of this. Avery had done a few things right, but Holly could've done as well, or better. Before he could say as much, a silky voice interrupted them.

"And what," said Jade, stepping into the lantern light, "are three lads like yourselves planning to do at this hour of the night?"

Chapter 46

The Crystal

The air was utterly still as night fell. None of the windows were open, but it seemed the chapel and her cell got damper and more cold the longer Holly sat there. Even the motion of the ship ceased.

Not that she cared much. The *Black Dragon* could go nowhere or sail away into the darkness; it wouldn't matter. The blow of losing Áedán had left a hollow pit in her stomach that might never heal. He had protected her, guided her, and she had let him down. A sacred creature of Anglielle was dead because of her. And, she thought bitterly, he had been her last chance, her secret weapon.

The only light came from a glint of moonlight and two torches set between the tall leaded windows. Though quite round, the moon was not yet full. Something about the moon's phase would strengthen Raethius's magic. But no matter what he wanted, she couldn't guide him to the Adepts' island any more than she could take the *Sea Witch* there. What would he do when he realized this?

Her only hope was that the *Sea Witch* would stay hidden far from here. At least no one else would get hurt. Holly wished she could get a message to Almaric and Ranulf somehow, tell them to send the boys home. She wasn't going to make it herself, and she was afraid they wouldn't leave without her. If only she could talk to them, just for a moment. But she could do nothing.

Her ankle throbbed. It was twice its normal size, and in the dim light she could see it had turned a dark purple. Her stomach turned as she recalled the Sorcerer's spindly neck shooting out to look her in the eye. He was almost like a changeling.

The changeling.

A hot blush suffused her cheeks. The time stones! She thrust her hand into the pocket of her jeans, praying the stones hadn't been washed away during her journey to the *Black Dragon*. If only she still had them . . .

She did.

She pulled them out one at a time: the fluorite, the crystal, and the obsidian. She had no wand, but she didn't need one. She could call on Ailith to perform a spell, to Vanish her back to the *Sea Witch*! Or Ailith would have another idea, surely she would.

Holly laid out the stones in order, the fluorite on

CLAIRE M. CATERER

her left, the crystal in the center, the obsidian at her right hand. She cupped the fluorite lightly in her palm. "Ailith of the Adepts," she chanted, picturing her, "come to me in this hour of need. Ailith of the Adepts, come to me in this hour of need. . . ."

She waited for the stone to grow cold in her hand.

Nothing happened.

Holly winced as a sudden knife-pain shot through her ankle. Of course she couldn't conjure Ailith. Almaric had told her: No one from the past could be brought into peril. Raethius had gone somewhere, but it was still dangerous here. Ailith could die, and then disappear from her own past.

Holly could call Almaric himself, she thought next, or Jade or Ranulf. But what would be the point? They couldn't fight Raethius. He would just kill them as he had Áedán. She didn't dare call the *Sea Witch*, even if it was possible to call an entire ship. If they weren't ready, she would put them all in danger.

She rubbed the tears off her cheeks. There was nothing for it: She would need to call Ben and tell him to leave her and go home. He would be stubborn and refuse, but she would have to convince him.

The chapel was empty. Ben would be safe for the few moments she would speak to him, and even if Raethius appeared, she could just send Ben back.

She put down the fluorite and picked up the clouded crystal. She pictured Ben on board the *Sea Witch*. She had never called someone from the present, but how different could it be?

"Benjamin Shepard of the brigantine *Sea Witch*, come to me in this hour of need. Benjamin Shepard of the brigantine *Sea Witch*, come to me in this hour of need. . . ."

Holly kept her eyes closed, the tears running down her face. *Please come, Ben,* she thought as she chanted. *Please come to say good-bye.*

Chapter 47

Vanishing

"Do not attempt to waylay us," Avery said to Jade in his most imperious voice. "'Tis a mission of honor we seek."

The cat sat down in the midst of their circle and curled his paws around Holly's wand, which he had brought with him. "Why would I waylay you? I am Lady Holly's familiar. I wish to accompany you." He eyed the prince's wand, which Avery held up as if ready to cast a spell. "You have not the mastery of that instrument."

"Of course I do," Avery snapped. "Now, cat, you will verify that I have the Vanishment incantation correct."

"I did *not* say that the Vanishment was the correct way to proceed," Jade said, "and certainly not without the *Black Dragon* in our sights."

"Nonsense! I can see it in my mind's eye; that is all that is required."

"And you say this considering your vast knowledge of Adept magic?"

"I feel funny," Ben said. His face was screwed up in a wince, and he shifted uncomfortably. One knee was touching Everett's.

"I believe I raise the wand and cry the word," said Avery, but before he could do anything, Everett grabbed hold of his wrist. "Unhand our royal person," Avery said, sounding very much like the prince Everett had first met a year before.

"Just wait," said Everett. "We've all got to agree."

Jade's tail twitched, flicking against the prince's other side.

"Really not good at all," Ben said, holding his stomach with one hand.

"Are you seasick?" Everett started to back away, but Ben grabbed him with one hand.

"No, it's—like a pulling. It's—it's—"

For that one moment, all four of them were touching one another.

Ben's words were lost in a loud, baffled sound like an enormous turbine, and the planks beneath them began to fade.

"Avery!" Everett shouted. "What're you doing? Stop it!"

"'Tis not I! I have not even used the wand!"

Everything around them began to turn. Everett felt what Ben had described—a tugging. All four of them began to whirl like one huge top. The brig, the pickle barrel, the lantern, all of it turned faster and faster until they were a colorful blur. It lasted nearly a minute, and then, abruptly, Everett felt a hard bump as he landed on his backside in the middle of what looked like a cold, dark, empty church.

Chapter 48

On Board the Black Dragon

"Benjamin Shepard of the brigantine *Sea Witch*, come to me in my hour of need," Holly whispered for the fifth time.

That's when she heard the *oof* and the *get off me* and the *what's this ruddy place* and the *you shouldn't have done that.* Her eyes flew open. Right in the center of the chapel was a tangle of arms and legs and one black tail. Holly was both overjoyed and horrified.

"What—how did you all get here?" she cried, and then lowered her voice at once. "You've got to get out! He might be back any second."

Jade extricated himself from the mess of boys and darted to her side. "Lady Holly, we are here to aid you. Has the Sorcerer done this?"

"This, and a lot more."

Jade eyed the stones spread out in front of her. "It

was you, not the prince," he mused, then raised his glittery green eyes to her with pride. "You called us. And without this." He dropped the wand through the bars of her cell.

"I tried to call Ben, that's all. I wanted . . . wanted to say good-bye. To tell him to get home as quick as he can. All of you. Stay out of Raethius's way. He wants me to take him to the Adepts' island, and I won't be able to. He'll punish you all."

"But we're here now," said Ben, running over, with Everett and Avery behind him. "We can get you out."

Holly shook her head, but Ben wasn't listening. "Avery, get over here with the wand."

"Where did *you* get a wand?" Holly asked.

"Never mind," said Ben. "First we need to spring this lock. What's that spell? Oh-says-me?"

"*Osclaígí,*" said Holly and Avery together.

The iron bars of the cell fell apart in a clattering heap. Holly gaped at the prince.

"Geez, you guys," Ben whispered. "You want to wake up everyone in this place? Where are we, anyway?"

"On board the *Black Dragon.* I know it doesn't look like a ship, but it is." Holly turned to the cat. "Jade, he took Áedán. He—he killed him." Somehow she thought Jade would be the only one to understand how awful this was, but all of them stared wordlessly back at her.

Jade recovered first. "Are you certain, Lady Holly? It seems unlikely."

"He gave him to his—his birds." She started to cry again.

"Stop that now," said Jade sharply. "Did you *see* Áedán harmed? Because Raethius has at least some Elemental blood himself. He would much sooner use Áedán than kill him. Where was he taken?"

"Jade, he's *gone*," Holly said, trying to calm her hitching sobs. "Raethius threw him against that wall, and the birds flew down. . . . I don't know. . . ."

"Show me the door." Jade darted to the far end of the chapel.

Holly limped after him, dragging the broken ankle. "I can't run. . . ." She gained the far wall and looked up at the yawning stone pedestals. "The birds kind of melted through here somehow."

"Then unlock it."

"But—"

"I shall do it," Avery said, at her heels. *"Osclaígí."*

The wall shimmered, then became gauzy, like a thin curtain. Through it Holly could see the deck of the schooner, where the thin, smokelike figures darted here and there.

"No, Jade, you'll get caught. I'll lose you, too," Holly whispered, her voice catching.

"I will return, Lady Holly. I promise." The cat darted through the veil. It closed over him.

"What's he doing?" Holly cried as the stone wall materialized again. Her tears dried on her hot cheeks. "How will we get him back?"

"One thing at a time," said Everett. "We need to figure a way off the ship. Maybe there's a longboat?"

"I . . . I saw one lashed to the starboard side." Holly started toward the leaded windows, then stumbled. Avery caught her.

"What has Raethius done to you, my lady?" he asked, wincing at the sight of her ankle.

"It doesn't matter. Just help me." Leaning on him like a crutch, Holly pulled up the painful foot and made her way to the window.

"He has always been so kind to me," Avery murmured. "I never knew he could be such a brute. Perhaps he is under a spell."

"He's the one *casting* the spells, you dimwit," said Ben.

Holly was aware of how quiet Avery was, what he must be thinking, turning events over in his mind. Was it possible Raethius had ever shown anyone kindness? She thought of Áedán and Jade; the grief dug at her insides, but she fought it down. "Careful, don't let them see you." She edged around the windowpane and spied the longboat. "Maybe I can Vanish the long-boat into the water without anyone noticing, but we can't leave without Jade. And I can't Vanish us to the *Sea Witch* unless I can see it."

"Never fear," said Avery confidently. "I am convinced that is all myth. It be simply a matter of reciting the spell, and—"

"Are you crazy?" Holly glared at him. "Magic has rules. I don't know where the *Sea Witch* is, which means I can't visualize a path to it. We'd end up in the middle of nowhere—maybe the ocean, maybe in pieces. Nobody does that spell but me, when I'm ready. Do you get that?"

She hadn't meant to speak so harshly. He had been awfully nice to her, but the idea that he would play with a spell like the Vanishment set her teeth on edge. He was still a prince; he thought everything was his right. Avery's face turned very red, and the boys on either side of him exchanged a nudging *I told you so* sort of look between them.

"Okay, then," said Holly. "Let's get—"

But she never finished that sentence.

The three torches between the windows suddenly sputtered and went out. Tendrils of black smoke rose from them, darkened, then thickened, ropelike. They burst from the torches and swirled around them. Holly had a sickening realization: The *osclaígí* spell had called them—the smoke demons. Their acrid, decaying smell made her nauseous.

"What . . . what are these things?" Ben asked in a small voice. They were stretching now, elongating, no longer looking like smoke so much as like humanoid figures. They lifted Holly's braids, ruffled through the boys' hair, and seeped into their clothing and down their throats. Ben began to cough.

"They're like the things that came out of the compass," said Everett.

"The torches," Holly said, coughing too. "They're . . . they're guards. He's coming. We have to go."

But the tendrils of smoke wove themselves into a black lattice like a spider's web encircling them. Holly tore at them, and Avery slashed with his wand, but the cage held. Everett kicked and shoved at the sticky strings; they gave, but only a little. Holly shouted the *osclaígí* spell, but the smoke demons only circled, contracting, as if circumventing her magic.

They were made of smoke, they were from fire, she thought quickly. She could control Elements too—well, one, anyway. But she couldn't conjure it. She could only move it.

Through the tall windows she could see a glint of the moon on the water. They were still at sea. Could she call the water from so far away, through glass, no less? She pointed the wand at the window. *"Tugaigí uisce!"* she cried.

At first nothing happened. Ben was turning red now and pumping his inhaler madly into his mouth. The others were gasping and choking; Avery had collapsed to his knees. He looked like he would throw up any minute. But then Holly heard it.

The growing, building *whoosh* that could mean only one thing.

A wave.

It was too black for her to see. When the wave reared over the starboard side of the schooner, it blocked the moon for a moment. It towered over the gunwale and hung for half a second before crashing to the deck, shattering the leaded windows.

The boys' mouths gaped. The wave washed over the stone floor and threw them off their feet. The smoke demons flew apart. Holly leaned on Everett, the only one of the boys who seemed strong enough to hold her up, and beckoned to the others. Their only way out was through the window.

But then—and Holly had not forgotten this—they would be trapped.

Chapter 49

Fire and Water

Everett was thinking the same thing as, one by one, they climbed through the window frame and emerged just below the schooner's poop deck. The ship was massive, with several quarterdecks and a hull that stretched down forever into the black sea. The crowded deck afforded plenty of hiding places, but it was too late for that. The smoke demons solidified into dark figures and swarmed over the deck and into the rigging. A flock of bloodred birds descended, screeching from the sky. Everett slashed at them with his sword. But where was the Sorcerer?

Holly positioned herself at the poop deck's railing and started throwing waves over the bow with her wand. They scattered the smoke demons, who were disorganized for the moment. But she was already tired; she couldn't keep it up for long. "I'll hold them off!" she shouted. "Just get the longboat."

He spied it lashed to the starboard side. "Ben, come help me!"

Avery stepped up to shield him and fended off the birds with his sword. He tried to churn the waves as Holly did, but his wand only emitted a few feeble sparks. Everett and Ben untied the longboat and hoisted it between them.

The splintered wood dug into Everett's shoulder. "On three, we'll toss it over," he said.

"What're we going to do then?" Ben asked.

"We'll have to jump for it."

"No way!"

"It's the *only* way, now come on!"

They gave a great heave. The boat fell an impossibly long way down, then splashed—upright, at least—into the sea. Immediately they began to drift away from it. The schooner was still moving. Everett and Ben climbed over the railing, clinging to the ropes. Ben's legs trembled as he straddled the railing.

"Holly, we have to go now," Everett said. "Avery, come on!"

"Take Ben!" she said. "I have to wait for Jade."

But just as she spoke, the cat came flying from the forecastle like a streak of black lightning, something clutched in his mouth. Behind him rose a figure, a *thing*, the likes of which Everett had never seen before.

CLAIRE M. CATERER

Its very presence stilled the crew as if they were caught in a game of freeze tag. The waves flattened. Everett, panting, was somehow frozen too, hanging off the ropes, Ben's sleeve clutched in his fist. When the figure spoke, its voice was like an icicle dagger.

"Adept," it said. "You have not fulfilled your contract."

Everett yanked hard on Ben's sleeve, pulling him over, and the two of them tumbled through the cold air, farther than Everett had hoped, waiting for the blast of icy water. It smacked them, then engulfed them.

At once, Everett's fingers went numb, but he tightened his grip on Ben's sleeve. All he could think of was how he'd nearly lost Ben in the castle moat, and he wasn't about to let it happen again. He hauled the two of them to the surface.

Everett could just see Holly over the curve of the great hull, standing her ground, her face set hard. Behind her back, she was waving the wand in tiny circles, and little eddies of water were swirling in their direction. Had she run out of strength at last? Was Raethius draining her somehow?

But then he saw what she was doing. The longboat, far adrift, was bobbing toward them on the tiny tide Holly had created.

She was shouting something at the Sorcerer now,

trying to distract him. Everett couldn't see Jade. He held Ben up by the collar of his shirt. He hung from Everett's grasp, his teeth chattering, too cold to flail about. That was a blessing; at least he wasn't fighting. Everett paddled toward the boat, and it glided to them. He shoved Ben up. "Grab it," he panted. Ben kicked, but he was too short and weak to pull himself in. "Hold on," said Everett, and dragged himself aboard. He grabbed Ben's arms and pulled him into the boat, then collapsed, breathing hard. He looked up at the deck of the *Black Dragon*.

He was glad he did, or he would've missed it: Holly, so small, but straight, her brown braids hanging down; Raethius, so tall and terrible, raising up his horrid black wings. Avery, huddled close to Holly, shouted at the Sorcerer, distracting him for a moment. Holly held something in her left hand. Everett couldn't see what it was, but she brought it to her mouth and kissed it; and then her hand blazed with a golden light, and a bolt of fire shot from it like a laser beam.

Beside him, shivering, Ben gasped. "That was— wasn't it?"

Áedán.

And even though Everett couldn't help thinking it was futile, such a little flame against such a prodigious foe, a warm hope filled him. Áedán struck again, and the protective fire sprang up around Holly. Raethius raised his fingers as if to counter the Salamander's spell, but Avery leaped at him, knocking him off-balance. Raethius roared and struck out a hand, sending the prince flying into the sea. Holly scrambled onto the poop-deck railing. Jade followed. They hesitated only a moment, Áedán's ball of fire a bright beacon against the black sky; and then they plunged.

Holly bobbed to the surface almost at once. The protective flames Áedán had cast were swallowed in the sea. Up on the deck of the *Black Dragon*, Raethius smiled, unconcerned. Where could they go now? He would just pluck them out of the water unless she did something.

Holly, Jade, and Avery, who was nearby, swam for the longboat as Everett paddled toward them. Her ankle gave a wrench as he pulled them aboard, but she felt it only for a moment. She scooped Áedán off her shoulder and cupped him in her hands. She blew on him to warm him, and Jade added his breath as well. The Salamander glowed.

"*Holllllly!*"

Her chin jerked up.

Ben wasn't in the longboat.

"Up there!" Everett cried, pointing at the sky.

She saw her brother silhouetted against the nearly full moon, suspended in a cyclone. On the deck of the *Black Dragon*, the Sorcerer stood extending his white fingers toward Ben. "I warned you, Adept!" he shouted. "Fulfill your contract and none shall be harmed. You have my word."

"His *word*," Avery said, his voice breaking. He raised his wand.

"No, don't." Holly caught his sleeve. "Let me."

Áedán's magic had already proved too weak against the Sorcerer's. And Raethius's command of the waves was better than hers too. She couldn't beat him with fire or water.

But fire *and* water?

Almaric had said it wouldn't work. Ailith had told her it couldn't be done. Even Jade had argued against it. They knew more than she did, but Áedán crouched in her palm, ready. He knew what she wanted.

"Together," she whispered to him.

Áedán shot the firebolt from his splayed, sticky foot.

Holly called the water with a flourish of her wand.

The sea churned around them, but she couldn't make it rise. The fire in her hand was fighting against it. She closed her eyes.

"Let the fire help you," Jade whispered.

She felt his warm paw on her arm. The wand trembled in her fist; she relaxed her grip, letting its power pour through her hands, down through her arm, until it filled her heart, gathered strength, and rebounded. She pointed the wand at the sky, pulling Áedán's firestream closer to her; then she threw it into the sea, and Áedán shot it aloft. The sea boiled; it spiked; a wave rocked the longboat, fell back, and finally rose alongside the firestream.

Her arms shook with the struggle to hold the two elements in place; the broken ankle throbbed. Sweat poured off her forehead into her eyes, despite the frozen wind and the ice chunks floating around them. In the air, Ben flailed on his back, his eyes round, his face as white as the moon. The Sorcerer drew the cyclone closer to the schooner.

"You can do it, Holly!"

She could barely hear him abovo the churning waves and the roaring wind. Or perhaps she only imagined him saying it, Ben who never doubted her, who thought she could do anything.

She had no choice but to prove him right.

The firestream shot to the cyclone and swallowed it with a greedy *thwump*. Right behind it, Holly's salt-water wave caught Ben and tempered the flames. The two streams intertwined in a slow dance, the silver water glinting in the moonlight, the orange fire dazzling her eyes. They interlocked.

A backblast rocketed to earth, heaving the schooner out of the water. The Sorcerer fell to his knees on deck. The longboat's bow shot out of the water and fell back with a smack as Holly guided the united streams toward them. The two streams cradled Ben and lowered him gently into the longboat. Holly collapsed against the gunwale.

But Avery tugged her sleeve. "A sail! Lady Holly, 'tis the *Sea Witch*—perform the Vanishment!"

For once he didn't try to cast the spell himself. Holly glimpsed the brigantine's lantern on the horizon. She could only hope that Avery was right; if he wasn't, she had no idea where they'd end up. But there was no time to think of that now; she seized Avery's hand as Ben and Everett grabbed on to her, and Jade's tail wound around her ankles. With one exhausted cry, they plummeted into darkness.

"Imigh!"

Chapter 50

Surfacing

The spell didn't feel as smooth as it had before. There was a good bit more jostling, and Ben squeezed her elbow so tight, her fingers went numb. She was cold, wet, and exhausted, and when the black curtain rose around them, she prayed she was seeing her own spell and not Raethius's wings. But a moment later the rough planks of the *Sea Witch*'s deck solidified beneath them and they fell in a jumble somewhere amidships.

Rowan, at the helm, clanged the ship's bell. "Captain, they're here!" she cried. Every hand appeared on deck, the Elementals stretched their webbed fingers, and the seawater sped away beneath the keel, driving the brigantine forward. Holly and the others fell over as the ship rolled, and a bolt of pain shot through Holly's ankle. But on her shoulder, spent and shivering, Áedán clung to her neck with his sticky feet, and that made everything bearable.

"Get below!" shouted Morgan from the forecastle,

and Holly dragged her foot to the hatch. When she threw it open, Almaric appeared at the ladder to help her down. The boys followed, and then the crew tumbled through as well. Everyone sat, cold and dripping, in the brigantine's lower deck.

Ranulf and Almaric couldn't stop hugging Holly. The centaur opened his lecture with, "These lads should never have—" But he was cut off as the ship plunged and everyone was forced to the floor.

Almaric clucked and *tsked* over Holly's ankle. "I cannot heal it," he muttered, "but I can make you more comfortable. This will help numb the pain." He rummaged in his knapsack and pulled out a linen cloth, which shimmered in a strange way. He tore it into strips and used it to bind her ankle. "A bit of my own magician's craft . . . Nothing to your own skill, obviously," he said, but Holly felt the difference at once. At least she could hobble on the ankle a bit now.

"Morgan's crew have been tireless," said the magician as he finished wrapping her ankle. "They have been driving the *Sea Witch* as if before a gale ever since you disappeared. And once we discovered the lads missing—"

"I should let it be known, Lord Magician," Avery cut in, "that I was indeed able to perform the Vanishment spell."

"No, you didn't," said Ben. "Those stones of Holly's got us to the *Black Dragon*."

Avery turned a little pink. "Well. With some assistance, no doubt."

Holly was so tired, she didn't bother arguing with Avery. The ship sank lower and lower. Almaric fussed with his bandages, muttering as he rolled them up. "Almaric? What's wrong?"

The magician swallowed, not meeting her eyes. "Your injury, Lady Holly. It is serious. I think it time we return you to your own world, where you'll be safe."

"We don't have to go. Not . . . not yet," Holly said. But she supposed Almaric was right. She couldn't navigate to the Adepts' island, and now that Raethius was after her, she was putting everyone in danger.

"We'll come back, Holly," Everett said. "We'll regroup at home, you can heal up your ankle, then we'll have another go, yeah?"

"Her ankle's broken," Ben said. "Anybody could see that. By the time it's healed, we'll be on our way back to America."

"Then you must stay in your own world," said Ranulf. "Until such is your time to join us again."

"But . . ." Holly hated the thought of leaving now that she knew what Raethius could do. She had no idea when she would be able to come back. Suppose no one was left to come back to?

Almaric's eyes also looked watery, but he rubbed them quickly. "What must be, must be. You will return to us, I am sure of it."

"Of course I will," Holly said at once. "The minute that I can. And so will Ben and Everett."

Both boys nodded. Avery sat next to Everett, gazing at the floor between his knees. Holly found it rather a relief that he was silent, but Everett nudged him. "You okay?"

The prince looked up, his eyes red. "What am I to do, Everett? My father's throne is controlled by a monster. He has seen me as a traitor. I cannot return to the castle."

Almaric and Ranulf exchanged worried looks.

"So, you'll come with us," Everett said.

"Is that wise?" Jade asked, staring pointedly at Holly.

Was it? Holly couldn't look at Avery, the question naked in his blue eyes. He had fought alongside her; she couldn't deny that. But how could they bring someone from Anglielle home with them?

"Where would he stay?" Ben asked. "We can't just say we found him in the forest. He's a kid. They'll try to find his parents. Plus, he talks weird."

"They wouldn't even understand him," Holly said. "We can, because the wand translates for us. But he doesn't speak the same kind of English that we do."

"I would make my own way," said Avery stoutly. "I shall live in the wood and hunt for my food."

"You've lived in a palace your whole life. You don't know anything about making your own way. Besides, you're not allowed to do that." The ship gave a shuddering jolt. It was ascending. "Almaric, where are we going?" asked Holly.

Kailani, who was sitting close enough to overhear, answered for him. "The captain has sworn to return ye to yer land. She'll take us as close to the Elm as she can, whence we fetched ye."

"In the forest?" Ben asked.

"Nay, she must surface in a body of water close by. From there she'll navigate to the Elm, as she did before."

Almaric groaned, no doubt thinking of his trees.

"But you know what that means, don't you?" Everett's voice sounded shaky. "You know where she'll surface?"

A silence fell as everyone considered this, and then a deeper one when they realized what he meant. Morgan knew of only one body of water near Almaric's Elm.

The castle moat.

"But the stream," Everett said urgently to Kailani. "The stream in the wood, where we came in from our world. That's where she should go. Can't we tell her?"

"She navigates the sea, not freshwater," said Jade quietly. "She has no point of reference for the forest stream. She emerged in the moat because you conjured her, and that's where she found you. She can return there, and there only."

"That's pretty much exactly the wrong place to take us," said Ben.

"It's all right," said Holly, thinking quickly. "I know the way from the castle to our portal. I'll Vanish us as soon as we surface and I can get my bearings."

"But not the entire ship, certainly?" Almaric asked.

He was right. She couldn't take the *Sea Witch* with her; at most she could take five or six people. It would take too much power.

"There's no need to be Vanishin' us," Kai said calmly. "We ain't afeard of the king."

"It's not the king we're worried about," said Everett.

"Raethius can't track us. We ain't got the compass. The captain flung it overboard as soon as she found the *Black Dragon*."

"He doesn't need the compass," said Ben. "The castle is his center of power. Of course that's where he'll go."

Kailani's brown eyes were steady. "'Tis an oath of honor. Morgan will take Her Ladyship home, Raethius or no. His ship is no swifter than the *Sea Witch*."

"She needs to take us somewhere else," said Holly. "Anywhere, it doesn't matter. . . . The middle of another ocean. A deserted island. Anywhere that Raethius wouldn't think to look." She pulled herself toward to the hatch.

"No!" Ranulf caught her arm. "Only Morgan can stay on deck while the ship is submerged. You would drown us all. Whither she goes, we must go with her. It is too late to turn back."

He was right. The ship was rising fast. Already the world through the portholes was getting lighter as they shot toward the sun.

"Another time zone, on top of everything else," Ben muttered. "It looks like it's day again."

A rather long day, as it would turn out.

"Adept!" barked the captain from above. "On deck! All hands!"

Holly climbed out of the hatch to find they had surfaced not in the moat, but in the river that fed it, just upstream of the castle itself. The moat half circled the castle, pouring into a creek that entered the wood on the north side. A cold autumn wind whipped around

Holly's face as the boys scrambled on deck behind her. The castle portcullis was raised, and a dozen armed knights swarmed around the gatehouse in the dawn sunlight, yelling and pointing at the *Sea Witch*.

Morgan motioned to Holly, who pulled herself up the poop-deck stairs to join her at the helm. "I'll sail the *Sea Witch* through the moat and down the creek into the wood. Then I'll have to run 'er aground and sail the rest of the way through the trees to the Elm, as we did before. The *Black Dragon* has no powers to follow us by that route."

Holly nodded.

"But hear me," Morgan went on. "I dare not keep His Highness for ransom now. I must get the *Sea Witch* somewhere safe and make repairs. I'll cut him loose here, then take you to the Elm."

"You can't do that! He's a traitor to the king."

"He is sure to be captured," added Jade, who had appeared at Holly's feet. Would the king execute his own son? Avery wasn't Holly's favorite person, but he had been helpful—lately, anyway.

"That's no problem of mine," said the captain.

"He can come with us," Holly said, then immediately backpedaled. "I mean, maybe. At least take him as far as the Elm."

"The longer he stays, the more of a danger he is to

CLAIRE M. CATERER

us all. Ye've been braver than I'd have thought, and ye've fought well. I'll give ye that." Crewso the parrot flapped his wings on the captain's shoulder, and she scratched his head. "To the Elm, then. *If* he's no trouble. In that case—"

But Crewso's screech cut her off. Morgan's face darkened as she looked over Holly's shoulder.

Holly turned around.

Raethius had found them.

Chapter 51

The Portal

The three-masted schooner burst from the river depths, water streaming off its black sails. The guards at the castle gatehouse fell into the shadow of its dark hull, but Holly could clearly see their gape-mouthed faces as the ship rose.

Raethius stood at the helm as his horrid smoke-demon crew swarmed over the deck. His bow was pointed at the *Sea Witch*; he knew exactly where she'd landed. Morgan's crew, exhausted as they were, stretched out their webbed fingers over the river, churning it to send the *Sea Witch* through the moat and downstream.

"Captain!" Pike called. He stood at the mainmast, pulling on the topsail braces. "It's the prince they want. Throw him overboard and give us a chance to escape!"

"No!" Holly cried.

Morgan shifted her gaze between Holly and Pike, then shook her head. "Bring him!"

Pike dropped the lines and seized Avery, who was

standing nearby. Rowan took Avery's other arm, and together they dragged him toward the poop deck. His feet scrabbled over the stairs, and his eyes widened as he struggled. "Lady Holly!" he cried.

She pulled on Rowan's sleeve, trying to get at Avery. "Stop! They'll kill him!"

"Stand aside." Pike shoved her backward, and she stumbled over her broken ankle. For a moment she couldn't focus on anything but the pain, which shot through the top of her head like a spike. But then she heard Jade hissing, and Ben and Everett yelling as they pushed their way toward the poop deck. Quelch stepped up and grabbed Everett, holding him back easily. Cook hooked one arm under Ben's and pulled him away, saying, "Stay out of it, lad."

They're pirates, after all, Holly thought.

Out of the corner of her eye, she glimpsed Ranulf, who was only now making his way through the hatch, but Pike and Avery had nearly reached the gunwale. Rowan's sword pressed against Avery's throat. Ranulf would never make it in time to help. Still splayed on the poop deck, Holly raised her wand.

But to do what?

"Stop!" she cried. "As an Adept, I"—she grappled for the word—"I command you!"

Pike turned to laugh at her, but his voice died when

he saw the wand. Rowan froze, her ropy arms poised to pitch Avery over the side. Even the prince himself stopped struggling. Everything halted, like a snapped photograph. The captain alone strode forward.

"This is *my* ship," she said in a low voice. With a rasp, she drew her cutlass. "*I* command it. And no Adept shall—"

Holly acted without thinking. In one swift stroke, she slashed the wand through the air, and a broad flash emitted from it, knocking the blade from Morgan's hand. She raised it next toward Pike, but she didn't need to strike again. Pike shoved Avery away from him. Quelch and Cook turned the boys loose; the captain staggered away from her fallen sword. Jade bristled at her feet. Áedán poised on her shoulder, gathering his power should she need it.

A heady warmth shot through Holly's fingertips and filled her core. Even the pain in her ankle dwindled. She was the captain of the *Sea Witch*, and everyone aboard knew it.

She pointed the wand at Morgan. "Take us downriver, to the Elm."

The captain studied her a moment, then retrieved her cutlass. She raised it over her head and shouted to the crew. "Downriver! All hands!"

Rowan and Pike rushed back to their stations. The

river bubbled into rapids, and the brigantine began to move past the castle.

Holly poised her wand over the starboard side to help, but she hadn't even uttered the spell before Ben, standing with Everett amidships, cried, "Look!" He pointed to the helm of the *Black Dragon*.

The Sorcerer's smoke demons weren't working to send their ship after the *Sea Witch*. Instead, Raethius fixed his eye on Holly, raised one taloned hand, and drew a jeweled dagger from his cloak. Then, with a strange combination of words, he plunged it into the deck of the schooner.

At once the earth began to rumble.

Holly thought at first that another ship was about to emerge. The tremor centered on the river between the *Sea Witch* and the castle, and the waves there rocked to and fro restlessly. Then suddenly they pulled away in a broad circle, clearing the way for something to ascend. Holly strained her eyes for a flagged mast.

There was none.

It was a head.

It was half as long as the deck of their ship, knobbed and triangular, elongated with a narrow snout. Huge lumps and boils mottled its brown reptilian skin, and its neck climbed higher than the foremast, higher even than the castle's gatehouse towers; and behind it came a foot the size of their mainsail with long, curving claws.

"It's a dragon," Everett said in a hushed voice.

But Holly didn't think so. Áedán huddled against her neck, hiding from the monster; he wouldn't be afraid of a fire creature.

The thing opened its mouth.

A torrent of water gushed from its maw with a gurgled roar. Ben gripped Everett's arm, and they scrambled up next to Holly and Avery on the poop deck. The monster belched a river of water like a burst pipe. Inside of a minute the moat flooded the banks and spread to inundate the trees.

"Lady Holly," said Jade at her feet. "The portal! We shall have to sail there."

"No, I can . . . I can Vanish us there." Why was she wasting time? She ought to have done the spell already, but seeing Raethius, she couldn't just leave the others to him. The boys huddled closer to her; Avery stepped up behind and held on too.

Holly looked up over the gunwale to get her bearings. She had to visualize the path to the portal if she was to do the spell successfully. And it was . . .

Which way?

A new sea stretched as far as she could see, in every direction.

The kingdom was gone.

Everett stood like a stone, watching Anglielle sink below the waves. The castle towers, the wood, the river . . . It had all disappeared. He almost believed they were on the high seas again, except that when he peered over the railing and into the depths, he could just make out the willows that bordered the river. It had happened so fast, even Holly hadn't been able to stop it.

Everett turned to Avery, only to find he'd raced down the poop-deck stairs. He stood at the mainmast, gaping at the creature. Everett followed and tugged on Avery's arm. "Okay, time to really use that wand."

"Why, what're you doing?" Ben asked, coming up behind them.

"Just watch," Everett fished in Avery's coat and yanked the wand out. He wrapped the red silk scarf tightly around it. It was time he did something real, time to redeem himself for stealing the wand in the first place, for lying to everyone about Sol. If he could get rid of the monster—

"The castle," Avery said in a hollow voice. "It has vanished. Everyone is drowned."

The sea serpent roared and raised its impossibly long neck. Everett pointed the wand at its head—he wished now he had the musket again—and flourished it, just as he had during his joust the year before.

Nothing happened.

The creature reared its tail and swept it across the stern of the *Sea Witch*. Holly pulled the captain out of the way as the poop deck collapsed, and the two of them tumbled into Morgan's cabin below.

"Holly!" Ben cried.

"She's all right," Everett said, though he didn't check to make sure. "We've got to get this wand working—Avery—"

The prince snapped out of his daze and seized the wand. His face was hard; his blue eyes blazed in his face. He lashed the wand like a whip at the creature, and a laserlike spark struck its neck. It howled, but the scales were like armor; Everett couldn't even see a wound.

"That's got it distracted, at least. Keep going!"

The sea serpent gave a furious cry and lunged at the bow, biting off the new bowsprit. Innes screamed as she tumbled into the sea, but the monster ignored her, focusing on the *Sea Witch*.

Avery aimed the wand at its huge, olive-green eye.

Morgan hollered orders as the crew moved the ship.

Avery's shot bounced off, but the monster opened its maw, displaying double rows of sharklike teeth.

CLAIRE M. CATERER

"Now you've made it mad," Ben said.

"Let me help," Everett said, grabbing at the wand.

"This castle is my home. I shall defend it!" Avery pulled hard the other way.

The sea monster threw its tail across the deck amidships only inches from their feet. A deep crack splintered the ship nearly in two, and seawater poured over the bow, flooding the deck.

"Give it to *me*," Everett said. "I've done it before!"

"I must defend the castle!"

"But I'm the better shot!"

"Cut it out, you guys!" Ben shouted. Something hard came down on Everett's arm, which was locked with Avery's, and he pulled away. Ben had butted them with his sword hilt. He wrenched the wand out of Avery's hand and pointed it at the beast. "Abra—blastifor—cowabunga!" he shouted, and another laser beam burst across the sea monster's tail, slicing off a large chunk of it.

Everett and Avery stood open-mouthed. How had *Ben*, of all people, managed to work the wand? And why, Everett couldn't help wondering, was Avery able to do what he couldn't? The red scarf—the lady's favor—should work for any of them.

Ben shoved the wand back at Avery and grabbed Everett's sleeve. "Come on, we gotta get out of here!"

Holly crawled out of the wreckage of the captain's cabin. She had blacked out for a minute, though she could have sworn she saw Ben fighting the sea serpent with a wand. And now Avery was throwing sparks at it—or was she having a dizzy spell?

"Here, Lady Holly." Ranulf was suddenly at her side, and he hoisted her onto his back. Jade leaped up behind her. The captain pushed past them and took up Innes's station.

"Over to the starboard side, Ranulf," Holly said. "I have to help Morgan get us to the portal."

Holly and the others swirled up eddies of water, propelling the ship away from the castle's towers, which poked a few inches above the water like toy boats. Morgan stood on the port side, trying to steer the brigantine with the water, now that its rudder was in splinters. But as soon as they started to move, the schooner did too. They simply weren't making good enough time toward the portal. The ship was too badly damaged, and the sea monster was still coming for them.

"Everything's ruined," said Holly, gazing out at the endless sea. "The whole kingdom . . . the Elm . . . How will we even find the beech tree?"

　　　　　　　　CLAIRE M. CATERER

Almaric, who had been pushing his way forward for some time, finally joined them on the poop deck. "Don't despair, Lady Holly. This flood is nothing but a spell, but it works in our favor. Now that she has water to work with, Morgan can open a sea portal at her last entry point."

"Aye," said the captain. "'Tis the only way."

"The last entry point. You mean your cottage?" Everett asked, and Almaric nodded.

"But what good's a *sea* portal?" said Ben. "It's not like we can just jump in there and get home."

"One portal will seek out another." Holly recalled Kailani's words with a sick feeling in her stomach.

"Indeed," said Almaric. "When Morgan opens the sea portal, you will dive into it. Your wand will find the beech tree like a homing pigeon and guide you the rest of the way."

"I can't just leave Raethius to kill you all," Holly said, her voice breaking.

"And we can't jump into a *sea portal*," Ben said again, but Everett shushed him.

"If I know the Sorcerer, he will follow you, not the *Sea Witch*," said Almaric.

Holly almost laughed. The floodwaters were pouring over the gunwale; the *Sea Witch* was sinking fast.

Morgan followed Holly's gaze and clenched her

teeth. "Things be not as dire as they seem. This is a ship like none other. I can make our escape if the Sorcerer deserts his vessel. He will not find us without the compass."

"Jade." Holly twisted around to see him on Ranulf's back. "Do you think it will work?"

"Have you not learnt to wield this wand?" asked the cat. "To control the water? This portal is naught but that, Lady Holly. Elemental water. It is what you have trained for."

"But . . . the rest of you . . ."

"Will make do until you return."

Holly turned back to the boys. Everett held Ben firmly by one arm, as if afraid he would bolt. Ben raised his wide, dark eyes to Holly's, and swallowed hard. "I guess you've brought us this far," he said.

Down on the fractured deck, the prince stood alone, throwing bolt after bolt at the monster with his wand. His shots were connecting, but the creature's armor was strong. Holly wondered how long Avery could hold out.

The *Black Dragon* loomed closer. None of the smoke demons were firing now; they were all concentrating on pushing the schooner faster and faster to catch up with the *Sea Witch*.

"We're closin' in now, milady," said Morgan. Her

black curls were dampened with sea and sweat. "I'm ready to open the portal. Once ye're overboard, use the wand. It will seek out the place where the veil between worlds is thinnest. But mind, I can't say how long it will take ye to find it. Ye'll be far beneath the sea, and ye're no Elemental. Yer lungs may not last."

Holly's heart fluttered. She gave Ranulf a quick hug and slid off his back. Everett caught her arm to steady her on her one good leg. There was nothing else to do. They would just have to make it work.

Jade laid a black paw against her cheek. "The wand will not fail."

"May Lunetia protect you," said Almaric. Holly nodded. She took Áedán from her shoulder.

"No, Lady Holly. Keep him with you this time. You may need him."

"But—"

"Now!" cried Morgan.

Below them, the sea opened to a narrow whirlpool, just like the one that had swallowed the schooner. Ben clutched her hand, and she saw him go green, then white, then green again, like a ridiculous blinking Christmas decoration. Everett had her other hand; Holly placed Áedán back on her shoulder. Out of the corner of her eye she could see the hulking schooner. At the other end of the deck, the monster's jaws gnashed at Avery, whose sword flashed in the dawning sun. Would he be all right? And what did she care? But he turned from the beast for a split second and grinned at her. "Go, Lady Holly!" he called, then faced the sea serpent and plunged his sword in between the damaged scales on the creature's neck. It roared as the wound spurted yellow blood. The monster was nearly finished, but she couldn't stay and watch. "Hold tight, everyone," she said.

They jumped.

CLAIRE M. CATERER

Chapter 52

Through the Sea

The worst part was the dark. They plunged into a hole that sucked them down into depths the sun couldn't penetrate. Holly wanted to call out to the boys, but she didn't dare open her mouth. She stuck out her right arm, willing the wand to find their tree portal somewhere in the murky sea.

The whirlpool closed over them.

She held Ben with her left hand; Everett grasped the belt on her right side, freeing up her hand to thrust forward with the wand. Áedán clung to her neck.

But just as they shot through the water, something grasped her left calf. It wasn't one of the boys. It was something with claws. The wand pulled them along through the dark hole of the whirlpool and under the sea.

It couldn't be him, no matter what Almaric had said. Holly told herself it was just Everett's other hand, holding extra tight to her leg, but the grip burned like tongs pulled from a fireplace. She could see nothing but the few things briefly lit by the wand's weak light in front of her as they flew by—a stand of trees here, a path there. She craned her neck backward. Behind her, all was a billowing blackness, and the glint of two narrow eyes.

A bird fluttered through the water, and a rabbit hopped to its burrow inside a fallen log, as if the world weren't underwater at all. The claws tightened around Holly's leg.

She kicked feebly, jolts of pain shooting through her broken ankle with every tug. Her lungs ached, burning through her stores of oxygen. Despite what she saw the woodland animals doing, she didn't dare draw breath. Ben's grip weakened. She tightened her fist around his shirt; she thrashed and kicked, but the clawed grip only hardened.

There, just beyond the next rise: The wand's light brightened, and the beech tree appeared on the bank of the swollen stream, which still tumbled along the seabed just as it had on land. But the wand wasn't slowing down. She had to shake Raethius now, or they would shoot straight through the portal with him alongside. Holly tried to turn her wand to direct it at him, but its forward pull was too strong. Beside her, Everett kicked at the cloaked form, but it floated in all directions like smoke, dissipating and then coming back together. The black pocket of silence made everything more awful, like a singer who had lost her voice and yet kept moving her mouth.

Holly was running out of air now. She had used too much strength struggling to dislodge Raethius.

She touched her shoulder.

It was ridiculous to ask Áedán to do anything, a fire creature submerged in the sea; it would be like striking a match underwater. She pulled Ben closer. Her chest burned; she couldn't hold out much longer. They slowed. As she weakened, the warm, strong connection between the wand and her own heart wavered.

They began to sink.

The wand's light flickered.

Her body fell gently to the seabed, which was really the forest floor. Bubbles floated up from her mouth. Finally she let the air burst from her chest, and her heart eased. The grass was warm beneath her cheek, as if the sun shone on it, and she thought she heard the tree's leaves rustle above her head. She was in the Northern Wood. Her right hand opened, and the wand tumbled out of her fingers.

It didn't matter anymore what happened. Raethius could not get through the portal without her, and she could stay here, beneath the beech tree, in the forest she loved. Water filled her mouth. She would not fight it. She and the boys, and Áedán, would stay here in the sun. She was tired; she had earned it. They would rest here together for a very long time.

A hand seized hers.

Not a clawed hand; a regular, ordinary, pudgy boy hand. The hand snatched up hers and wrapped it around the wand; and then, from somewhere else, another hand appeared holding something long and shiny. It glinted in the wand's dim light. And in languorous slow motion, Holly's wand hand and the sword pointed together behind her. The Sorcerer's narrow, beaklike maw opened in a silent scream. His talon raked at her calf; his other hand grasped toward Holly's face.

The wand's beam broadened. Holly could feel a power moving through it, a magic that had nothing to do with her; her own heart had nearly stopped beating. The wand shot an orange light that grazed the grasping claw. The talons pulled back from her face, though the other claw still clung to her leg. Then the sword came down, slowly, so slowly, as a screech burbled through the underwater wood. The claw edged away, but not before the sword found it. Two of the talons fell away from the desiccated hand.

It released her.

CLAIRE M. CATERER

Suddenly the wand leaped back in front of them, propelling them forward through the trees. The portal stood ready for them. Just a few more feet, just inches to go now. The wand's renewed power burst through Holly's chest and pumped air into her lungs. The pudgy boy hand was still wrapped around her own; together they touched the tree trunk with the wand, and three tangled bodies fell into it like water through a sieve onto the cold, damp, muddy ground of England. Holly lay in the muck, gasping at the air, aware of the sun that had finally come out of the clouds, shining full upon them. The forest, though dripping with recent rain, was starting to dry out. But the beech tree wasn't. Even as Holly clutched at it, a geyser of water sprang up from its roots, engulfed it, and pulled it into the earth.

Beside Holly, Everett lay coughing. Áedán clung to her shoulder. And bunched up on her other side, his plump little hand clutching hers, wrapped around the wand, the sword still in his fist, was Ben.

Chapter 53

Tea and Ice

First, Everett said—and everyone agreed that he was quite right—they needed a bath, a nap, and a cup of tea.

Holly did have a hot shower and she donned fresh clothes, but the nap, she decided, could wait. She knew where to go for the cup of tea.

Indeed, it was ready for her before she even knocked on the door of Number Seven.

Mr. Gallaway smiled and beckoned her inside. He set the tea in front of her, and wrapped and iced her ankle. He set it gently on the chintz-covered ottoman in his front room while Holly nestled into the comfortable chair. The day was so damp, he had lit a fire in the grate.

"You just happened to have all this stuff ready?" Holly asked, sipping her tea.

"I find it best to be prepared for any contingency." The old man settled back into the cushions of his settee. "Are you going to show him to me?"

She reached up to her shoulder, and Áedán crawled into her palm. He turned his golden eyes to hers questioningly, but when he saw Mr. Gallaway's lined hands, he crawled into them willingly. Mr. Gallaway turned him this way and that, the glittery scales reflected in his deep-set blue eyes. "He is quite wonderful," said Mr. Gallaway at last. "Would he like a warm-up in my fire, do you think?"

Áedán crawled happily into the burning hearth and turned around three times before settling down with his tail curled around his feet. He snoozed while Holly told Mr. Gallaway everything that had happened, though she had the oddest feeling that he didn't need telling at all.

"You learnt quite a lot this time," said her host, when she had finished.

Holly nodded. Her heart trembled as if it had slipped its mooring in her chest, and her palm ached. "I've just left them in a really bad way. Again. Worse, even. The kingdom's underwater. . . ."

"But you heard your magician friend. That was temporary magic. Even the animals in the forest weren't affected."

"I guess that's true. But what about the sea monster? And Morgan and the others on the *Sea Witch*?"

"Well . . ." Mr. Gallaway fetched a shortbread from

a tin decorated with a tartan print. "It sounds as if the prince—what was his name?"

"Avery."

"It sounds as if Prince Avery had the monster finished off, in any case. Perhaps he's changed his ways. Or his loyalties."

"I doubt it," said Holly dryly. "He was in as much danger as the rest of us. I don't think he was trying to save anyone but himself." She thought of the last sight she'd had of him, grinning as he plunged the sword into the sea monster's neck. "Still. I hope he's okay."

"His kind usually are," said the old man. "They find a way round most consequences. Not really fair to the rest of us, is it?"

"It's Ben I can't get over," said Holly. "He used to panic in water, and he was the bravest of all of us when we went back to the portal. Somehow I was able to get some power back into the wand, but if he hadn't helped me . . ." She shuddered.

"People will surprise you. None of us knows what we're made of till we're tested." Mr. Gallaway tottered off to his kitchen and returned with a fresh ice pack for Holly's swollen ankle.

At some point Holly would sit down with Ben and with Everett, and the three of them would talk about what had happened. She would think of a way to explain Áedán to her parents and devise a plan to get him onto the plane back home. Ben would join the fencing club, which pleased his mother, who attended every tournament. Everett would congratulate Ben for his bravery at the portal, and contemplate whether Raethius's talons would regenerate like a halved earthworm, and he would force Holly to spend time with him and not wander off by herself into the woods every day.

The village of Hawkesbury withstood what went on record as Britain's coldest, soggiest summer, but it gradually warmed as August waned. The stream slowed down, and the beech trees and the oaks and the silver birches rewarded a sodden, weary nation with brilliant hues and an uncommonly dry autumn. Holly and Ben returned to America as the fall drew near and thoughts of school supplies and the subtle dance of lunchroom socializing filled their heads. But part of their minds—and part of their hearts—stayed tucked away in the heart of a British wood, warm and safe until their return.

Acknowledgments

The Wand & the Sea is the first book I've ever written on a deadline, which creates a unique vortex of madness that can only be tamed with the support of others. And so I thank—

Marjorie Caterer-Clark, my pal at ALA Chicago and my sister everywhere else.

Sally Caterer, who tells all her friends about me, whether they want to know or not.

Ruta Rimas, who edits my work and helps make every scene count and every word better.

Tracey Adams, the kind of agent who makes you feel you won the lottery when she signs you up.

Mary E. Kelly and her tireless extended family of Wrights, Werps, Hazlewoods, and Hertzes. My own family isn't large, but you've always made me feel welcome in yours.

Jennifer Ann Mann, a fine writer who always reminds me that I'm not a freak, just a debut author.

And as always, Chris and Melanie Bohling, who put up with mood swings and piles of laundry and too much takeout food. I love you.